No Help for the Dying

Adrian Magson

CRÈME DE LA CRIME

First published in 2005
by Crème de la Crime.
Crème de la Crime Ltd, PO Box 523, Chesterfield,
Derbyshire S40 9AT

Typesetting by Yvette Warren
Cover design by Yvette Warren
Front cover photography by John Powell.
Image supplied by Ace Stock Ltd, London, SW19 4EZ
www.acestock.com

Printed and bound in England by Biddles Ltd, www.biddles.co.uk

ISBN 0-9547634-7-5

A CIP catalogue reference for this book is available from the
British Library

www.cremedelacrime.com

About the author

Adrian Magson is a novelist and freelance writer, and lives with his wife Ann in Oxfordshire.
www.adrianmagson.com

To the tireless folks at Crème de la Crime, for their recognition that crime does pay, and to Christie, a brilliant and kindly editor.

Most of all, to Ann – chief stalker, publicist, fan, minder, accountant and cheerleader. The best.

The white van made two slow circuits of the block.

It drifted like a shabby ghost beneath the street lights, a curtain of rain rippling down the windscreen and out across the tarmac, lending the road the sheen of molten liquorice. A digital clock in a shop window read 01.45.

The vehicle's bodywork looked tired and scuffed under a layer of dirt, a sharp contrast to the precision sound of the engine beneath the bonnet. But while this and the heavily tinted windows might have seemed unusual, to a casual onlooker it was simply another white van, doing what white vans do.

At the end of the third circuit, the vehicle switched to side lights and slowed, swinging sharply into a side street. The tyres crunched across the nightly debris of fast-food cartons, discarded cigarette packets and greasy chip wrappers, and a plastic Malvern water bottle resisted briefly before spinning away into the darkness.

"Anywhere here." The man in the passenger seat took a bible from the dashboard, holding it against his chest and caressing it absent-mindedly with his thumb.

The driver stopped across from a travel shop and a photo boutique. Wedged between them was a narrow alleyway like a gap in a row of teeth. No light reached into this recess, and whatever lay inside had been swallowed in a dark soup of shadow.

After a few moments the passenger door clicked open and the man with the bible stepped lightly to the ground. He stood for a moment, his breath vaporising in the cold air and quickly snatched away by the bitter March wind. A few minutes walk away lay the colourful glitter of Piccadilly, with its bright lights and fluorescent advertising panels, a relentless flow of people and noise. But none of that reached here.

The man was tall and thin, with rimless spectacles perched on a pale, bony face. His shoulders were loosely wrapped in a long coat covering dark pants and a black silk shirt with a mandarin collar, and on his feet he wore black, rubber-soled boots. He reached back into the van and lifted a silver metal flask from a box on the floor, then nodded to the driver and moved away. Seconds later he was swallowed by the dark.

He paused for his vision to adjust before stepping forward. He passed the windows of a pub, long shuttered and dead, and a network of scaffolding interlaced with ladders and boards. A row of wheelie bins waited with their accumulation of refuse. The smell was sharp and strong, a mix of old food, stale water and something unidentifiable. He ignored it and continued into the gloom, favouring the wall to his right where the darkness gathered like molasses. There were stirrings from the shadows and an empty can clattered away from his foot. Something drummed against cardboard, and further on someone coughed, a brief bark of sound quickly stifled. Another voice cursed in a soft protest, blurred by the effects of alcohol or drugs or the bitter cold.

The man stopped alongside a battered skip, its solid presence indicated by the glow-worm speck of a warning lamp. He transferred the bible to one coat pocket and the flask to the other, and took out a slim, black Maglite torch. Bending easily, he reached out with his free hand, finding the slippery texture of a sleeping bag, the fabric stiff with ingrained grease and dirt. He ran his fingers along the top and located the zip pull. It snagged briefly before running free with a faint purr. The smell from inside was sharp and feral. He flicked on the Maglite.

The bag's occupant came awake with a cry of alarm. The man was ready; placing one knee on the sleeper's torso, he clamped a strong hand over the mouth, killing any sound.

When the struggles ceased, he shone the torch on the white face and fearful, blinking eyes. It was the right one.

He put the torch down and withdrew the silver flask. As he unscrewed the cup one-handed, a heady aroma of tomato filled the air around him. He bent close to the sleeping bag. "I've got some soup for you, kid," he whispered softly. "Nice hot soup." He squeezed the occupant's face, cupping the mouth into an elongated O. The skin was soft to the touch, as yet untainted by dirt or infection. He tipped the flask in one movement, using his body's weight to stifle the sudden violent eruption of movement from beneath him, a hideous parody of a lover's embrace. He ignored the choking sounds and what might have been the beginning of an agonised scream, and placed his hand back over the mouth. A spot of soup forced its way between his fingers and stung his cheek, but he ignored that, too. He continued pouring until the flask was empty and the body lay still. When he removed his hand, there was a gloop-gloop as the last of the thick liquid found its way down, followed by a pop of an air bubble rising to the top. He checked the pulse. Nothing. He zipped the sleeping bag and replaced the top of the flask, then stood for a moment like a priest over a grave.

"Tough luck, kid," he said softly. "Seems Daddy didn't want you back badly enough." He brushed the spot of soup from his cheek, then turned and walked back the way he had come, stopping at the mouth of the alleyway. His eyes flickered across the dark recesses one last time, then he took out the bible and, clutching it once more to his chest, walked back to the waiting van.

1

The telephone was insistent and annoying, jarring its way into Riley Gavin's subconscious. She mumbled into the pillow and rolled over. One of these days, she thought, I'm going to invest in a machine that rings only in daylight. She opened her eyes and blinked. It was still dark, but with a faint blush of dawn sneaking across the ceiling. A car hissed by in the street below, heralding another day of dull, March weather. The clock radio, a birthday present from her mother, flashed a blurred 05.00 on to the wall above her bedside cabinet in green gothic figures.

She kicked off the duvet and stumbled out of bed, stepping instinctively over a large tabby cat sprawled fast asleep in the living room doorway. "Fat lot of good you are," she mumbled, and scooped up the handset.

"Riley, sweetie." The syrupy tones of her agent Donald Brask slid down the line, and she forced herself to overcome the last few mental steps between sleep and wakefulness. Donald, God bless his mercenary heart, was all that stood between income and poverty, and whatever hour of the day or night, being nice to him guaranteed continued work.

"Donald, don't you know what time it is?" she pleaded half-heartedly, and moved on auto-pilot into the kitchen, homing in on the kettle. Coffee. No, tea. No, dammit – coffee. Donald only rang when he had an assignment for her, and he preferred perky and wide awake, otherwise he got snitty and went into a camp sulk.

"What's up, dear heart? Did I drag you out of someone's loving arms?"

"I should be so lucky. What do you want?" She watched as the cat wandered through and sat by the cupboard, cleaning itself with an air of casual patience as if time was of no consequence. It was all an act; the animal had once belonged to a former neighbour in Fulham, but had assumed squatter's rights and eventually moved in once it knew where Riley kept the tins of food she'd bought in for its occasional visits. It was a subtle form of psychological bullying for which she had fallen big-time, and a habit that had stuck when she moved to Holland Park. Luckily the neighbour had given her the cat and her blessing. One day she might get as far as giving it a name.

"Do you know a man called Henry Pearcy?"

"Wait a second." She switched the handset on to loud-speaker and dropped it on the worktop, then busied herself with getting a tin out of the fridge and forking meat and jelly into a bowl. Amazing how a tin labelled rabbit could smell so much like a trawlerman's armpits. The cat stopped licking and waited, its tail quivering like an antennae, then dived forward like a missile as she put the bowl on the floor. That was one problem solved.

"Riley? Hello?" Donald's voice ventured richly out of the handset.

"I hear you. I'm thinking." She dumped ground coffee into a filter pot. The rich aroma pervaded the air of the small kitchen in seconds, making her shiver with an odd feeling of comfort. "Henry Pearcy... that's going back a bit. He's a journo - or was. How did his name come up?"

"He called me yesterday evening. Said he had something to pass on to you, but didn't know your number. The editor of *Diaryline* told him you worked through me." Donald sounded unusually patient considering he was being used as a message service, and Riley wondered why.

As a busy agent for a string of journalists, media slaves and a clutch of entertainment personalities, he rarely bothered wasting time on calls which didn't promise a commission for one of his clients. And while he professed to have a soft spot for Riley, for whom he dredged up investigative assignments from contacts in the trade, as far as Donald Brask was concerned time was money and favours were an intrusion.

"So what are you not telling me, Donald?" said Riley. "You only remember my number in the middle of the night?"

"Actually, sweetie, it's nearly daytime. I wasn't going to call until later, because I thought this was another one of your army of admirers trying to get back into your favours. Then something odd happened." He paused and added, "I must say, he sounded a bit... well, old for you, if you don't mind me saying."

Riley smiled at the deliberate ploy. One chink in Donald's businesslike demeanour was his incurable thirst for gossip, about celebrities, politicians or even his own clients. Drop him a morsel of information and he'd damn near salivate over it, teasing out every last detail like meat from a crab's claw. Now here he was trying to figure out her innermost secrets.

"He's old enough - although there's nothing wrong with the more mature man, as you well know." She waited for a riposte but there was none, so she explained: "I worked with Henry for a short time a few years ago on a commercial radio station. He was their head newsman and was looking towards retirement even then. I was learning the broadcast ropes after a stint on a local rag. He taught me a lot."

Henry, she recalled, had been a kindly but unhappy

man. She dredged up an image of him, more college professor than newsman. He wore old, once-expensive suits that had seen better days, and carried with him a palpable air of melancholy. It showed in his manner and his eyes, which rarely offered a full smile. Yet he had never allowed it to affect his work. She'd heard rumours about a dead wife, but to a young reporter learning the ropes it wasn't a subject to broach. In the end it was Henry's love of the bottle that saw them part company as colleagues. Caught driving while three times over the legal limit, he had been sacked. The last Riley heard he was holding down a desk job on a tabloid in the Isle of Dogs, although she couldn't recall which one.

"You haven't seen him lately, then?"

"No. We shared office space occasionally, but that was it. He wasn't into socialising much. What did he say?"

She heard paper rustling in the background and pictured Donald at his desk, ergonomic headphones on and a green night-light casting spooky shadows across his office. She'd been to his home a couple of times; the business part was a hum of activity, with an array of state-of-the-art technology, and the home part was as clean as a pin, with the air of an Ideal Home show house: no mess, no drink rings on surfaces, no discarded magazines, no impressions on the cushions. Donald's contacts in various branches of the police, the media and government were legion, but if he had any kind of love life, it didn't appear to involve overt signs of passion.

"He told me he had some information for you. Something about a girl named Katie Pyle. He gave me his number then rang off. Somewhat abruptly, too." Donald made it sound like a deplorable breach of etiquette.

Riley put down her coffee and felt the atmosphere go

cold around her neck. Katie Pyle? The name rang a distant bell. It had been years ago, back when she'd just started out on her first small newspaper. *The Reader* had been a local freebie on the rim of London, lasting about four years before it zoomed from stuttering start-up to terminal obscurity. Its problem, she recalled, was that it had been neither rural nor urban, hovering in limbo between city and Hicksville, a collection of cheap adverts and 'Under a Fiver' columns, with a few grudging inches for news.

She closed her eyes, trying to re-assemble the details while Donald waited patiently. Then it came to her, slowly taking form as her memory kicked in through the residual fog of sleep. Ten years ago. A missing girl – a teenager – had walked out of her home one day and disappeared. She remembered feeling powerfully affected by it; it was one of her first stories as a twenty-year-old wannabe reporter and the echoes of it had followed her for a long time afterwards. In fact, it had probably been the one thing which had driven her towards freelance investigative journalism, rather than a staff job. She had ditched the notes on it long ago, but something told her there had been no resolution to the story. Just another disappearance, unexpected and unexplained, in a long line of missing people who chose to walk away from what they had, with no explanation, no note… and often nothing in their family history to account for it. But then, as she had learned since, most families kept a tighter hold on their darker secrets than the Bank of England.

But if it was still a live story, why would an old news-hound like Henry Pearcy be willing to pass on information to another reporter, especially after all this time? That would be like Donald inviting some grubby computer nerd to hack into his PCs and have their wicked way with his files.

"OK, sing it out."

As Donald called out the number she snatched up a marker pen and scribbled it down. It looked like a mobile number. "Did he give an address?"

"No, but I have a sweet bit of caller ID software which did," said Donald smugly. He was very proud of his gadgets, all of which were designed to allow communication with clients and contacts without ever leaving his office. It gave him the image of a giant spider, tugging away at the various strands of his convoluted web. "It confirms the subscriber as one Henry J Pearcy at 12, Eastcote Way, Pinner, Middlesex. Nothing else, though." He sounded faintly disappointed, as if the equipment had failed him in some way by not including a raft of juicy details.

"Right." Riley wrote down the address. "I'll try that number. If he comes on again, tell him I'll be calling." She hesitated. "You said something odd happened. You mean connected with Henry?"

"Yes. I got a call from a contact in the Met twenty minutes ago. The body of a young woman was found along the Embankment yesterday evening, in a memorial garden between the Albert Bridge and Cheyne Walk. She'd been dumped behind a statue called 'The Boy David'. About mid-twenties, well-dressed, ordinary, she appears to have died of asphyxiation – or more accurately, of choking on her own vomit. No purse, no ID and no obvious signs of assault. Apart from a crucifix, the only item of value on the body was a bracelet. One of those cheap silver things on a chain, with her name on the inside."

Riley didn't want to ask, but the awful inevitability beckoned. "What was the name?"

Donald paused. "I know this is unusual, Riley," he warned her sombrely. "But I sense a story here. So, I think, will the editor at *Diaryline*. You don't need to pursue it if you don't want to, bearing in mind the personal angle. But I know I can sell it."

Riley let a second or two tick by. This wasn't their customary way of working; usually Donald secured an assignment from an editor and Riley either agreed or not - so far, always the former. But this time things were different. "Personal?"

"The woman's name was Katie Pyle."

2

Riley switched off the phone and sat down, her coffee forgotten. The cold feeling was back and she shivered slightly as if something had touched the back of her neck.

She wandered back into the bedroom and slid beneath the covers. The cat followed, curling up on the foot of the bed and flaring its claws with pleasure.

Katie Pyle had been her baptism of fire. Pitched in at the deep end by an editor who was short of staff and impatient with mundane things like equal rights in the workplace, she had been assigned to cover a story way beyond the traditional newbie jobs of weddings, births, deaths, flower shows and local good works. As far as her boss was concerned, when news beckoned a reporter reported and neither gender nor lack of experience was a barrier.

Armed with only the vaguest instructions and the police report to go on, Riley had dashed off with crusading zeal, anxious to put the world to rights and dig below the scummy surface to reveal The Truth. Her main problem – something her editor had seemed to have neither the time nor inclination to tell her – was trying to trace someone who either didn't want to be found or was simply beyond reach.

She had begun by talking to the police, the most immediate experts. They had been by turn cautious, factual and professional. They had pointed out that according to the available evidence, Katie, barely fifteen years old and a single child, had left home voluntarily, taking some money, a shoulder bag and a change of clothes, but little else of value. As a subsequent visit to her shell-shocked parents had shown, even her favourite teddy had been left behind, propped up on the bed-head and staring blankly at the opposite wall as if hiding all the girl's secrets behind its frozen, glassy expression.

A helpful desk sergeant, perhaps sensing Riley's inexperience, had acquainted her with the statistics of missing persons each year. It now stood, she knew, at a staggering two hundred thousand plus.

"Most of them are back within days, weeks or months," the sergeant had informed her. "Usually none the worse for it other than needing a good wash, some grub and a kip."

A more senior officer had been more analytical, suggesting that many wore the signs of their experience like a new coat, recognisable only by those closest to them. Some were deeply secretive about what they had done and where they had been. Sometimes they lost these new affectations and reverted to type, sometimes not. The unlucky ones, he'd added gravely, turned up dead, mostly at the hands of somebody known to them.

"Shit happens," one DCI had commented before hurrying away on a call. As she had subsequently learned over the years, those two short words had proved a brutally accurate summary of life's more unpleasant events.

Riley was about to close her eyes and give in to sleep when the door buzzer sounded from downstairs. She tried to ignore it but it kept on ringing until she scrambled out of bed again and angrily punched the button in the hall. "Who is it?"

"Ouch," came a familiar male voice. "So, no chance of a coffee, then?"

Riley sighed and buzzed the door open. Ever since she

moved in three months ago, her sometime colleague, private investigator Frank Palmer, had been promising to drop by for a tour of her new flat. He hadn't said it might be at this ungodly hour of the morning, though. They had forged a friendship of mutual understanding after working on a couple of assignments, but pleading insane waking hours evidently wasn't going to put him off.

"Nice gaff," said Palmer, putting his head round the kitchen door. If he was startled by her rumpled blonde hair and the sight of her in grey sleep joggies and top, he hid it well. Riley ignored him and spooned fresh coffee into the filter pot. Palmer had seen her looking a lot worse, and frankly she didn't care if he approved or not; it was far too early in the day for standing on ceremony. If she carried on drinking coffee at this rate she'd be as high as a kite by lunchtime and unable to sleep tonight.

"Glad you like it," she muttered, slightly mollified. "I don't want to sound unwelcoming, Palmer, but what are you doing here at this time of the morning?"

"Work, as usual. Why else?"

"What kind of work?"

"I'm babysitting a Saudi business type for a couple of days. He's down the road at the Kensington Hilton. You sound cranky."

"Oh, well spotted. Donald wakes me at God knows when, and just as I'm dropping off to sleep again, you turn up on the doorstep expecting instant service. How does being cranky *not* come into it?" She gave him a suspicious look. "Hang on a minute… did Donald get you to come round here?"

"I don't know what you mean." Palmer gave her his best vacant look, the one he used when he didn't want to give anything away. Bloody Donald; he was making her paranoid. He had a bit of a thing on the quiet about her safety, which was how she'd first met Frank Palmer. Co-opted as backup on an assignment involving some unpleasant gangster-types the previous year, and with a background in the Military Police, there was nobody better than Palmer to have on her side. But she doubted he would come out and admit he'd been told to stop by. She let it go and watched as he wandered off to prowl around the small series of boxes which comprised her latest home. The cat followed his progress with a watchful tilt of the head, but didn't seem the least bothered by the man's presence. Riley wasn't surprised; Palmer had a way about him which was both unthreatening and reassuring, guaranteed to set old ladies and animals at ease in the middle of a firestorm.

"Not bad," he congratulated her again, returning from his scouting mission. "So what was wrong with Fulham that made you move to sunny Holland Park? Or is this Notting Hill?"

"Depends who you talk to. Mr Grobowski downstairs reckons Notting Hill, but the old dowager upstairs says Holland Park. I'm just Confused of West London and don't really give a damn. I felt like a change of scenery." It had also been a practical and timely way of despatching ghosts after her previous flat had been burgled by a psychotic thug named McManus. Somehow a thorough cleansing hadn't been sufficient to rid herself of the feeling of vulnerability afterwards, although McManus was long gone to whatever hell awaited him; in the end, the desire to move had become irresistible.

Palmer nodded but said nothing. He too had known McManus, and understood Riley's need to shake off the past. He drifted over and poured coffee into two mugs, then leaned across to the fridge and rooted around for the milk. Riley allowed him the familiarity, pleased he felt at ease. He was wearing, she noted, his usual comfort-before-style tweedy jacket and jeans, of a sombre colour guaranteed to blend in wherever he went. After a career in the Military Police, Palmer, now somewhere close to forty, had developed a healthy dislike of formal wear of any kind. He also wore his fair hair slightly longer than Queen's Regulations would have permitted; it seemed to suit his tall frame and angular face.

"So... nothing to do with broken hearts, then." He handed Riley a mug and spooned three portions of sugar into his coffee.

She scowled at him. "It's not socially unacceptable for a girl to be single, you know." He was referring to her arms-length relationship with John Mitcheson, by coincidence also a former soldier. They had met on an assignment in Spain barely a year ago, and so far had struggled to maintain momentum while he was building up his security business in San Francisco. Due to a misunder-standing with the law, Mitcheson was not currently welcome in the UK, so much of their involvement took place over snatched weekends in out-of-the-way places. Exciting and head-spinning at first, the relationship had suffered from a lack of regular care over the months, a fact both of them acknowledged. And all the while Frank Palmer had observed them with detached interest, watchful of Riley's welfare, a good friend but nothing more. His opinion of John Mitcheson had originally been uncomplimentary, but had changed with time. Now, she guessed, he remained merely cautious on her behalf.

"What did Donald have to say?"

She led the way through to the living room and slumped

on the sofa, the cat bagging the place next to her and staring at Palmer in disdainful triumph. Palmer stuck his tongue out and opted for the armchair, whereupon the cat lifted one leg to a lithe ninety-degree angle and licked its bottom.

Riley told Palmer about the message from Henry Pearcy, and how she had first met the newsman, ending with Donald's news of the discovery of the body on the Embankment. "It could simply be a bit of final house-keeping on Henry's part," she said. "He probably heard of the girl's death the same way Donald did and wanted to tip me the wink."

"For old times' sake?"

"Why not? Henry was OK. I'm surprised he's still around, though, let alone in the business." When Palmer looked puzzled, she explained: "He suffered from depression… and he drank a lot."

Palmer nodded. "Bit unusual, though, this girl – woman – turning up dead after all this time. What was it – ten years? Didn't her parents ever hear from her?"

"I don't know. I lost touch years ago." Riley hoped they had made contact, even if only for their peace of mind. Apart from offering a reward for information, they had put up dozens of posters wherever they thought it might do some good. The search had been carried out, she recalled, almost as an act of self-protection rather than hope, as if it might somehow alleviate the awful pain of realising their daughter had chosen to leave of her own accord, with no explanation. It was painfully obvious even then that the event had permanently marked their lives, numbing them into a state of paralysis from which they seemed unlikely to recover.

She gave Palmer a keen look. "For a coffee-break visit,

you're asking lots of questions."

"Am I? And here I was thinking I was just being matey. Are you going to follow it up?"

Riley shrugged. After all this time she wasn't sure she wanted to get into Katie Pyle's life again. It had affected her enough the first time round; she didn't need another dose of family sadness and grief to deal with. Besides, hadn't she moved on from that kind of news trail? She was now, if her recent track record was any guide, more into high-level fraud, gang-busting and political chicanery than family tragedies and missing teenagers.

"Hey-ho." Palmer drained his mug and stood up. "Time's a-flying. Better get back to his Highness the Prince of whatever."

"He's a real prince?"

"So they tell me. His lackeys seem pretty impressed." He looked at her. "What is it?" Her attention had drifted away while he was speaking and she was staring out of the window with a faint frown.

Riley shook herself. "Sorry – I was just remembering something about the Katie Pyle case. It's not important."

"OK." He waved and drifted towards the door. "What are you working on at the moment?"

Riley looked at him. The question had been almost off-hand, but there was something not so relaxed in the way he had put it. "I've just finished a piece about forged papers and phantom airport workers. Why?"

"No reason. Just asking." He waved a vague hand at the four walls. "Nice. Who else lives in the house apart from you and the other two?"

"Jeez, Palmer. If you must know, just the three of us. Mr Grobowski helps out at the Polish Community centre, and the old dowager type upstairs, whose name I don't know and is a spit for Miss Marple, comes and goes at odd hours. I think she might be a vampire. Satisfied?"

"Great. So, no chance of any wild parties, then." He smiled and left.

Riley listened to his footsteps fading down the stairs and shook her head. Palmer was getting paranoid. He'd spent his life watching people and probably couldn't drop the habit. New faces and new places meant somebody else to keep an eye on, just in case.

She scooped up the phone and dialled the number she'd written down. With full wakefulness, her mind had started working on Donald's information. Activity was the only way to get to the bottom of it. Who knew, it might lead to a decent story.

As the phone rang at the other end, the thought that had been bothering her suddenly crystallised in her mind. It was so obvious she wondered if she had got it wrong. But she knew she hadn't.

Katie Pyle had disappeared a full twelve months before Riley had left *The Reader* and begun working with Henry Pearcy. Twelve months in which the story had faded and died, superseded by a thousand other events that changed lives and claimed public attention. In many ways, Riley felt that her inability to discover what had happened to the girl had been a failure on her part - certainly too much to want to talk about it a year later with an experienced hack like Henry. Which meant that in news terms, as far as Henry Pearcy was concerned, any connection between her and Katie Pyle had simply never existed.

Frank Palmer walked down the path from the front door and paused at the gate to look back at the building. He was just out of sight of Riley's window. He was already holding his mobile in his hand, and leaned down next to a street lamp just outside the gate and pretended to talk to someone. He rubbed at the ID plate, stared up at the lamp and made gestures towards the house, then shook his head and put the mobile away. With a bit of luck it might convince any watchers that he was a conscientious official from the lighting department going about council business.

Especially the two men in the white van with tinted windows fifty yards away.

He walked past the vehicle, noting the registration, and wondered why they were scoping Riley's building.

3

The area around Heathrow airport was busy, the lights hazy through an impenetrable early-morning drizzle steadily turning the roads to a slick, shiny gloss. A large jet thundered in, trailing twin lines of vapour from its wingtips, and Riley mentally crossed her fingers until it touched down with a squeal of rubber and disappeared into the mist.

She peered through the windscreen of the Golf, trying to recall the locations of the main hotels along the Bath Road. Her infrequent trips to Heathrow usually ended at the car parks, with little or no reason to familiarise herself with the surrounding geography other than a passing awareness of alternative roads in and out.

She spotted the building she wanted on the north side of the road, its presence anchored in the grey light by a large blue-and-gold logo. Nosing beneath an open chevron barrier, she found a parking space not far from the main entrance between two growths of berberis. As she flicked off the lights she caught a glimpse of movement in the glass-lined foyer and a flutter of curtains on the first floor. Evidently some guests were already up and about, no doubt preparing for imminent travel and trying to suppress nerves and catch an early breakfast.

When she had dialled Henry's number from her flat, she'd got his answer machine. But in place of the normal request for callers to leave a message, Henry's plummy voice had spoken directly to Riley. "*Remember me? It's been ages, I know. I'm on the move and have to switch this off for a while. It's important I see you, so please call me later.*" The message had clicked off without another word, leaving her staring at the phone in puzzlement. Was that a slur in his voice... or simply the toll of the years? From the note of urgency it was obvious he'd been waiting for her to call, and had left the direct message to make sure she kept trying.

She had given it another twenty minutes before dialling again. This time he'd picked up on the first ring, wasting no time on catch-ups, his words spilling out with urgency. "Riley, are you mobile? Sorry I couldn't speak earlier – I had to switch off the phone. I must speak to you, but there's not much time." His voice had been clearer, the cultured drawl coming back to her over the years. Henry had been expensively educated, she remembered hearing, with a good degree from Oxford, although it wasn't something he had ever talked about.

"What's this about, Henry?" she'd asked him. She probably sounded equally terse to him, but it was difficult not to match his urgent manner. "You mentioned Katie Pyle."

"I'm near Heathrow," he said, as if that would explain things. "At the Scandair."

She knew the hotel vaguely; it was a refurbished concrete-and-tinted-glass block catering to mid-range travellers, a stone's throw from the airport's chain-link perimeter fence.

"I'm... ummm... flying out tomorrow – sorry, this morning," he continued. "Rush job, covering for someone else. You know the way it is. Can you come here? I'd meet you halfway but I can't get to my car easily at the moment."

"Why not tell me over the phone?"

He hesitated. "It's difficult. A man's been looking for you."

"A man? What man?"

"He wouldn't give details. I heard about him through a… colleague. He's been asking questions about where you might be… how he could contact you."

"What does he want?"

"I'd best leave that to him. He wants to talk to you about… Katie."

"He said that?" This was becoming bizarre. What kind of peculiar twist of the gods could simultaneously bring back a name from the past now turned into a dead body, an old news-hound from outside the circle, and a stranger with information?

"Henry?" Riley wanted to shout at him to open up and stop messing about. But she told herself to be patient. There was no telling how fragile Henry might be, and the longer she kept him talking, the more likely he was to tell her what was going on. On the other hand, spook him and she might never find out. The pause stretched for a few more seconds. "What did he say about her?"

"Riley… it would be better if I saw you. I'm in room 210. This chap – the caller – has your name. But that's all. I said I'd try to get in touch with you, that you'd moved on and so forth, and he said he'd call again."

"And did he?"

But Henry had gone, leaving a heavy silence. Riley hung up and stared at the phone, trying to make sense of his words. Whatever was bugging him involved this mystery man who was trying to contact her. But why not just tell her who he was, instead of acting as if the whole thing was a state secret? She couldn't recall him ever being so evasive.

She'd gathered her things and slipped into Kickers, jeans and a warm jacket, then headed for her car and west London. The journey had taken an hour because of a

22

spillage of timber on the westbound carriageway, leaving her raging in silence until the traffic cops and highway crews in their wet slickers managed to clear a path through the debris.

Riley got out of the car and approached the hotel entrance. A flatbed luggage trolley loaded with bags stood near the doors. One of the bags, a large, blue, canvas-sided piece with gold locks and a reinforcing strap hugging its middle, had fallen off the trolley and lay in a puddle like a beached whale.

A clutch of figures stood behind the misted glass under the ceiling lights, deep in conversation. Two of them wore police uniforms. Riley scanned the car park and saw the nose of a squad car partly shielded by a delivery van, steam drifting off the bonnet.

The double doors opened with a hiss, discharging a current of over-warm, recycled air. On the wall behind the desk a clock reminded everyone that it was nearly 7 a m.

Riley was accustomed to coming under the scrutiny of cops; approach a crime scene often enough and it became something you could almost ignore. A mixture of suspicion, interest and wariness. It was probably the same the world over.

"We help you?" One of the uniforms stepped away from the group and into her path. He was built like a prop forward and the brim of his cap was spotted with rain. He had the assurance of someone who was beyond directing traffic or filling in forms. Or maybe it was the creased black leather holster on his hip, which, Riley reflected, unless things had moved on dramatically in the past few hours, was not standard issue for traffic patrols.

"I need a room," Riley responded instinctively. It probably sounded lame, but on the other hand, asking to see a male guest at this time of day sounded even more unlikely. "What's going on?"

For a second the cop said nothing. He looked down at Riley's hands. "Travelling light?"

Riley bit back a reply and wondered if it was the gun which made him so pushy. "I'm on my way into London," she explained. "I thought I'd check availability first. If that's all right with you?" His eyes narrowed at the tone in her voice, but instinct told her sarcasm would be a natural response for someone tired and fractious and facing a nosy cop at this time of the morning when all she wanted was a room.

It worked, but only just. He shook his head. "Sorry, but we've had an incident here. You might like to find somewhere else." The way he said it meant: *Leave now, we're busy.* Over his shoulder she saw the other cop watching, while a man and a woman who looked like hotel employees gave the impression that they wanted to be somewhere else.

"Like where? And what sort of incident?"

The cop's response was a flat stare, so she turned and walked back to the car, wondering what was going on. Maybe one of the guests had run amok with a meat cleaver. Or maybe there had been a terrorist scare. Whatever it was, it seemed to have everyone on edge. What struck Riley as odd was that armed police didn't normally attend incidents unless there was a report of firearms or other deadly weapons. In which case, where was their backup and incident unit?

She was about to climb in the car to call Henry when a youth appeared round the corner of the hotel. He was tall and skinny and dressed in a white shirt and porter's waistcoat, hunched against the cold and jingling a large

24

bunch of keys. A plastic badge gave his name as Andy. Riley stepped in front of him. "Do you know what's going on? Why are the police here?"

He glanced towards the entrance, then back at Riley, his eyes doing the up-and-down trip but without conviction, as if his mind was hovering elsewhere.

"Beats me," he offered. "I only got here fifteen minutes ago. The place was all lit up. Someone said there'd been a fight. The night manager said to go round and check all the exterior doors, and not to talk to anyone." He gave a half-grin at his small show of defiance. "I'd better get back."

"Wait." Riley needed to know what was happening inside the hotel, and at the very least get inside to see Henry. But she could hardly go back to reception while the police were there. This youth might be the only answer. "Pretty unusual, though, isn't it – armed police at a fight?" She was hoping he'd respond with a bit of speculation, leavened by some gossip or a piece of solid detail.

"I suppose." He shrugged super-cool, like it was old news and all too boring. "They're most likely one of the armed response teams from the airport. They'd be the nearest. The night manager would have dialled 999. It's what we have to do, when there's trouble. There are more upstairs, only not in uniform. Maybe somebody died."

Riley was surprised. This was all moving too fast. First the call from Donald, then the hesitant runaround from Henry and his directions to this hotel. Now this – and with plain-clothed officers to boot.

She dug out her mobile, along with a £10 note, the smallest she had. "Hang on," she said to Andy. "Please." He said something but didn't move, anchored by the sight of the money. Riley hit redial, and Henry's mobile number came up. After five rings it was picked up.

"Who's this?" The voice was a man's, solid and official sounding. In the background came a buzz of other voices and the hollow slam of a door, before somebody made a shushing sound. All she could hear then was the hiss of somebody breathing into the phone. She cut the call. Henry's phone but definitely not Henry's voice. Weird.

"I've got to go," the youth was saying. He was gesturing towards the entrance and beginning to sidle away, but still with one eye on the note in Riley's hand.

"This is yours if you get me inside." The words came out impulsively. Riley was reacting on the hoof with no clear thought of how this might pan out, but her instincts told her that whatever had happened inside the hotel was connected in some way with Henry Pearcy. "Just get me in, that's all. I'll take it from there. Don't worry, I promise I won't steal anything."

He shuffled his feet, greed fighting for supremacy over fear of being caught out. "Are you a reporter?"

It was either a lucky guess or the kid was smarter than he looked. "That's right. I happened to be in the area."

The promise of immediate cash evidently made up Andy's mind; he turned and walked back the way he'd come, leaving Riley to follow him round to the back of the hotel where the rooms overlooked a second car park and the lighting was sparse enough to throw pockets of gloom everywhere. He stopped at a side door and fiddled with his keys, then turned and held out his hand.

"You never saw me, right?" He was staring at her intently.

"What floor did it happen on?" Riley asked, parting with the note.

"Sorry – you're on your own." He pocketed the money and unlocked the door. "Close it within ten seconds or the alarm will show on the security board." Then he turned and hurried away.

Harry Poustalis, manager of the SnapFast photo boutique, ducked off the exposed stretch that was Piccadilly, shoulders hunched against the squally rain. His hand clutched a polystyrene mug of extra-strong coffee, his preferred method of kick-starting his day, and in his head was an image of sun-blessed Kefalonia, his family island home. He wished he were there rather than here in cold, wet London. As he stopped outside the shop door, he found his way blocked by a misshapen bag of rubbish, its sides torn and pulled apart in a familiar fashion. He supposed it was one of the urban foxes that lived in the neighbourhood. Setting his coffee aside, he gathered the spillage of torn paper and plastic wrappings, grasped the bag and walked with it down the adjacent alley, stepping carefully over more scattered debris. The wheelie bins were already full, so he walked on towards the builders' skips at the back.

As he swung the bag over the lip of the skip, he almost stepped on a huddled form encased in a grubby nylon sleeping bag. He cursed softly, wondering how anybody could sleep out here among this filth. Every morning it was the same. If this soul didn't move soon before the contractor's lorry came round, he or she stood a good chance of being crushed beneath the wheels.

Harry stooped and shook the sleeping bag. The occupant felt small and slight – most likely a kid. Maybe this one needed the coffee more than he did. The way they lived, it was no wonder some of them ended up in the local A and E. He shook the person again and tugged the zip down, and the fabric fell away. In the same moment that he registered a strong aroma of tomato soup from inside the bag, Harry found himself looking at a deathly pale, pinched face and two sightless eyes staring up into the grey morning sky.

4

Riley expected to find herself in a corridor leading towards the centre of the hotel complex. Instead she'd landed in what felt like a large stock cupboard. It was about six feet square, heavy with the mixed aromas of cleaning fluids and polish. By inching her way around in the dark, she found two walls lined with wooden shelves holding cleaning gear and some metal containers. The third was taken up with vacuum cleaners and buckets, and the fourth wall included a door with a thin crack of light showing at the edges. It wasn't much, but sufficient to give her some bearings. She nosed up to the door and listened. If there was anyone out there they were being very quiet.

She felt for the door handle. It was a standard doorknob with a small locking mechanism in the centre. She snicked it open and a wave of warm, musty air flowed through the gap, carrying a faint smell of carpets and damp.

Riley slid off her jacket and draped it over the handle of one of the vacuum cleaners. It left her in jeans and a plain white shirt. Might as well try and look like a guest, just in case. As an added extra, she messed up her hair and rubbed her eyes with her knuckles. It was unlikely to be flattering, but this was business.

When she stepped outside, she found herself in a dead-end corridor lit by overhead strip lighting, with a heavily patterned carpet underfoot and an occasional bland print on the bare brick walls between rooms. She walked towards the far end, where a sign indicated stairs one way and reception the other. At a guess, 210, Henry's room, would be on the first or second floor, but until she spotted a sign, she'd have to run blind. She just hoped it didn't turn out to be next to the one where the fight had taken place.

A sudden clatter made her jump. It was an ice-making machine and drinks dispenser set in an alcove. It gave her an idea, and she retraced her steps to the cleaning cupboard, where she took down one of the containers she'd noticed on a shelf. It was an aluminium ice bucket, standard issue in every hotel room from Alaska to Zanzibar. She walked back to the ice machine and jammed it under the dispenser.

The noise was horrendous, making her jump. When the bucket was full, she headed for the stairs. Fortunately no one seemed to have been disturbed by the clatter, and everything was quiet save for a vague murmur which could have been a television or the grumbling of the heating system.

Riley walked up to the first floor, where the signs indicated rooms 101-199. Second floor it was, then. As she turned to go up the next flight of stairs, a uniformed PC stepped out of the shadows off the landing and stood looking down at her.

Riley brushed her hair back and peered at the signs on the wall, then gave what she hoped was the goofy smile of the terminally jet-lagged. "This place is like a maze," she said, stifling a yawn, and climbed the stairs, moving to step past him. But he reached out an arm and barred her way. Riley felt her stomach go cold.

"Which floor are you on, then?" he asked, adding, "Miss."

"Three, I think," she replied, trying to recall if there was a three. "The ice machine up there looked dirty, so I came looking for another one." Before the officer could react, she peered up at him and said: "Look, what's all the noise about? It's worse than Oxford Street. And why are you lot asking everybody questions?"

She was counting on playing the aggrieved and disturbed guest to work, and it did. His eyes slid from her red eyes and rumpled hair to her boots, taking in the ice bucket on the way. He didn't appear to see beyond the illusion that she was simply another guest.

He dropped his arm and gave her the benefit of a half smile. "There's been an incident involving a guest on the second floor," he explained. "Nothing to worry about. I take it you didn't hear anything unusual?"

"No, sorry. Like I told your colleague, I had the television on. I couldn't sleep." She rattled the ice bucket. "Thirsty, too."

"Colleague?"

"That's right. Tall man... looked like Wild Bill Hickock." When the PC frowned she added: "Not the moustache – the gun."

He relaxed and stepped aside. "In that case, you'd better get back to your room, Miss. We don't want another guest disappearing, do we?"

Riley walked up to the second floor and checked the corridor, then pushed open the door, flinching at the sucking noise made by the draught excluders. Voices came from a room just a few doors down on her right, followed by a short bark of laughter. As she approached, a man stepped out and walked towards her. He wore a rumpled suit, with the tired expression of someone who had been up all night and didn't expect to get to bed any time soon. Riley yawned, but didn't catch his eye. They passed each other without speaking, ships in the night. Well, morning.

As she drew level with the open door, she saw the

number and felt her stomach lurch. *210. Henry's room!* What the hell was happening here? She paused and looked in, and saw a man standing by a television set in one corner, scribbling in a notebook. He wore a suit and his heavy shoes were surrounded by shards of broken glass. Near the door was a roll of coloured crime-scene tape.

The bathroom light was on, spilling out into the room and illuminating a section of pale wallpaper, and Riley could hear a ventilator fan humming noisily in the background. But what caught her attention was a shocking smear of dark red running down the wall and across the white doorframe.

"Excuse me, Miss."

She turned. The first man was watching her from the open door at the end. She waved apologetically and continued walking away from him, but he called again. *"Hey – Miss?"*

It was time to go. Another ten steps took her to the far end of the corridor, with a fire exit on the right-hand side. Using her shoulder to thrust it open, she ran down a set of bare concrete steps coated with a non-slip surface. She heard muffled footsteps pounding heavily along the corridor she had just left, and an exchange of voices.

She hit the next landing on the run and continued on down. She probably had a few seconds before someone thought to use a radio to shut off the downstairs exits. If she could get back to the cleaning cupboard, she had a good chance of getting out and clear before they got organised.

A glance through the glass panel showed the bottom corridor was deserted. As she hit the door a volley of shouting echoed down the stair well behind her. She sprinted along the final stretch of carpet, praying nobody chose this moment to come out of their room. She dumped the contents of the ice bucket in the dispenser then ducked into the cupboard, where she wiped the bucket with a piece of paper towel before replacing it on the shelf and retrieving her jacket.

The rear car park was clear. She shut the door behind her and hurried back to the car. She felt exposed and vulnerable under the rows of windows, but there was no burst of shouting and no heavy footsteps to intercept her. As she reached the Golf and fumbled with the keys, an engine burst into life on the other side of the car park and a white delivery van nosed out past the barrier. Riley tucked herself in behind it and followed it out on to the Bath Road, joining an already growing convoy of commuter traffic heading into central London.

Back at the flat, as if taunting her with the idea of a day not yet done, the answerphone light was blinking to announce a waiting message. She hit the button and began to take off her jacket. A familiar voice filled the room.

It was John Mitcheson.

"I told you she wouldn't be back." Madge Beckett watched as her husband George did a tour of the flat. It didn't take long. It wasn't much more than a glorified bed-sit, really, with a separate kitchenette off to one side through a sliding door. American kitchen, the builder had told them when he'd shown them the plans; everyone was having them. A bathroom was just along the passageway with a toilet next to that. It wasn't much but their tenant had never asked for more. She'd seemed happy, anyway, and stayed here over seven years in all. Most tenants moved on long before that, always saying they'd found something better, something they could call home; a real step up, was

33

the implication, as if this was merely a staging post. But with most of them you knew that wasn't true. This one had seemed different, though. Settled, she'd been. Like she'd found her place in the world.

"But just like that? It doesn't sound like her." Madge thought George sounded dismayed, as if the young woman had been his own daughter and she'd run off with their life savings. He flicked at some of the personal objects around the room, on the sideboard and the dressing table, brushing them with his fingertips as if they might tell him a secret. "Why would she just leave?"

Madge didn't know. She shrugged and stared past him out of the window at the rooftops of Chesham. If she squinted hard, she fancied she could almost see the shimmering haze of traffic pollution off the M25 round north-west London.

Jennifer Bush had wandered in one day in answer to an advert in the local newsagents, and she'd taken the flat, as they'd grandly called it, without a murmur. She'd brought in a few things; a CD player with a stack of Asian-sounding music, a small trunk and a load of books, but that was all. A special needs teacher, she'd let slip one day when Madge asked her what she did for a living. For autistic kids and the like. And here she'd stayed, quiet, self-contained and never a noise or a cross word for anyone. Until two days ago. Madge had heard her go out in the early morning, while it was still dark. She'd bumped against something on the way down the stairs, which was unlike Jennifer, her usually being so considerate. Seconds later Madge thought she'd heard a car door slam, but it could have been her imagination.

"A man, you reckon?" George said, picking up an object like a small drum on a stick, with some tassels attached. He tapped it against his hand but there was no sound so he put it down again. He sniffed loudly and picked at a partially burned incense stick, stuck into a small pot of white sand. "Stuff stinks, doesn't it? What good does it do?"

"It never harmed us," said Madge quietly. She felt sad looking around this room, with its neatly made bed, its few scattered ornaments and books. She'd only been in here a couple of times, to sort out a problem with the blinds and another with the heater. There had never been any need, otherwise. But suddenly she knew the girl wasn't coming back. She could feel it. She reached out and took George's hand. "It's only incense... joss-sticks. Smells quite nice to me. And so what if it was a man? She's entitled, isn't she, a nice girl like that? Maybe she was just waiting for the right one to come along. Same as I've been doing all my life."

George looked at his wife with raised eyebrows. "Very funny. I know you don't mean that." He moved past her, shaking his head, but kept hold of her hand. "So what do we do, then - wait for her to show up? She's left all her things here."

"We'll give it a few days." Madge turned to follow him, wondering where Jennifer, their quiet, sad, untroublesome tenant, burner of joss sticks and lover of mystical, eastern music had gone. And, not for the first time, where she had come from.

5

Mid-morning was a good time to hit the local coffee franchise, after the rush of take-outs had gone. Following a restless couple of hours sleep, in spite of her flagging energy, Riley took a selection of newspapers round the corner in search of warmth and bustle. It was where she liked to do most of her reading, in between people-watching and chatting to any of the other regulars who happened along in search of a caffeine boost and a friendly face.

Right now, though, all she was interested in was sinking a strong latte and trying to shake off all thoughts of John Mitcheson. Forced to stay out of the country by the threat of possible arrest because of his unwitting ties to a criminal gang, his message had capped a long line of other missed calls, abandoned dates and clinical emails with all the romantic appeal of a wet flannel. So much for enforced separation, she thought. She dumped a portion of brown sugar in the latte and stirred it with feeling. What was it they always said? Absence makes the heart grown fonder?

"My eye," she muttered out loud, and glared at a man in a suit at the next table, who looked startled at the comment.

To help with the process of Mitcheson-banishing, she scoured the newspapers for reports of crime in any hotels near Heathrow. It didn't take long. If an assault had happened, it evidently hadn't been gory enough to make the early editions. She wasn't sure if events at Heathrow would make the London evening papers, but it was worth checking, even if only to confirm that her description wasn't splashed across the front pages as a possible suspect. She was almost into the sports sections and giving up when something about the Scandair made her stop and think: amid the uniforms and the woken guests and the obvious police presence, there had been no evidence of paramedics or an ambulance. Which was odd. Given a body or a serious injury – and the blood she'd seen indicated the latter – most people would summon an ambulance before they called the police. Unless, of course, there was no body.

She went through the papers again, page by page. What Heathrow lacked in mayhem, the capital had more than made up for. A suspected arson attack on a house in Acton had claimed a trio of asylum seekers from Iran; a drive-by shooting which had killed two and wounded five was being put down to a resurgence of Jamaican Yardie activities in north London and Birmingham; two pensioners had managed to beat each other to death simultaneously over an offending Leylandii hedge, a new drugs turf war was warming up in the East End and, according to one report, another young street-sleeper had been found dead in central London. With no obvious attempt at irony, the report suggested the dead teenager was a victim of contaminated drugs.

With half her mind busy trying to figure out what to do next, Riley allowed herself to be drawn into the story, intrigued by the headlines in spite of her concern over Henry. Not that it was anything truly fresh. The author of the report reminded readers with dramatic over-statement that the number of young street sleepers who had died in the past three months stood at seven. Most, like this last one, were thought to have been down to drugs use, rather than deliberate or suspicious causes, although it was evidently of low interest, judging by the lack of further details. Rough sleepers died all the time, was the cool tone; it was a high-mortality lifestyle, and if the cold, disease or drugs didn't get them, some other faceless monster with no conscience would. In other words, what could you expect? The thumbnail photo accompanying the reporter's name showed a fresh-faced brunette with a winning smile. Her name was Nikki Bruce.

Riley studied the photo with a vaguely professional interest. Not a bad shot if it was recent. But she didn't look the sort to go trawling the streets in search of a good story. She wondered cynically if Nikki Bruce had actually stepped outside her office to cover this one or whether she'd done it over the phone.

She put the newspaper to one side and tried Henry's phone again, but either it had been switched off or the battery was dead. Next she rang Donald.

Her agent listened in silence as she related the morning's events, but she could feel his excitement down the phone. If there was one thing that warmed his wires more than gossip, it was the sound of a good mystery. Mysteries meant news; reporting them and exposing any criminal activity involved led to repeat fees.

"Stunning, sweetie," he purred. "I just love the idea of you vamping around hotel corridors with mussed hair and an ice bucket, chased by strapping policemen. I didn't realise you had such hidden depths."

"Stop it, Donald," she chided. "One day your imagination will get you into trouble."

"If only, dear heart. Now, what do you need from me?" He was back to business, the complete professional.

"I need to know who Henry was working for. I could ring round, but it would take me ages. Someone might know what he was working on. It's a long shot, but it's the only thing I can think of at the moment."

"So you don't think he was… umm…" Donald hesitated diplomatically.

"Drunk? On drugs? Search me. But I doubt it. He sounded – I don't know – strange. Stressed." Which, if the sign of blood had been any indication, she thought, he had every right to be.

"All right. I'll check. I'll also see if I can pick up any gossip from the Met. Call you back."

Riley had almost finished a second coffee when Donald called back. "Pearcy's current registered work is with an international agency here in town. Showbiz stuff mainly, for the glossies, looking for anything juicy. Tits, bums and black eyes, mostly."

"What does Henry do there?"

"Odds and sods. Editing, by the sound of it, but nothing major, and nothing outside. Sounds as if he's at the end of the track, career-wise." Donald gave her the number of the agency and Riley cut the call and re-dialled.

"Sorry – who?" The voice that answered sounded young, female and bored.

"Henry Pearcy," Riley repeated carefully. "Guy in his sixties… sad face?" She struggled to think of anything else recognisable about Henry. "Oh – and a fruity voice."

"Hold on," the girl muttered, and Riley was left listening to something classical while the girl probably took a tour round the office, had a coffee and came back to say something like, "No dice."

Riley re-folded the used newspapers and slid them on to the next table. Somebody else with time to kill would find them useful. As she leaned across, she noticed a sheet of paper on one of the chairs. She picked it up and read it, wondering how many such items she'd seen over the years.

It was a missing persons flyer. Like the death of the street-sleepers she had just read about, it was a reflection of the times. The flyer was a standard A4 sheet with a six-by-six black-and-white portrait and heavy block lettering underneath. The photo was of a sullen looking girl with a mass of hair and a down-turned mouth. Maybe the original snap had been taken by someone she didn't much like. The text underneath was simple and depressingly familiar.

MISSING:
ANGELINA (ANGEL) BOOTHE-DAVISON
- 15 - 5′ 6″ - 110LBs
BLONDE HAIR, BLUE EYES, PALE SKIN.
LAST SEEN MARBLE ARCH ON 15TH FEBRUARY.
THOUGHT TO BE SLEEPING ROUGH IN AREA.
IF SEEN, PLEASE CONTACT:

There was a contact number but no name. Riley wondered how many Angelina Boothe-Davisons were currently lurking in the capital, favouring an existence on the streets rather than the alternative of living at whatever passed for home.

It reminded her of the posters distributed following Katie Pyle's disappearance: one of the reasons Riley was drawn to reading them; not because she thought it might help, certainly not after all this time, but because it was something she shared with others, albeit from a distance.

The paper was cheap, all-purpose stock, and the text composition basic and heavy, designed solely to draw attention. Since most of these flyers ended up on the floor, torn down and discarded by disgruntled and uncaring locals, quality wasn't a consideration.

The snitty operator returned and dragged her back to the present by announcing tiredly, and without checking first if Riley was still online and had not died in the process: "Sorry. No one of that name here."

"There has to be." The words were out before she could stop them, fuelled by puzzlement and a tinge of anger at the girl's lack of conscience or interest. This was insane. Donald didn't get his facts wrong, and if he said Henry worked for this agency, it was cast-iron solid.

"Well, I'm sorry. I did check, you know." The response was sharp and resentful, the 'sorry' a verbal parry in place of a genuine apology, like a child caught out for not doing her homework. Then there was a mutter of voices before a male voice came on the line.

"Can I help you? My name's Murdoch – I'm the office manager here."

Riley repeated her request. "I've been assured he works for you, Mr Murdoch," she said, "but your switchboard girl doesn't seem to know what I'm talking about."

"I'm not surprised," said Murdoch. "She's a temp. Thinks fame is a birthright and probably wants to be an actress or model by the time she's eighteen." He paused, then continued, "I'm sorry, but you're out of luck. Henry did work here, but not for two weeks now. He didn't turn up for work one day. We've tried contacting him, but without luck. Nobody's seen him. If you speak to him, ask him to get in touch, would you?"

6

Murdoch hung up without saying goodbye and Riley felt the air contracting around her. This was getting odder by the minute. Odd that Henry had specifically said he was on his way to a rush job, which was the kind of terminology someone would use to a colleague. Former colleague.

She checked with a couple of directory enquiry agencies to see if Henry had a separate home phone listed. With a bit of luck he had a private number. But both enquiries turned up a blank. No surprise there. Next she rang Donald and asked him to repeat Henry's address, which she wrote down on the back of the missing person flyer.

Number 12 Eastcote Way turned out to be a detached Georgian house in a quiet street a stone's throw from Pinner station. The building seemed in danger of being consumed by a tangled mass of dying ivy, although the leaf-strewn gardens were mature and neat, enclosed by weathered fencing and a growth of spiky greenery. Riley tried to recall if Henry had mentioned a wife, but the information wouldn't come. Perhaps he employed a gardener instead.

She left her car along the street and crunched up a gravelled drive, where twin ruts showed the regular passage of a vehicle leading from a garage set on one side of the house. The twin green doors needed painting, as did the front door of the house, but here, even age seemed to have its place, adding to the feel of solid comfort and prosperity. She found a doorbell and thumbed the button.

If it rang she didn't hear it. She gave it another ten seconds before pressing again. Still nothing. She turned and surveyed the road outside the gate, and the houses either side with their tastefully netted windows. Suburbia at rest. Though not without eyes, she guessed. She looked at her watch in the manner of someone with an appointment and puzzled by the lack of response.

Riley wandered casually over to the garage and tugged at one of the doors. It opened a fraction and revealed an empty space, save for a metal tray in the centre of the floor and a workbench against the back wall. The air smelled musty and oily, and by the amount of black sludge sitting in the tray, whatever he drove leaked like an old sieve. If Henry had come and gone recently, it was without leaving any wet tyre tracks.

A gravel path ran from the garage to the side of the house. She pushed through a wrought-iron gate heavy with snakes of dried honeysuckle and found herself in a garden only marginally smaller than Hyde Park – or so it seemed to Riley, who didn't even possess a window box. She studied the generous sweep of neat lawns and borders and the selection of spindly cherry trees, and wondered how Henry Pearcy had managed to hang on to this house if his career was going so badly.

The gravel path continued across the rear of the house, skirting a patio tinged green with moss. Against the wall stood a wrought-iron table with a glass top and four matching chairs. The glass was puddled with rainwater, the surface stained with dirt and the remnants of dried blossom. A few mouldy leaves clustered forlornly around the feet of the furniture, trapped and waiting for a heavy broom to sweep them free. It resembled an abandoned stage set, and Riley guessed it had been a long time since

Henry had last hosted any kind of gathering here.

A set of French windows stared blankly on to the garden, with a heavy set of lined curtains cutting off any view of the inside. Further along, a small extension jutted out from the main line of the building. This proved to be a kitchen, with a glass-panelled door set in one wall. Riley stepped over and peered through the glass, but all she could see was an ordinary kitchen: cooker, table, sink, fridge, pot and pans. But no sign of recent activity. She put her hand out to try the door when something made her freeze.

The glass pane close to the handle was missing.

She peered through the hole, and saw broken glass glinting back at her from the floor inside.

Then a voice said: "Can I help you?"

The white van with the darkened windows idled through traffic on the outskirts of Staines, to the south-west of London. The driver was killing time and waiting for instructions. He glanced sideways at the man in the passenger seat, who was fiddling with a mobile phone and humming to himself. A bible rested on his knees, the leather covers worn and shiny, and the top of a silver flask protruded from one pocket of his long black coat.

"He's taking his sweet time," the driver muttered, easing around a Fiat Uno turning right into a one-way street against the traffic. His accent was American. He stopped right behind the Fiat as the woman driver realised her error and turned to see if she could back out. She was now blocking a surge of oncoming traffic led by an enormous petrol tanker, and with no way back. The driver of the van grinned as the woman became aware that she was completely vulnerable if the tanker driver chose to exercise his right of way. "Serves you right, bitch," he whispered nastily. "Should learn to keep your eyes open." He sniggered and looked at his companion who was shaking his head in disapproval. "What? Is it my fault she's stupid?" He gave a heavy shrug of his shoulders before easing the van forward a few feet.

The passenger's phone rang. He answered with a curt: "Here."

"Is it done?" The voice from the other end was smooth and softly-spoken.

"Yes, it's done. What next?"

"You're sure you weren't seen? I don't want any repercussions."

"There won't be." The man looked at the driver and urged him with an impatient gesture to drive on.

"Good. What about our package?"

"We've got it." He turned and looked behind his seat, where a cloth-covered bundle was laid out on the floor. It had rolled once when the driver had negotiated a roundabout too quickly, but other than that it was stable.

"Fine. If you've cleared up any other signs, you'd better get back here. We've got a function to prepare for."

The passenger opened his mouth to acknowledge the instruction, but the man on the other end had already cut the connection.

7

It took Riley a massive effort of will not to run. The voice wasn't Henry's and the owner wasn't standing inside the house. She turned and saw a face watching her from over the top of a larch fence adjoining the next property. It belonged to a woman in her late sixties, and from the look she threw Riley, interlopers were watched very carefully around here.

"Mr or Mrs Pearcy," Riley called across to her, just to let the woman know she wasn't spooked. "Are they in, do you know?"

The old woman looked panic-stricken for a moment, as if Riley had spoken in Swahili. Then she drew herself up so her chin was on a level with the fence. "There is no Mrs Pearcy," she said politely. "May I help?"

Riley stepped over to the fence, moving slowly so as not to alarm the woman. Up close, she saw she had been generous with the years; the woman must have been eighty if she was a day, thin and brittle as an old stick. She was dressed in a faded but once stylish cardigan, pulled close around her thin shoulders and pinned with the sort of silhouette cameo brooch you rarely saw outside antique shops. Behind her, in complete contrast to Henry's immaculate garden, lay a profusion of colour and disorder, with a jungle of browned, withered plants and very little grass, mown or otherwise.

"Henry called me," Riley explained. "We used to be colleagues at the paper. When I tried to call him back there was no reply." She waited, but when the old woman said nothing, continued: "I was told he might be going abroad.

I hope it's not in that old car of his."

The mention of the car seemed to act like a password, and the old lady relaxed visibly, although she didn't move any closer. "I'm sorry, young lady," she said. "I can't help you. Henry took the Rover out the other day and I haven't seen him since. I'm keeping an eye on his cat for him, though. First thing in the morning, last thing at night – and I check during the day." The last was delivered with a faint hint of warning, as if Riley should take note and pass it on to every cat thief in London and the Home Counties so they would know somebody was on the job.

It was clear the old lady hadn't noticed that a pane of glass had been removed from the kitchen door. She was either blind or the break-in had occurred since she last fed the cat.

Riley thanked her and walked round to the front and back down the drive. There was little point in going inside, even if she could sneak past the neighbourhood watch unit. Whoever had removed the glass must have taken a chance on daylight entry, which meant they'd probably watched the old lady leave before going in. Still, she wondered what they'd been looking for.

She headed south towards Ruislip and Hayes and dropped down to the A4 Bath Road. Traffic was busy, the usual stop-start build-up to what would be gridlock in a couple of hours. A pass along the front of the Scandair Hotel revealed no obvious police presence, so she doubled back and turned in off the main road, tucking the Golf into a space in the rear car park. She studied the other cars. Most of them were fleet-type vehicles, shiny and uniform, and the sight of a man unloading a flip chart and a couple of briefcases from a Nissan confirmed it was a landing-pad for company meetings and conferences. Riley waited until the man was struggling across the tarmac towards a single swing door in the main building, and caught up with him in time to hold it for him.

"Give you a hand?" she said with a smile, and offered to take one of the briefcases. If there were any kind of police presence inside, it would help if she could merge into the scenery.

"Oh. Cheers." The man looked grateful and surprised, and gave her a quick once-over. His eyes seemed to waver a little at the jeans, but he still managed to pigeonhole her as one of his own kind. "You must be from the south-west team. I'm Mike Hutton." He stuck out his free hand. It had the sweaty, over-strong grip of the professional hand-shaker. "I hear we've pretty much got the whole place this afternoon. Should be noisy in the bar tonight." He grinned at the prospect and gave her the kind of sideways look which was clearly a come-on for later.

Riley gave a meaningless smile and nodded, and followed him along the ground-floor corridor to a conference room. Outside stood a pile of boxes containing glossy sales catalogues and scratchpads. There were two men in the room, both in shirtsleeves. They were laughing at something in a newspaper. Hutton breezed straight in, evidently on familiar territory and keen to join in. His bulk conveniently blocked her from view, so she set the briefcase down inside the door and ducked away before he could make introductions. On the way, she snatched up one of the catalogues.

Up on the second floor she peered through the landing door towards room 210. There was no sign of activity, so she gently eased the door open and padded along the carpet, ready to flap the brochure and play lost if a uniform appeared.

The door to 210 was slightly open, with a strip of crime-scene tape stretched across the gap. Riley checked over her shoulder, then pushed the door back until it bumped against the wall. No lights, no movement, no sign of a forensics team. But perched on the bed was a policeman's peaked cap. No doubt belonging to a uniformed plod left here to watch the place. He'd probably sneaked off for a fag break. Thank God for easygoing cops. It was decision time.

She knew there was a risk that the policeman might come back at any time, but she figured she had to take the opportunity while it was still off-limits to the cleaners. The place would have been searched carefully by the forensics team - if one had been called - but without a body, the procedure might not have got as far as a full scene of crime unit investigation.

She ducked beneath the tape and stepped into the room, clicking the door shut behind her. If anybody asked, she'd play dumb or tired. Failing that, she'd have to run again.

The room was standard - double bed, twin bedside cabinets, table and two chairs, television, dresser with hospitality tray and kettle, and wall-hanging space for clothes. With its royal blue carpet, curtains, bedspread and seat covers, it looked like a thousand other hotel rooms from Bangkok to Bolton. Only the smears of blood on the wall and doorframe were non-standard.

Riley checked the bathroom first. It had been emptied but not cleaned, and one glance was enough to see it held no clues. Back in the bedroom, the nearest bedside cabinet revealed a soft leather bible and a paperclip, but nothing else. The other cabinet held a hotel notepad and another bible. This one had a simpler, paperback cover bearing a logo of an oil lamp with a flame. She recognised the emblem of The Gideons.

The dresser held a copy of Yellow Pages, a guest information book and a plain polythene laundry bag, and a glance at the hanging space showed nothing but a bunch of the hangers nobody considers worth stealing because they can't be used at home.

She stood and mused for a while, conscious that the longer she stayed, the greater the risk of discovery. Plainly there was no obvious clue here as to why Henry had called her, or where he had gone. And if he had brought any clothes or papers with him, they had already been taken away for examination. Only the blood on the wall and the fact that his mobile phone had been picked up by a policeman showed something disturbing had happened.

A metallic clatter echoed along the corridor outside, and she went to the door and listened. If the cleaners had been given the OK to come in and do their thing, now was the time to move. She opened the door just a crack and peered through as the rear view of a service trolley, pulled by a woman in a green overall, disappeared down the corridor.

Riley ducked out beneath the tape again and walked the other way. She was nearing the door at the end when a movement behind the glass pane revealed a dark sleeve and a flash of a metal shoulder tag. At the same time, she heard a man's voice and a woman's answering laugh echo up the stairwell. Fag break over, then.

She began to turn back, then noticed one of the doors nearby was unlocked. She nudged it open and slid inside, praying she didn't bump into a male guest in his chuddies. To play safe, she called: "Room service". But all she got was a strong smell of air-freshener and the clinical feel of a room recently tidied and ready for occupation.

Heart pounding, she closed the door and sat on the nearest bed, waiting while the policeman walked slowly past the door and went into room 210. Then she heard the blare of a television and a burst of canned laughter. Great. She'd chosen to coincide her visit with one of London's finest bunking off work and watching an afternoon game show. She peered through the spy-hole in the door, but couldn't see if he'd left the door open behind him.

She flicked through the brochure and waited. The general sales pitch was something to do with seating systems for conference venues and about as interesting as having her teeth filed. She dropped it on the bed and checked through the nearest cabinet for something else to read.

There was nothing other than another Gideon. This one was another plain paperback, and other than a pencilled smiley face on the flyleaf, showed few signs of having been used. Must be a budget room for low-cost heathens. Riley rolled across the bed and checked the other cabinet in case anyone had left a magazine, but it was empty.

She picked up the sales brochure again and was halfway to the door when a thought struck her: why was there a leather-bound bible in one room and a cheap paperback in another? Would the Gideons really use leather-bound bibles? There were at least three hundred rooms in this place alone; to repeat that in every hotel in the country would be hugely expensive.

But why was this suddenly an issue? After all, a bible was a bible was a bible.

Suddenly, the television went quiet and heavy footsteps passed the door. She waited until she heard the door close at the end of the corridor, then slipped out and headed back to 210.

The bible query had taken root, and was suddenly too

insistent to be denied. As she drew level with 210, she cursed herself for extending the risk level and flipped a mental coin. It came down heads.

The door was still open, although the tape had now gone. The police must have finished with it. Riley was inside and back out again in seconds, this time with the leather bible concealed inside the sales brochure. She wasn't sure what the laws were on removing evidence the police had overlooked, but she was pretty sure the courts had a ruling for it somewhere. Apart from that, if she was stopped now, she was going to have to do some quick thinking to explain the relationship between seating systems and food for the soul.

Back in the car, she stared at the bible, turning it over and riffling the pages. Unlike the paperback versions she'd seen, this one was heavier, the leather covering soft and pliable, like an expensive calfskin. The only decoration was an indented scroll in each corner; no title, no picture of an oil lamp and flame. She flipped it open. The paper was thin, and held the sort of text you would expect to see, with one exception: there was no mention of the Gideons. Instead, stamped across the flyleaf in rich, blue ink were the words:

CHURCH OF FLOWING LIGHT. WELCOME ALL
WHO ARE UNLOVED AND ENTER HERE.

In one corner were the initials HP. Henry Pearcy.

8

The bold text of the welcome message was followed by a telephone number. Riley stared at it, trying to gauge if there was something she was missing, or if she was trying to read too much into it. It was a bible, that was all. Not a Gideon exactly, but so what? But unless the uncanny arm of coincidence meant someone else with the same initials had passed through recently and left behind their very own copy, this bible had to belong to Henry Pearcy. How had the police overlooked it?

Riley turned to the greeting on the flyleaf. It was different, certainly, but hardly unbiblical in tone. Still, a hell of a way to get inside the heart of a lonely resident of an airport hotel: to appeal to the unloved side of their nature. She wondered how they approached the terminally depressed or the deeply suicidal.

A shadow suddenly loomed up at the car window. It was Mike Hutton, the salesman with the flip chart. He was mouthing something at her through the glass. She lowered the window a crack. "What is it?"

"I said, the boss wants to see you. He's a bit pissed off, to tell you the truth. Says if you're with us you should have reported in earlier. You'd better get your business suit on, too, he's a stickler for that." His gaze dropped to the bible on her lap and faltered slightly, as if he'd found her doing something unwholesome.

"Thanks," she told him, turning the ignition key. "But I'll pass. Tell him I've just been made a better offer by the opposition."

By the time she got back to Holland Park, it was late afternoon and a chill was descending, lending a sharpness to the emerging street lights. She parked the car in a nearby street and walked back to the flat, head buzzing with unanswered questions. After all this she was no nearer knowing whether Henry's bible being left in a hotel room was significant or not. As far as she could recall he'd never voiced religious leanings, although few people of his age ever did. Religion was the third side of the conversational triangle along with sex and politics, and only the young seemed intent on discussing them openly with little or no embarrassment and precious little in the way of experience.

"Miss Gavin?" The voice carried the familiar air of tired authority, and Riley felt her stomach flip. A man stepped out from a plain car parked at the kerb in front of her building. He was tall and stocky, with the look of one who knows not to take anything or anyone for granted. A uniformed officer stood on the other side of the car, idly flicking raindrops off the roof, but watching her carefully.

"That's me," she confirmed, and saw curtains twitching in the flat below hers. Mr Grobowski, no doubt keeping an eye on things. Give it a couple of hours on the local grapevine and this was going to do her street cred no end of good.

The policeman nodded but made no move towards suggesting he wanted to go inside out of the weather. He had a fleshy face and an unfashionable moustache that looked as if it had begun life as a dare and become a fixture. He flashed his card but in the poor light she couldn't read it closely. "DS McKinley. I'd like to ask a couple of questions, if that's all right?" The way he said it meant her agreement was actually immaterial. He looked as if he'd had less sleep than she had. He consulted a small notebook. "You made a phone call at oh-five-thirty-one this morning to a mobile belonging to one Henry Pearcy. This was followed by another at oh-five-fifty-three, then again at oh-seven-ten. Would you care to tell me why you were calling him?"

Riley felt her stomach tighten. Of course, Henry's phone would have revealed her number. It would have taken the police no time at all to get her address. The fact that McKinley had gone straight to the question of why she was calling meant they had enough information to bypass the bit about did she know him and where they had met.

"That's right," she said, deciding on as much of the truth as she dared use. "He left a message for me earlier, saying he was on his way overseas and suggested we have a drink. He wanted to tip me off about a story he'd picked up. I arranged to meet him, but when I rang again to confirm where, I had trouble getting through. Is something wrong?"

McKinley stared at her while chewing his lip. His face was a careful blank, and Riley couldn't tell if he believed her or not. On the other hand, what was he going to accuse her of?

"I said –"

"I heard what you said, miss," he murmured. "Bit early, though, isn't it, to be talking about having a drink?"

She shrugged. "He probably meant coffee. I didn't think about it at the time."

"And you were quite happy to get up and drive out to meet him, were you?"

"Why not? I've been up earlier and driven further for less."

"Further than where?" His eyes glinted as he stared at her, suddenly leaning forward slightly like a gun dog spotting a kill.

Riley swallowed. *Shite. That was a stupid slip.* She told herself to play it calm. "To Heathrow. Some hotel on the Bath Road, he said. And before you ask, DS McKinley, I was already up when I got his call."

"How come?"

"I don't have to answer that. What hours I keep are my business."

McKinley nodded. "Fair enough. Well, being a reporter, you'll know all about crime investigations, won't you?" The warning was as clear as a clap of thunder: *Don't mess with me, otherwise I'll turn your life upside down.*

"Of course. But what's that got to do with me? And what crime? Has something happened to Henry?"

"Have you been in contact with Mr Pearcy since your last call?"

"No, I haven't. Look, what's happened?" Riley decided to act out the part, since if she clammed up and tried to brush him off, he'd probably go to town on her.

"Have you been out to the Heathrow area at any time in the last eighteen hours?"

Something told her McKinley was waiting for her to say more, and she guessed he knew that she – or someone very like her - had been to the hotel where Henry had disappeared. It was time to come clean. Well, clean-ish. "I went out there this morning," she admitted, putting on a sheepish look. "I was halfway there and forgot which room he'd said he was in. So I rang – to find out."

"Which room did he say?"

"Two-ten."

"You went into the hotel?" The question was casual, like it didn't really matter and he was only going through the motions. He even looked off to one side, as if his heart wasn't in it. But his eyes were too sharp.

"As far as the foyer. I was stopped by an armed officer. He suggested I leave, so I did."

"And you haven't heard from Pearcy since?"

"No. I told you. I rang him again, but got someone else – a wrong number. Look, why is it so difficult to tell me what happened?"

The detective chewed his lip some more as if debating the issue with himself. "The hotel management called to say a fight had taken place early this morning in one of the rooms. A passing patrol found signs of a struggle having taken place in a room registered to Mr Pearcy. His passport was under the bed, so it doesn't look as if he caught his flight out. But we're checking on that."

"What sort of signs?"

"Evidence of an injury. We have reason to believe Mr Pearcy either left in a hurry or was forced to leave by a third party."

"Was anyone seen going to his room?" Riley suddenly realised she had completely overlooked the presence of security cameras and felt the blood drain from her face. The thought that they had her on film skulking around the corridors made her feel sick.

McKinley didn't appear to notice. He nodded. "We're checking all that. Do you know if Mr Pearcy had any enemies – anyone he might have had a disagreement with?"

It was a standard question but she couldn't think of an obvious answer. Reporters picked up their fair share of hate mail, but she couldn't envisage Henry being on anybody's hit list. "No. I can't. He wasn't the sort."

"The sort?"

"You know what I mean."

He shrugged and handed her a card with his name and

number on it. "Please call if you hear from him." He climbed back into the car and was driven away, leaving her with a feeling that in spite of his casual attitude, he hadn't taken anything she'd said at face value.

She went inside and paced around the flat for a while, watched by the cat. In the absence of anyone else as a prime suspect in Henry's disappearance, the police had her. She not only knew Henry, but had phoned him earlier, just prior to his disappearance. She had also turned up at his hotel shortly afterwards, compounding the problem. Even a raw recruit fresh into Hendon wouldn't need long to make a connection out of that.

She sat down at her laptop and fed in what she knew so far. As a possible story it held precious little in the way of solid facts; an unconnected jumble of detail surrounded two main points. One was the disappearance of Katie Pyle, which had now become her return and death, ten years later. The second part was the disappearance – possibly violent – of Henry Pearcy, who claimed to have information about Katie, and seemed to know that her name was familiar to Riley. Yet how could he know anything about her, unless he had reported on it at the time? It was a slim possibility, but one she couldn't ignore.

She stared at the bible, which was the only clue she had. It pointed to Henry definitely having been at the Scandair last night, a fact confirmed by the police. Yet if he'd gone to the trouble of carrying a personal bible with him, would he leave it behind voluntarily?

She flicked through the pages and came back to the flyleaf. It was just possible the Church of Flowing Light might have heard from him, or knew where he might be. She picked up the phone and dialled the number on the inside cover.

"Is he sedated?" The speaker watched with distaste as the two men deposited a bundle on a single bed in an otherwise bare room. It was a man, with traces of dried blood at the corner of his mouth and nose. He was limp and frail looking, and freshly dressed in a pair of old pyjamas. On the floor by the bed lay his recently discarded trousers and shirt, creased and dirty from the floor of the white van parked out front.

"He's out cold," said the man with the glasses. "Don't worry – he won't bite."

"He'd better not," muttered the speaker. "When he comes round, I want to know what he's done and who he's been in touch with." He walked to the door, then turned and gave the unconscious man a malevolent glare. "And I don't care how you get it out of him."

9

Broadcote Hall, the UK headquarters of the Church of Flowing Light, was located in a rambling mansion fifty miles outside London on the fringes of the Cotswolds. Oxford was only twenty minutes away, close by the M40 to London and Birmingham, but civilisation could easily have been a thousand miles beyond, such was the feeling of isolation. Set in several acres of rolling fields and woodland, the property was delineated by a high dry-stone wall bordering the edge of a narrow country road with little regular traffic and few other signs of human life. After the fury and gridlock of London, it was like driving off the edge of the world.

Riley's call the previous afternoon had got a recorded message, telling her that due to an important function nobody was free to take her call, but that callers should leave a message. The voice was male, soft and rich, exuding peace, love and tranquillity like a warm balm.

She hated leaving messages, and once she had traced the address, decided to drop in unannounced first thing next day. There was nothing like catching people unawares, and anyway, weren't church people renowned for their open door policy and ever-simmering pot of tea?

It was ten in the morning by the time she arrived at the twin pillars marking the main entrance. As she turned off the road, she passed the first sign of life since leaving the main road several miles back. A drab, dusty Nissan was parked by the gates, with the bonnet up. The driver, a tall, thin man in a sombre suit and tie, was staring down into the engine cavity. He looked up as she turned in, but gave no response to Riley's nod and sympathetic smile, so she eased on by.

Accustomed to the growing paranoia of the city, Riley had expected some kind of entry-phone arrangement, but other than a small, stone-built lodge which looked unused, and a set of gates standing invitingly open, there was no obvious barrier to simply driving inside.

She followed a rutted driveway towards the main house, passing beneath a straggly canopy of trees just beginning to show signs of budding. There were no signs to greet visitors apart from an arrow directing drivers along the track. The verges on either side were a twin wilderness of tangled grass, dotted with rotting leaves and twigs. Beyond the grass a double band of mature trees formed an effective backdrop which, her suspicious mind noted, even without their covering of leaves, would help keep prying eyes from seeing into the grounds.

After three hundred yards, the track spilled out on to a large open circular area housing a collection of cars. Most looked to be in the luxury class, the paintwork gleaming and polished to a high shine. Riley was surprised. She had been half-expecting a tone of utilitarian restraint governed by calling and necessity, but evidently the people here were well-heeled and not shy of displaying their wealth. She stopped next to a large new Lexus and climbed out on to a stretch of smooth gravel leading up to the main house.

As she reached back into the car to pick up Henry's leather bible, she heard a scrape of movement behind her.

"Welcome to Broadcote Hall."

It was too early for surprises. Riley spun round and saw a tall, gaunt man in a black coat and a charcoal shirt buttoned to the collar, standing against the dark background of trees. His near-skeletal face was the only pale detail, highlighted by flashes of light from a pair of rimless spectacles.

"You shouldn't do that," she told him. "You could give someone a heart attack."

The man tilted his head to one side, a gesture of apology. It was an oddly bird-like movement. For bird, Riley thought, studying the thin frame, read vulture.

"I'm sorry. I didn't mean to frighten you." He didn't look sorry and his words were too cold and precise. He reminded Riley of a particularly spooky dentist she had once known. "I'm Mr Quine. Do you have an appointment?"

Riley shook her head. "No, I don't. But I'd like to talk with the person in charge, if possible. I've driven out from London."

His eyes had fastened on the bible in her hand. "I see. It's a long way to come. I'm afraid we're very busy today. We have an important function in progress." At least that explained the fancy cars. "But it may be possible." He held out one hand, palm upwards. "If I could have your car keys for safekeeping?"

"That won't be necessary. I'm on a flying visit."

His face remained expressionless. "I'm sorry – house rule. All keys are held in reception. It's a precaution in case of emergencies."

"What sort of emergencies?"

Quine shrugged. "I don't make the rules, Miss. It's in case we need to move a vehicle quickly. The car will be perfectly safe, I promise. I'll give you a receipt if you wish." The hand crept forward, insistent.

Riley debated refusing, then thought, what the hell. If she got snitty over her car keys, this might be as far as she got. And this character looked as if he'd enjoy bouncing her right back out of the gates. She needed to find out about Henry. With as much good grace as she could muster, she handed over the keys and received a numbered ticket in exchange. The man nodded and directed her with an open-palmed gesture towards the house.

Up close, the building was bigger than she had first thought, but with the solid, squat appearance of a fortress rather than a home. Architecture wasn't her strong point, but she noted that the house appeared to be composed of a mixture of styles, with little regard for any overall sense of design or continuity. The tall windows overlooking the parking area revealed high-ceilinged rooms and enough wattage from inside to light a small town. The 'important function' was clearly in progress.

Inside the main entrance, Riley found herself in what she took to be the general reception area. It housed a huge oak desk with elaborately carved legs and a worn leather top. On top stood a telephone and a guest book. There was no other furniture and no sign of a receptionist. The walls were covered in dark panelling, with a carpet the colour of dried blood underfoot, though the overall impression lacked warmth. If the rest of the building was like this, she could understand why they needed the lights on during the day.

Riley was about to lift the telephone for directions when a door opened and a large figure appeared. He nodded to her in acknowledgement, leaving a steady buzz of conversation and laughter in the room behind him. After the austere atmosphere of the reception area and the strange man in the car park, such geniality seemed suddenly at odds.

Riley guessed the man was in his late fifties, with a broad

expanse of stomach artfully concealed beneath a well-cut blue blazer with gold buttons. Smart slacks topped highly polished black shoes. She noticed he had small feet. The overall figure was topped by carefully-coiffured hair and a rather fleshy face with several chins rolling over a stiff collar and tie.

She had expected a degree of puzzlement at her unscheduled appearance, but he was smiling as if they were old friends. She half-expected him to make some effusive comment about how long it had been. She also had the feeling he'd been informed the moment she'd arrived, and presumed Quine, the man in the car park, had called ahead.

"Welcome," said the man heartily, holding out his hand. Even with the single word, she instantly recognised the voice from the recorded message. "Welcome to the Church of Flowing Light. It's so nice to have more visitors. I am Pastor de Haan, head of this facility. How may I help you, Miss -?"

"Riley Gavin. I'm sorry for intruding." Riley nodded towards the sound of conversation behind the door. "I've arrived at an awkward moment."

"Oh, no, not at all," he said, almost dismissively. His fingers were warm and dry to the touch, like old leather. He eyed the bible Riley was carrying in the same way Quine had done, although with a slight lift of one eyebrow. "A conference, that's all. We're just enjoying a coffee break. Perhaps you would like some?" He held out a hand and gestured towards the door, moving smoothly for a man of his bulk.

Riley had no choice but to follow as he led the way into a vast, panelled room with ornate plaster cornices and heavy brocade curtains. At the far end was a podium with a microphone and lectern overlooking rows of chairs, and a large banner on the back wall bearing the Church's name and motto. The room was filled with people, some standing, some sitting, but all holding coffee cups and chatting the way crowds do when they have been released from the rigid confines of listening to a speaker.

Pastor de Haan eased through the crowd, patting a shoulder here, pumping a hand there, plainly at ease. He stopped at a heavy oak table where a young man was pouring coffee and milk from silver jugs and offering plates of biscuits. Riley took the coffee but decided against the biscuits. She was already juggling the bible and a handful of bone china. She didn't need to add to her anxiety.

"Now," said the pastor, skilfully edging her to a quiet spot against the wall. "It's true I haven't much time, but I promise I will help as much as I can. That is our mission in life, after all." His smile was open and the voice was carefully modulated. For a brief moment, Riley felt as if she could tell this man almost anything, and reminded herself that she was probably in the presence of an expert at gathering funds and support for his good causes.

"I'm looking for someone," she told him. "A friend called Henry Pearcy. I was hoping you could tell me where he is. He seems to have gone missing."

10

Just for a fraction of a second Pastor de Haan's genial expression wavered, and he appeared to adjust the way he was looking at her. Whether it was the mention of Henry's name or the realisation that she was not about to dip her hand in her wallet and bestow a new wing on his elegant building, Riley wasn't sure. But she had the feeling she was being deftly slotted into a different compartment to the one she might have occupied moments earlier.

"I'm sorry – that's not possible." The refusal came smoothly, the smile easing back into place. For the first time, Riley detected a slight American accent which had been buried earlier by something more overtly European. She had guessed Dutch, because of the name, but now she wasn't so sure. "Not because I wouldn't want to, Miss Gavin," he continued. "It's our policy never to divulge details of our members' activities… or whereabouts."

"So you do know him, then?" Alongside her rush of relief, Riley noticed a change of accent again, this time more American. She wondered which one was the original.

"Yes. We know Henry. What seems to be the problem?"

"I think he might be in danger."

"Danger? Surely not." De Haan's eyes widened at the very idea. Riley couldn't tell if it was meant to convey alarm or scepticism – it was a close call. "What makes you think that?"

"We had a meeting planned. Henry didn't make it." Riley told him about finding Henry's bible in the hotel, and his sudden disappearance. She didn't mention the police or crossing the crime scene tape. His eyes dropped to the bible again and he nodded. "I wondered about that." Before she could stop him, he reached out and plucked it deftly from her hand, flicking back the cover to check the inside. "Our senior members value these highly, Miss Gavin. None of them would willingly leave them lying around, I assure you." The way he said it sounded terse, as if the very crime was punishable by death.

"Senior members?"

"People we value highly for their hard work and efforts on behalf of the Church."

"Financial supporters, you mean?" Riley put the question carefully, one half of her brain trying to analyse the crowd gathered here. She was already wondering how the church managed to maintain a building like Broadcote Hall. It would cost a fortune in heating alone. Neither was possible by simply passing around a silver plate once a week among the faithful. Not unless the faithful were all afflicted by huge wealth and stonking generosity.

De Haan gave a patient smile. "They are few, but nonetheless a solid core of blessed help. We rely solely on the charity and good works of others, you see." He beamed with what might have been gratitude, although to Riley's cynical soul it looked more like an inner core burning with the heat of self-satisfaction.

"And these people?" She nodded towards the crowd. From what she could see, they matched the opulence of the vehicles in the car park. Of varying ages, but with a preponderance of middle years, they all had the groomed appearance of people secure in themselves and their place in society, and there was an abundance of expensive jewellery on display . Among the smart suits and dresses she thought a couple of faces seemed vaguely familiar.

"Indeed. Like these good people. But without supporters

like Henry to focus on reaching out to the right quarters, we would have nothing and be nothing. Tell me, what is your… relationship with Henry?"

"I used to work with him. We were friends, but haven't seen each other in a while."

This seemed to satisfy him. "Yes. We all need friends, don't we? Did Henry tell you about us?" He offered another coffee and Riley wondered if she was being shuffled back gently towards the box marked 'potential donor'.

"Henry didn't talk much about his private life," she replied truthfully. "But then, neither do I."

"Very wise, too. All too often we become labelled by what we do, don't we? It shouldn't matter, of course, but it does. Being in business doesn't preclude being charitable, after all." There it was again: the nudge towards the possibility of being one of the generous few. She decided to turn the conversation back to Henry.

"Can you tell me if Henry is OK? I'm worried about him."

"Of course," de Haan replied. "In fact I'll do better than that – I'll get him to call you. I'm sure he didn't mean to alarm anyone… he'll be most upset at the idea." He studied a fingernail, tilting his hand to catch the light as if suddenly finding an unexpected blemish. "Although I can't guarantee he'll respond. He has been under a great deal of stress lately. But then, as a friend, you probably know about that?" A raised eyebrow accompanied the questioning tone at the end of the sentence, a gentle signal meant to reassure her that she was among mutual friends and could safely unload all her secrets. Riley ignored it.

"I didn't. But I do know he left his job recently."

"So he did. It was all part of the… umm… problem. A difficult time for anyone – especially at his age. But I'm sure he'll come through it with our – and God's – help." He flicked a glance upwards in deference to the higher authority. "For sure we have plenty of work for Henry to do." He smiled again and by the briefest of gestures, managed to turn Riley back towards the door to reception, a clear signal that it was time for her to leave.

"This work," Riley said, sensing she wasn't about to get anywhere further with Henry's whereabouts. "What do you do, exactly?"

The pastor seemed surprised by the question and appeared to relax slightly, relieved, perhaps, to be on more familiar ground. He held the door as though unwilling to pass through. "That's right – you said Henry didn't tell you. Well, among other things, Miss Gavin, we bring help and succour to those in need, in any way we can. A necessary result of our times, I'm afraid." He replaced his smile with a more sombre expression. "We help the disaffected," he continued, with a sudden rising note in his voice, the energy if not the volume catching the attention of people nearby. A born showman. "The lost, the weak and the disadvantaged – we hold out a hand to the ones who can't help themselves. To the ones who have been rejected, the ones who are unwanted, we offer the hand of friendship. After all, if we don't, who will?"

A woman nearby clapped enthusiastically in appreciation, causing de Haan to raise a hand in modest acknowledgement. A tall, hawkish man beside her looked less impressed, while other listeners seemed poised to come nearer and join in. But a sudden crackling and thumping sound from the speaker system signalled that it was time to resume.

"You go out looking for them?" Riley asked, as the crowd shuffled back to their seats. The dewy-eyed woman cast a backward glance as if she would have preferred to stay and listen to de Haan rather than whatever discussion was on offer from the speaker. "That can't be an easy task."

"We rarely need to do that, Miss Gavin." He placed a soft hand beneath her elbow and steered her through the door, letting it swing shut behind him. "They come to us. They seek us out, you see, and when they find us, they know they have found salvation. For we can give them something their families have been unable to." His grip hardened on her arm and she decided that whatever lard covered Pastor de Haan's body was based on an ample foundation of muscle. "Or maybe unwilling."

"Love, you mean?" This was ground she had trodden before, when she felt herself drawn into the cloying atmosphere surrounding the disappearance of Katie Pyle. The questions were invariably the same: was it lack of love that had caused her to leave? Had her parents and friends been negligent in some way? Could they have done more for her?

De Haan looked almost affronted. "Oh, no, Miss Gavin. We don't offer love. That would be too simple… and in the end, meaningless. What we offer is something much more lasting."

"Really?"

"Too often these unfortunates have had no place, no status, no meaning. They have been educated, it is true – sometimes very expensively. Clothed, of course, even indulged, if mere possessions can be termed an indulgence. But in the end they have been all too often rejected, ignored and, very often, treated with indifference… or worse." He blinked, his mouth curling in a faint expression of distaste at the idea. "Far worse, some of them, poor souls. What we seek to do is redress the balance, either by bringing them back to their families in a caring and beneficial way when they have strayed, or if they have chosen their own path, by giving them a place in another, wider family. It's the least we can do."

Riley wasn't sure what to say. Position rather than love; status within a group instead of caring. It was certainly a different approach from the norm, and who was to say they weren't right? But before she could comment there was a crackle of electronic feedback in the room they had just left, signalling the resumption of the conference, and de Haan clapped his hands together with a smile. Riley could have sworn he looked relieved. "Now, I really must apologise, but I need to get back. We have a very busy programme to get through."

A movement of shadow made Riley turn her head. Mr Quine was standing just inside the entrance, feet apart and hands clasped in front like a praetorian guard. Against the relative gloom of the wooden panelling, his dark clothing made him look even more like a bird of prey.

"Thank you," Riley said. She wondered if knowing about de Haan's organisation would have helped Katie Pyle. Something told her, maybe not. She extended her hand, but instead of taking it, de Haan stepped away. Clearly the audience was over.

Riley suddenly remembered Henry's bible. She turned back and retrieved it from the pastor's grasp. He looked dismayed for a moment, glancing quickly past her towards Quine, who began moving across the floor towards them. In that instant, Riley felt a sudden flicker of menace in the air. Then de Haan coughed and waved a quick hand, and Quine stopped in his tracks.

Riley had no idea what had just happened, nor why having the bible back was important. But she figured when Henry did turn up, she wanted to be the one to return it to him. *If* he turned up. Suddenly she was no longer sure that would ever happen.

She stopped in front of Quine and held out her hand. He stared at her without expression, then slowly handed back her car keys. She got the feeling he was imprinting her every facial detail on his mind for future reference, and the idea made her feel uncomfortable. She nodded coolly and walked past him out on to the drive.

She got back into the car and drove out to the main road, turning towards London. She felt unsettled by what had just happened; she'd been in the place little more than twenty minutes, and had learned precious little, save that pastor de Haan wasn't quite what he pretended, and Quine was too spooky for words. What she had confirmed was that Henry belonged to a charity and had been under some stress lately. Or maybe it was just more of the stress he had carried with him all those years ago. It might explain his odd behaviour, such as leaving his job without telling anybody. But it still didn't explain why he had wanted to see her so urgently, or how he came to know Katie Pyle's name. Odder still was that, in spite of doing good works, the charity caring for him wasn't about to let her anywhere near him to find out. It was mildly irritating but she could hardly force the issue; if he was one of them, it was presumably normal for the organisation to want to protect one of their own. She debated the point with herself for a couple of miles of narrow road, then pulled into a lay-by and took out her mobile. As she did so, a familiar car drove slowly by, the driver turning to give her a long look. It was the motorist she had seen staring into the engine compartment of his Nissan at the entrance to Broadcote Hall. Maybe he'd tried the power of prayer.

De Haan and the man called Quine stood in the doorway

and watched Riley drive away. The pastor shook his head with a hiss of disapproval. When he spoke it was with a chilly tone of accusation.

"It's beginning to get out of hand. How did she get this far?"

Quine shrugged, unruffled. "Pearcy must have spoken to her after all."

"But you said he hadn't!" A bubble appeared at de Haan's mouth. He checked himself, aware that anger achieved little. "If Friedman gets to her as well, everything will be ruined."

"He won't." Quine casually rearranged some pamphlets on a windowsill. One was slightly damaged. He tore it slowly in two, then put the two halves together and tore them again, before dropping the pieces in a waste bin. "I've got it covered."

"How?"

Quine smiled, his demeanour that of an equal. "He won't get to her. That's all you need to know."

11

Frank Palmer's office in Uxbridge hadn't changed much since the last time Riley had called. In spite of a lick of paint which had freshened things up slightly, it still exuded a faint air of gloom, as if the walls were in need of a good chuckle. Or maybe it was the ancient, battered furniture and the fluorescent lighting which killed any potential atmosphere at birth. Palmer was standing at the window overlooking the street. He seemed unusually thoughtful and waved a vague hand towards a mug of coffee already waiting for her on his desk. She guessed he had seen her arrive.

Riley joined him at the window. As views went, she couldn't see what he found so enthralling.

"What's the problem?" Palmer turned and sat down.

"This is surprisingly good coffee, Palmer. Did I say there was a problem?"

"First, thank you for the compliment – the Kenyans will be deeply chuffed. Second, I could hear it in your voice when you called."

"Clever dick." Riley had called Palmer soon after leaving Broadcote Hall. He had just finished escorting his Saudi prince through check-in and was on his way back to the office clutching a cheque and trying to think how to spend it.

She told him about the phone call from Henry, the follow-up, the events at the hotel at Heathrow and the brick wall she had run into at the Church of Flowing Light. When she told him the background about Katie Pyle he looked sombre.

"Sad business," he said. If he was surprised by the fact that she had never mentioned it before, he didn't say. In fact, he said very little, absorbing everything like a sponge and occasionally drumming his fingers on his knee. She recognised it as one of his old de-briefing tricks, leaving her to do all the talking and probably saying far more than she might have intended. In the end he waved his hand in the air. "This… Henry Pearcy bloke," he said. "You said you didn't know much about his private life; for instance that he was a bible basher. Does that mean he wouldn't have known much about you, either?"

"We were colleagues, not bosom buddies."

"And Katie's disappearance?"

"I never told him. It wasn't something I talked about. It was hardly my best journalistic moment."

"You were young and inexperienced. Don't beat yourself up over it." It was Palmer's usual pragmatic approach: change it if you can, if not, get over it and move on. "Not that I'm saying you're not still young."

"How tactful."

"Yet this Henry calls Donald in the middle of the night, looking for you because there's a mystery bloke trying to contact you. During which, he mentions a missing girl by name – a name you say he couldn't – shouldn't – have known." He looked at her apologetically. "Sorry – I need to spell out the blindingly obvious. It gets the grey cells working. Going over old ground often yields surprising nuggets."

"Henry mentioned Katie by name, yes. But when I asked if this mystery caller did, he said not. I think that was a mistake."

"Unless he actually discovered you had been assigned to the story originally."

"I don't see how. I only met Henry about a year afterwards. By then it was history. And the paper closed years
ago."

"I see. And this bloke… the one he said was looking for
you; no clues about what he wanted other than to talk
about Katie?"

"That's right. Henry said he'd tell me about it face to
face. He sounded stressed."

"Maybe he realised he'd said too much." Palmer held her
look with a steady gaze, doing what he did best, which was
to question everything and tease it apart. She suddenly
knew how wayward members of the British army must
have felt when he was in the Special Investigations Branch.

"But why would he lie?" Now she was doing it, only she
wasn't yet convinced that Henry had done anything
wrong. It was becoming clear that he'd not been entirely
truthful, either about still working or telling her
everything he knew about the caller. But maybe his
intention had been simply to meet up with Riley and tap
her for work.

"Good point. But without him to tell us, or this mystery
man turning up, we're never going to know." He yawned.
"So where do we go from here, boss?"

"You mean where do I go. I wanted to pick your brains,
that's all. I can't pay you. And as stories go, this might
fizzle out into nothing."

"You don't have to pay me. Call it reciprocal co-operation.
I might need your help one day. We'll work something out.
Cook me a meal, iron my socks… something menial." He
grinned and stood up. "I've got some contacts in the Met.
I could ask around, see if they've got anything on the dead
woman. Might be worth having a look round Pearcy's gaff,
though."

"On the grounds of?" Riley didn't bother arguing with him; he'd insist on sticking his nose in whether she wanted him to or not. Besides, he was good at this sort of thing.

"On the grounds that if somebody else found it worthwhile paying a visit, then we should, too. Anyway, people rarely disappear without leaving something behind."

"But he hasn't disappeared. He's with the Church of Flowing Light."

Palmer looked cynical. "Yeah, right. And whose word have you got for that?"

Riley felt a rush of relief. At least Palmer shared her feelings about de Haan and Quine – and he hadn't even met them. She had previously dismissed the idea of going back to Pinner. But Palmer brought with him a wealth of experience and a fresh perspective, and might uncover something she would have missed. She recalled writing Henry's address on the missing person flyer, and showed it to him.

He looked at the address long enough to memorise it, then glanced at the photo on the front. He was about to pass it back, then did a double-take. "Christ – I know this kid." He checked the name. "If it's the same one, her old man was an Air Commodore in the MOD. He'd been given a desk jockey job… something to do with procurement."

"Are you sure?"

"Definite. I remember the name. He brought her down to a test firing on the Salisbury ranges a few years ago. I was there to boost security and he asked me to look after her while he was out watching squaddies make banging noises. She was a nice kid."

"According to her family, so was Katie Pyle."

12

Riley returned to Holland Park to find another message on her machine from John Mitcheson. Maybe the fates were trying to tell her something.

"Riley? Sorry I've missed you again…what a pain. I'm off to Florida for several days on a job. Pity you can't make it over here. We need to talk. I miss you. My mobile number's —"

She punched the stop button with a degree of venom. Was this his idea of psychological torture? What would be next — the sound of him singing in the shower? The rattle of his snoring? She wished she could tell him about the assignment. He would have had a way of reducing things to their bare essentials and cutting though all the froth. A bit like Frank Palmer, only less deliberately irritating.

She booted up her laptop and focused on what she had so far. If she didn't get something in to Donald soon, to show there was a story, he was going to start bothering her. But after five minutes of typing, she had pathetically little on the screen in the way of hard facts, with more conjecture than solid, provable detail. It wasn't enough, any more than her feelings about de Haan and his spooky colleague, Quine. And trying to construct a story which confessed to her invading a crime scene at the Scandair Hotel was a sure way of committing professional suicide. She leapt up and roamed the flat, making coffee and letting it go cold while the cat vied for her attention, head-butting her whenever she came within range until she got the message. In between strokes, she mulled over what was puzzling her most. If there was a link between Katie and Henry and his subsequent disappearance, she still couldn't

78

see it. The two events were totally disconnected by time and circumstance. Yet there had to be something.

She was also bugged by the idea of someone looking for her. Was it someone she had met while working on Katie's story? If so, he had left it a long time to try and make contact. Unless he knew something about Katie's disappearance. With Henry out of the picture, would he continue looking for Riley or would the necessity to find her wither and die?

She picked up the leather bible where she had left it on the coffee table and idly fanned through the pages, hoping perhaps that some divine inspiration might fall from them. But other than the musty book-smell of print and paper, nothing did.

Something about it was bothering her. It was tugging away at her consciousness like a fish pulling at bait on the end of a line; you know something is there but until it surfaces, you have no idea what it might be. It was something familiar… yet it stayed just beyond reach. The last bible Riley had seen was probably in the church at her father's funeral.

After a while she gave up and went for a walk, leaving the cat to finish cleaning itself. Maybe some fresh air would help clear her mind. The sky was the colour of dirty sheets, and it was grey and cold enough to keep people indoors, which suited her fine.

Riley crossed Holland Park Avenue, dodging with casual ease through a gap in the traffic, then cut through to the park. As usual it was like entering another world – one of tranquillity and continuity, with the whisper of the trees and the scurrying sound of wildlife in the undergrowth. Along the trails between a stretch of beech trees were the usual baby walkers and doggie freaks, today hunched under umbrellas against drops of water falling from the branches overhead. Most were tucked inside fleeces and thick jumpers to ward off the cold wind, the exception being a group of four women, apparently impervious to the elements and chattering away in Russian, pausing only to dart off and retrieve an errant child making a bid for freedom in the bushes. She skirted the pond with its statue of Lord Holland and crossed an expanse of green towards the gardens and Orangerie. A jogger flitted between the trees on a trail to her left, moving with an easy gait. He was sporting a long coat rather than the usual designer wear favoured by local jogging freaks, but Riley doubted anyone would notice; stranger things were seen every day in this area.

She walked through the Arcade with its nineteenth century murals, and wandered out to the sports field, where she stood and stared across the open space. Another shower of rain was gusting towards her, so she went back and bought a cup of tea from the park café and stood under one of the archways, sipping it and watching two old men playing chess. They seemed frozen in place, staring at the board as if eyeball contact alone would move the pieces into a winning position.

The air was cold enough to chill salmon. She dumped her empty cup in a bin and began walking across the park.

She emerged on to a damp, wind-swept Kensington High Street with no clear thought of where to go next. Home seemed a good idea. She had walked enough. Time to get back and do something constructive.

As she turned to retrace her steps, a rectangle of pale paper taped to a street light caught her eye. It had the forlorn, wet look of another 'missing' flyer with a photo and contact details. This time the subject was a small

Yorkie named Ralph. It wasn't only humans who went missing.

Then Riley felt as if she'd been punched in the chest.

The flyer.

Of course. The flyer she'd found in the coffee shop about Angelina Boothe-Davison, and the leather bible from Henry's room. Suddenly the connection was blindingly obvious. She wanted to race back and confirm it with her own eyes before it slipped away.

Her mobile rang. It was Palmer. "Walk across the main entrance to the park and don't look round," he said calmly. "Turn up Abbotsbury Road and keep walking."

"Why? What the hell are you talking about, Palmer? Anyway, I've just thought of something."

"Never mind that. You've got company."

"What?"

"A white van's been dogging you since you left home. Two men inside, and neither of them looks friendly."

"What?"

"One of them followed you through the park on foot… a tall bloke in a long coat. I don't think they're after your autograph."

13

It took Riley a real effort of will not to turn her head and stare. The jogger she had spotted through the trees earlier? But what the hell was Palmer doing here? He must have been behind her all the way from the flat. Or Uxbridge.

Riley followed his instructions and turned to her right, walking along the pavement past the park entrance. The traffic flashing past on her left was a muddle of cars and buses, with a sprinkling of bikes and revving scooters weaving in and out to gain extra yardage. No white van, though.

"Could they be police?" Riley wondered if DC McKinley had decided to put a tail on her to check her story.

"Nah. They'd find a spot and let you come to them, then double ahead. These two jokers like to keep on the move, as if they don't want to get caught on a double yellow." He chuckled with evident satisfaction. "Seems you've perked up someone's interest. This is good."

"Good? How the hell can it be good, Palmer? Did you get the number?"

"Got it, logged it, phoned it in." He didn't say where he'd phoned it in to, but her guess was a contact with a finger on a reliable vehicle-licensing database.

She continued walking with the phone clamped to her ear, pretending to ignore everything around her but scanning the surrounding traffic. She had a hint, but that was all: white, as Palmer had said, and nondescript, with no markings. You could see a hundred like them any day of the week, anonymous and unremarkable apart from their apparent disregard for traffic regulations and anyone else on the road.

"Keep going," said Palmer calmly, as she took the first road to her right after the park. "If they keep to their pattern so far, they'll turn off in a minute and go round the block, then come up behind you and play catch-up." He gave a snort of disgust. "It's criminal. I mean, if they're going to play silly buggers, they could at least do it properly." He sounded genuinely offended, as if they were letting the side down. Then he told her to get ready, because as soon as they were out of sight, he was going to do a drive-by and pick her up. Riley crossed to the left-hand side of the road to make it easier for him.

Moments later a scruffy Saab 95 slid into the kerb alongside her and Palmer popped open the door. She slid inside and he took off again immediately. He drove fast and with a deceptively casual air, slowing only to negotiate speed bumps in the road. Then it was foot down on the accelerator, the engine humming so smoothly Riley could have balanced an egg on the bonnet. The thup-thup of the windscreen wipers filled the silence.

After dropping her off outside the flat, Palmer disappeared to park his car a couple of streets away, then trotted back. Once inside he stood at the window facing on to the street, studying the traffic. A few minutes later he nodded with satisfaction. "Right on cue."

Riley peered past him just as a white van drifted slowly past the front of the building. The windows were too dark to see through, but the passenger side window was lowered, showing a section of narrow, pale face and close-to-the-bone cropped hair. "They know where I live."

"Yes. I first spotted them a couple of days ago. I came round for coffee but you were out. Yesterday morning I saw them again. What they won't know is how you got back here so quickly. It'll have thrown 'em for a bit."

"They'll assume by taxi." She looked at him. "If they've been out there a couple of days, why didn't you mention it before?"

"So you could do what – go out and kick their door in? I wanted to be sure first. I think it's safe to assume they've been following you for some time, and they might know about me, too." His mobile beeped and he took it out and listened. Riley handed him a notepad and pencil, but he waved it away before thanking the person on the other end and switching off. "Well, well. Sometimes we find out more by what we don't know than what we do." He didn't explain the cryptic comment but looked hopefully towards the kitchen, rubbing his hands. "Coffee, I think."

"Help yourself," said Riley and left him to it. She knew he'd soon tire of the smug act and tell her what he was thinking. She didn't really care how he got his information, as long as he didn't keep her in the dark.

"All right, so who are they?" She felt annoyed at being the first to give way.

"You first."

"Sorry?"

"You said earlier you'd thought of something. What was it?"

She picked up the missing persons flyer from the coffee shop and passed it to him. He studied it for a moment, front and back. "I saw this before. So?"

Riley pointed to the phone number underneath the pic-ture of Angelina Boothe-Davison. Then she picked up the leather bible. When she flicked open the cover and pointed to the stamp inside, he looked puzzled.

"The bible is from Henry's hotel room," she explained. "The flyer was in a coffee shop down the street from here.

Look at the phone numbers."

He did. "It's the same." He was staring at the bible with an odd expression on his face, as if genuinely surprised. That was another first. "Isn't it usually the family who put out these flyers?"

"Usually." She had helped Katie's parents do the same, tramping around the streets pinning posters to anything solid. They'd probably been breaking all sorts of by-laws, but at the time she figured a missing teenager trumped regulations any day. She took over making the coffee while Palmer studied the piece of paper. While it brewed she took out her phone and dialled the number inside the bible, then pressed the button for loudspeaker. After three rings, there was a hiss of static, then a click, and de Haan's familiar and theatrical voice echoed richly around the room to a faint soundtrack of organ music. This time, instead of the announcement about the important function, the words were more traditional:

"You have reached the message service of The Church of Flowing Light. If you have information about our missing persons, please press two and leave a message. If you require further information about our services, please press three and leave your name and address. We will get back to you. Thank you for calling."

She switched off the phone.

"Pretty one-sided," said Palmer, "for a church that relies on sponsors. You'd think they would need to grab every caller first time round."

Riley nodded. "But it answers the question about that phone number and confirms what de Haan told me; they trace missing kids."

"Yes. And most likely on behalf of the families. Must be worth a few quid to some people." Palmer looked sideways at her, a glimmer of a smile on his lips.

"You're an old cynic."

"You bet. It keeps me young." He stared at the ceiling. "Right, logic time. You never came across this church before?"

"No."

"So, it's a coincidence. They help people in need, they distribute bibles in hotels and they search for runaway kids. It's not illegal and they're not the only ones. And Henry is a member, supporter, whatever. Good for him."

"Except I can't understand why de Haan wouldn't let me speak to Henry."

"Maybe he was telling the truth, and Henry had some kind of breakdown. It happens." He waited while she digested the logic. Common sense dictated that if de Haan and his Church were truly looking after Henry and concerned with his welfare, she didn't need to concern herself about him any longer. The presence of the bible was a clear indication that they already had some kind of relationship, and were probably the best people to care for him. But were they? Her suspicions, already stirred by de Haan's changing accent and Quine's palpable aura of menace, were increasing steadily.

"Henry might have asked him to keep callers away," Palmer continued. "Breakdowns and stress affect people in different ways. Some let it all out, others just want to find somewhere to hide."

"Well, thanks for that input, Doctor Palmer," Riley said dryly. "And here was I thinking you were going to tell me my suspicions were absolutely correct and the whole thing was a conspiracy. Why do you think the men in the van know about you?"

"Because when you came to the office, I got a tingly

feeling in my neck. Never fails me."

"Tingly as in –?"

"The white van. It stopped along the street after you arrived. Same colour, same tinted windows. Where I come from, only people with something to hide use tinted glass."

"But it was just a van. The streets are full of them." Even as she said it, she knew it wasn't as simple as that. People like Palmer seemed to operate on a different wavelength from the rest of humanity. In this case he had been right. It explained why he had seemed so thoughtful when she walked into his office.

"The passenger window was down a couple of inches and the bloke inside was watching your car. He was trying to look casual but he got careless." Palmer made it sound like a criminal offence. "When they took off after you, I decided to follow. They tailed you right back here. Definitely suspicious."

"I didn't notice."

"No reason why you should. Spotting a tail in busy traffic is a tough job. But I've had the training," he added smugly.

Riley was annoyed; she had been so fixated on finding out what Henry could have known about Katie, she had totally missed the procession behind her. She went back over her movements for the past two days, trying to work out how long the van might have been there. Nothing came to mind. "Thanks, I owe you," she said, and meant it. Such carelessness could have been serious. "What about the number… did your friend in the ministry of mystery registration numbers find out who it belongs to?"

Palmer shook his head. "The number fits a Fiat Punto written off seven months ago."

Riley frowned. "I thought you said you knew something

about them."

"I do. I know that whoever these people are, they're definitely not legal. Now all we've got to do is find out who they are and want they want."

A hundred yards away, the white van idled at the kerb, shielded from Riley's flat by a large removals lorry. The driver, Meaker, looked at his colleague for instructions. He wasn't empowered to make decisions, and was quietly hoping he wasn't about to get the blame for losing the woman outside the park.

"She had help." Quine spoke dispassionately. He kicked some leaf mould from one boot, where he'd been running through the trees. "She had to, disappearing like that."

"Should we go and look? They could be up there," Meaker ventured, eager to encourage the deflection of responsibility.

Quine shook his head, his jaw muscles moving. "No. She'll keep for later. Her and whoever helped her."

14

Henry's house looked undisturbed and empty, with no obvious signs of activity. Riley eased the Golf into a space eighty yards from the entrance and waited. It was late afternoon and the suburban road was quiet and deserted, apart from Palmer, who was checking the area on foot. It could have been her imagination or the effects of the dull weather, but she thought the house now wore the unique air of desolation which seems to cloak deserted buildings when their human occupants are not coming back.

She joined Palmer on the pavement as he came abreast of the car.

"This should do," he said. They were close enough to the house to pick the car up in a hurry, yet sufficiently far away for it to be missed by anyone keeping watch on the front door. "If anybody has got the place under surveillance, they'll expect us to park up close."

They had decided earlier to hit the two houses – the neighbour's and Henry's – simultaneously. They each carried clipboards and were trying to look like canvassers working the street. Privately, Riley didn't think Palmer looked like any canvasser she had ever seen, but no doubt he would argue that he would get by on charm. Part of the plan was for him to work that charm on the Neighbourhood Watch supremo, while Riley got inside Henry's place. She hadn't been able to think of a logical reason for coming back so soon after her last visit, so it would be better if the elderly neighbour didn't see her.

Riley turned down Henry's drive, the gravel crunching loudly underfoot. If anyone was watching it would look too suspicious if she kept to the grass, so she gritted her teeth and marched along as if she had every right to be there. Off to her right, Palmer was doing the same. She reached the front door and pressed the bell. Count to thirty. Press again. Count another twenty for luck. No sounds from inside and no sign of movement through the slit windows either side of the door. The corner of an envelope was protruding from the letterbox, which meant the post hadn't been touched today. She heard Palmer pounding on the door on the other side of the fence and whistling cheerfully, already playing his part to distract attention from Riley.

The garage doors were still shut, so she walked over and looked through the crack. It showed the same empty space and the same oil tray with its glutinous black deposit, the surface now covered by a scum of dust and bits of leaf. She walked round to the back and peered through the honeysuckle-clad gate, one ear cocked for noises. It would be crass to go charging through the house only to find the old neighbour giving the cat an early tea.

She crossed the patio to the kitchen door. The same shards of glass were on the floor, except now a faint outline of a dried footprint showed alongside them. It had probably been there on her first visit but it had been too damp to see clearly. Judging by the size, which was at least a nine, it had not been made by the old lady.

Riley tried the door and, surprisingly, found it open. She wiped her feet carefully on a small brown mat, stepped over the slivers of glass and looked around. A fork was lying in the middle of the work surface, with remnants of what looked like cat food stuck to the prongs. An empty dish stood nearby, licked clean save for a smear of dried jelly.

She did a rapid scout of the ground floor. Out of the kitchen down a carpeted hallway, into a living room on one side and a dining room on the other. A downstairs cloakroom opened off the entrance lobby on one side, with stairs nearby, and across from it and looking out on to the front, a large study. A room to come back to.

Back out and across the lobby and up the stairs. There was a double twist in the staircase leading to a landing. She didn't like the idea of that open space above her, but there was no choice other than to keep going. Wimping out now wouldn't achieve anything. Four bedrooms, ranging from master to smallish, with no signs of regular occupancy in the first three. A toilet and a bathroom, then an airing cupboard. A faint trace of soap or air-freshener. And something else she couldn't place. Musty, like the inside of an old wardrobe.

A sudden flash of movement made her start and a black and white cat streaked past her on the way downstairs. It had come skidding out of the last room facing the rear of the house. Riley felt the hairs on her neck move and stepped quickly up to the open doorway, holding her breath. She had momentary visions of the old lady coming out, having chased the cat to stop it soiling the carpet, and screaming the place down when she saw an intruder.

But the old lady wasn't going anywhere, and any screaming had probably been done earlier.

She was lying on the room's double bed, her face turned to the ceiling, arms by her side. She looked oddly elegant, but a shadow of her former self. Her skin was as pale as parchment, and any wrinkles she'd possessed seemed to have smoothed themselves, as if fate had decided that death was bad enough, without being old too.

Riley couldn't see any signs of a struggle, but the old

lady plainly hadn't got here by choice. Her clothes were neat, and her dark cardigan carried traces of white hairs where the cat had been nestling against her side. Riley thought about the fork on the kitchen work surface and guessed that was where she had been surprised. Carrying her up here afterwards would have been no problem; there was almost nothing of her.

Riley made her way downstairs and called Palmer. When he answered she told him to come round the back through the kitchen and to wipe his feet.

"No answer next door," he said, when he joined her moments later. "Maybe she thinks I'm a Mormon." He sniffed the air and frowned, then noticed Riley's face. "What's up?"

She nodded at the ceiling. "It's the old lady. She's dead. Last door on the left. I'm going to do the study if you want to have a scout around up there."

He nodded and disappeared upstairs. Riley entered the study, trying to dismiss the mental image of the old lady on the bed upstairs and concentrate on the task in hand. The room was a typical male preserve, dark and solid in furnishings and tone. A heavy antique desk and a club chair stood squarely in front of the window, the surface holding a clutter of papers and a coiled black power cable. Bookcases lined the walls, and other than a side-table holding a small combination television and VCR, the only other items of furniture were a sofa and a recliner chair with a week-old copy of the *Radio Times* on the extended footrest.

The desk drawers yielded little other than the usual household items; bank statements, old bills, a few assorted batteries and a bunch of pens and pencils held together with an elastic band. Judging by the hotel names, Henry liked to collect souvenirs on his travels. In the bottom drawer she found a small stack of pamphlets showing a traditional biblical scene of fishermen in the Holy Land staring up at a ray of light coming from the heavens. The picture was topped by heavy lettering in black and gold, with the now familiar words:

THE CHURCH OF FLOWING LIGHT. WELCOME ALL WHO ARE UNLOVED AND ENTER HERE.

Behind these were some old leaflets announcing a fete in support of funds to set up a drop-in centre in Southampton. It was dated two years ago. Next to it was a stack of envelopes with the same title on the back flap, and underneath these was a box of lapel badges with the name of the church in neat, gold lettering. On the very bottom was a photograph of a group of grinning youngsters standing round a picnic table. They looked self-conscious and awkward, and one or two had even turned away or raised their hands in protest. The shots were slightly blurred and grainy, as if they had been taken from a film or video reel. In the background Henry was grinning and holding aloft a sandwich and a glass of drink. He looked as if he was the only one happy to be caught on camera.

There was no indication on the reverse side of where or when it had been taken. From the subjects' clothing, Riley guessed it could have been any time in the last five years. She peered closely at Henry, but he looked no different from when she had last seen him - tall and gaunt and somehow effortlessly comfortable.

Riley took one of the leaflets and the photo, then checked through the bookcases. Henry's library seemed to be big on biographies, which came as a surprise. She couldn't tell if they had been read or were simply there for shelf yardage. He also seemed to have a keen interest in company information, with an extensive collection of business directories covering the UK and Europe, and a carefully stacked section of business magazines such as *Fortune, Business Week* and several volumes of *Who's Who*.

The side table holding the small television and VCR had a couple of videos in cases and one empty case. On the spine of each were titles in Henry's spidery hand, proving he was a *Newsnight* and *Panorama* fan.

She couldn't see anything which helped and went back into the lobby just as Palmer was coming downstairs. He looked as cool as always, but she knew he would have been thorough, ignoring the dross and inspecting anything that seemed promising.

"Nothing up there," he said. "If I was a betting man, I'd say the place has been sanitised."

"Any guesses?"

"About how she died?" He shrugged. "She must have disturbed them when she came round to feed the cat. There's some bruising around the mouth, but that's all. She couldn't have put up much of a struggle."

Riley showed Palmer the pamphlet and the photo of Henry. "It looks like he's a fully paid-up member of the Church after all."

He nodded and checked the cloakroom, expertly flicking through coats and jackets and humming softly while he did it. He found a slip of paper and handed it to Riley. It carried a familiar phone number and name: Donald Brask.

"He went out without his coat." Beneath the coats was a small padded case, the kind used for carrying a laptop. He nudged it with his toe but it was empty. "Did you see a laptop anywhere?"

"No. But there's a power lead on the desk."

"Point one for the killer. He – or they – probably came

here for the same reason we did and picked it up on the way out."

"Why not take the case?"

"Less obvious…easier to hide a laptop under a coat… couldn't be bothered. Maybe they panicked."

Riley stepped across to the front door, where the white envelope she had seen from the outside was hanging from the letterbox. It was junk mail. She looked around; there were no other envelopes in evidence, which meant either the old lady had moved any recent mail or the killer had taken it.

As she moved away from the door, she heard the crunch of gravel outside. She peered through the side window. A police patrol car had pulled up in the driveway.

15

The two of them reacted simultaneously, grabbing their clipboards and running for the back door. For whatever reason the police were here, Riley guessed they weren't collecting for the Annual Policemen's Ball. They had been tipped off, possibly by the old lady's killer.

Palmer led the way down the garden and over a fence, showing a surprising turn of speed. They ducked beneath some ancient apple trees and walked down a narrow path between two properties, out on to another street lined with trees and cars.

"Someone," breathed Palmer, when they were safely back in the car and heading south, "knew we were there."

Riley nodded. Either that or another nosy neighbour had seen them. "I vote we take a look at the Church. Soon."

"Seconded and unanimous."

By the time Riley dropped Palmer off at his car and made her way back home, the light was fading and traffic was heavy. If anyone was following her, it was going to be virtually impossible to spot them. And the fact that there was now no sign of a white van meant nothing; the men inside could have changed vehicles.

When she opened the front door, she discovered a folded wad of newspaper pushed through her letterbox. She was about to toss it in the bin in the hall when she noticed someone had scrawled a vivid red circle on the outer sheet. She unfolded the wad and saw there were two separate cuttings: one a single paragraph about a woman's body found along the Embankment near Chelsea, the other a report by Nikki Bruce, the author of the previous report Riley had read about dead runaways. Both cuttings were from the early editions of the *Post*.

The report on the woman mentioned only that the body wore a crucifix and a bracelet and that the police were investigating. There was no mention of the victim's name. The Nikki Bruce piece was on a different subject and more informative.

A further addition to the street mortality statistics was revealed today when photo shop manager, George Poustalis, arrived at his premises just off Piccadilly and discovered the body of a young man beside a nearby builders' skip. There were no indications of the youth's identity, but police put his age at approximately 18 years. It is thought the youth may have been one of the regular homeless sleepers living rough in what is arguably one of the capital's most exclusive postcodes. A post-mortem is expected to reveal that the death is drugs-related, although an officer at the scene suggested there were signs that the victim had died of choking. The death is not thought to be suspicious in nature. This now brings the number of deaths of street-sleepers in the capital to eight, most of which appear drugs-related. Local drugs counsellors working with the homeless community have confirmed that contaminated drugs are circulating, and are warning users against taking further risks by buying supplies from unfamiliar sources.

Riley went upstairs and peered out of the front window, wondering who had left this for her. Other than the usual street traffic there was nobody in sight. If someone was out there waiting for a reaction, they clearly weren't standing out in the open to advertise their presence.

She read both cuttings through again, feeling a prickle of discomfort. Why had somebody chosen to push these cuttings through the door? Was this meant as some kind of pointer about what had finally happened to Katie? Had her death down by the river after all these years been simply as a victim of a drug her body had been unable to withstand?

Riley didn't think so. The Katie she had known of had shown no interest in drugs. Her parents had sworn it, her closest friends had confirmed it and there had been no indications in her room of a leaning towards the temptations of narcotics or alcohol. Even ten years ago, there were some 15-year-old kids who already knew their own minds and what they would or wouldn't touch.

She went downstairs and rang the bell to the flat below. She knew that Mr Grobowski, a Pole who ran a community centre down the road, always sat by his front window and watched the world go by. It was his idea of Neighbourhood Watch when he wasn't organising social events for his fellow Poles. Not that his vigilance ever resulted in him catching anyone, but he routinely claimed that was because they knew he was there.

"Yes, miss. How are you?" he yelled with a generous smile when he saw her standing there. In spite of her repeatedly asking him to use her name, he insisted on calling her 'miss'. Built like a concrete block, with a craggy face and hair which looked as if it had been ironed on, he was slightly deaf and so figured the rest of the population was too. His accent, unchanged after more than sixty years in London, mangled his words into a stew, from which, if she was fortunate, Riley got the general gist of what he meant. If she frowned, he simply shouted louder.

Riley showed him the cutting. "Did you see anyone put this through the door? It would have been in the last couple of hours or so."

He snatched the cutting and tilted his head back to

catch the light from inside, mouthing the words as he read carefully. Then he shook his head and handed it back. "No. I too busy doing thinks. What you think, miss, I got time to sit here and dreams all day?"

"Worth a try," she said, wondering if he was having her on; everyone knew he used his window like a watchtower. She turned to walk over to the stairs, but his next words stopped her dead.

"The other mens, though, they sittink out there a lot. You should maybe talk to the polices, I think."

"Other men?"

"Sure. Mens in a white van. Bloody gangsters, probably. Why else they have those dark windows, huh? You tell me."

She told him she had no idea, her attention suddenly distracted by a nagging thought.

"But don't to worry, miss," he continued, waving a meaty hand. "I look after thinks." He grinned proudly and pointed towards the front of the building as if it was his field of fire and therefore of no more concern.

Riley smiled gratefully. "It must have been one of them, I suppose. Thank you, Mr Grobowski."

"No worries, miss. And if the other mans come back, I get his names, you bet."

"Other man?" Jesus, this was getting confusing. "You mean my colleague?" She described Frank Palmer.

"No, not hims. Hims I know look of. This mans he walk by several times. Last two days, he was here. Maybe three times. Smart suit, like banker, only look tired."

"He looked tired?"

"No. Suit. Clothes good but tired like charity shop. Like he worn too long. Good stuff, though. Nice cut. I used to be tailor once... I know good clothes."

"What did he look like?"

"Tall mans, maybe six foot. Thin. Look hungry."

"When did you see him last?"

"Yesterday. He walk by but don't come near." He jabbed two fingers towards his eyes. "But I know he is looking at this house." Something hissed and spat in the background, and Mr Grobowski turned his head. "Excuse, miss… my dinner boil over. Moment." He disappeared, and Riley heard the clatter of a saucepan lid. He came back shaking his head, bringing with him an aroma of spices and a bead of moisture on his forehead. "I should get better timing clock. Recipes say only cook for ten minutes. Very specific, otherwise shit for food. Sorry, miss."

"You've been cooking?" Mr Grobowski's kitchen was at the back of the building, overlooking the communal gardens.

"Sure. I very good cook. I chef once. Many times I do food for old mens at Polish Community centre. They have kitchen, but… " He waved a contemptuous hand. "I prefer my own thinks. All afternoon in kitchen. Bloody hot, I tell you. Good for losing weight, like sauna." He laughed and patted his stomach to show it wasn't working.

Riley thanked him for his help and asked him to let her know if the mystery watcher came back, then went back upstairs. Faced with what she had just seen, she wondered how much of the day's events right outside the front door Mr Grobowski had missed. Enough, it seemed, for the mystery postman to have sent her a message without being spotted.

She checked the telephone directory, then made a call. It rang twice before a voice answered: "Evening Post." She asked to speak to Nikki Bruce and was treated to a piece of modern classical music while she waited.

"Bruce." The single word snapped down the line, as if

she had just been caught on her way out of the office on important business.

Riley introduced herself. "The piece you ran about the dead runaways," she said shortly. "I might have some information for you."

Thirty yards along the street, a shadow detached itself from the gateway of a house under renovation and walked away. The owner was tall and wore a suit, and as he passed beneath a street light, the glow briefly highlighted a gaunt, tired face, before he vanished into the next pool of shadow.

16

Nikki Bruce in the flesh turned out to be older than her picture in the *Post* suggested. Tall and bony, with pale skin and a brittle smile, she wore a burgundy designer suit with knife-edge creases. A wristful of gold preceded her as she pushed through the door of the coffee shop and stared around at the pre-lunchtime crowd.

Riley waved and indicated the chair on the other side of the table. The *Post* reporter sat down and gave Riley a wary once-over before reaching inside a leather bag for a pack of cigarettes. "Well," she said dryly, "this is different." The coffee shop was an independent, situated just off Wardour Street, and what it lacked in big-chain glitz and bustle it more than made up for in atmosphere.

"Sorry it's not the Savoy," said Riley, wondering if this had been a mistake. She had met many reporters in her time, and found most were generous in the help they would give to a fellow journo. Others jealously guarded every scrap of information as if the next acquaintance was going to wrestle it away and sell it for a small fortune. Time would tell which category this woman fell into.

"You said you had information," said Bruce, flicking back her sleeve to reveal a slim gold watch. "I've got twenty minutes." She had agreed to meet Riley with no particular curiosity or enthusiasm, and then only if it was in the Soho area.

Riley ordered coffees, then said: "I was intrigued by your story about the dead kids. It might tie in with something I know, and I wondered how far back it goes."

"Not far. Why the interest?"

After setting up the meeting yesterday evening, Riley had wondered how much to tell her. If the *Post* reporter was generous, it would be no problem. But right now she wasn't so sure. "It's a personal thing... a story I worked on some years ago. A fifteen-year-old girl walked out of her house one day and disappeared. It seems she did so voluntarily, but it made no sense at the time. There was nothing in the family background and no obvious reason which drove her away. The usual stuff, on the surface. Your story set me thinking about what might have happened to her, that's all." She smiled. "I'm not after your story, by the way."

Bruce looked faintly sceptical, but shrugged as if it was no big thing. "My stuff doesn't go back that far. My boss put me on it weeks ago because he thought it would run. In my opinion they're just rough sleepers being fed poor quality shit by dealers who couldn't care less. To be honest – " She lit her cigarette and blew out a puff of smoke, allowing a hard smile to edge around her lips – "it's not as if I need to worry about it any more. Not after today."

"Really?" Riley felt a flicker of irritation at the woman's coldness. She was dismissing those dead kids as no more than detritus cluttering the streets of the capital.

"Because I'm moving into telly. The pay's fantastic and my contract means I won't be scratching around with all the other cruddies for stories nobody wants to read. Sorry – no offence – but give it a few more days and I'm out of here."

"Good for you." Riley kept her temper, though she felt like throwing her coffee over the snooty bitch. She'd never been called a cruddy before. "So who's the lucky channel?"

"Star Central. You won't have heard of them, darling,

they're an offshoot of a Japanese/Aussie tie-up. They cover society and celeb news anywhere between here, LA and the Pacific Rim." She smiled coolly, her eyes drifting off centre for a moment as if picturing the future. "And that's a hell of a lot of society, believe me."

"So you can't help me." Riley felt an odd sense of deflation and got ready to leave. If Nikki Bruce had any interest in news, it no longer mattered unless it carried the glitzy tag of fame, wealth and fortune. "Can I ask why you agreed to meet me? You obviously know what I do."

Bruce shrugged again. "Habit. Curiosity. Professional interest… I wanted to see what you were like." She looked Riley squarely in the eye for the first time. It was a bit like being studied by a feral cat. "I've heard your name quite a bit recently. Is it true you nearly got dusted in Spain a while ago? Gossip mentioned a bunch of mercenaries and a mine-shaft. Sounds hideous."

In spite of herself, Riley was surprised. She never gave much thought about her standing in the business; as far as she was concerned she did her job and others did theirs. Reputations were hard-earned but transitory, like the news itself. "Gossip got it wrong. The Spain bit was right, though. Listen, I appreciate this is old news for you, but I'm just trying to make sense of a situation. I thought you might have some information I could use."

Nikki Bruce stared at Riley with raised eyebrows. "What are you offering – a trade-off? I show you mine if you'll show me yours?"

"I haven't anything to trade."

"Oh, that's right – it's personal. Listen, that's professional suicide."

"Maybe. But can you think of a better reason to follow a story?"

Bruce conceded the point. "Fair enough. Look, I've picked up a lot of stuff over the last few weeks. Some of it makes sense, some not. Most of the deaths were explained away, like dirty drugs or infection - or both. That's it."

"Most of them?"

"Well, two, maybe three were borderline. There were possible natural causes like choking - this latest one, for instance – or pneumonia, stuff like that. They could equally have been helped along; a fight, maybe… being in the wrong place at the wrong time – a spat over drugs. It happens all the time."

"I know. I've been there."

Bruce raised her eyebrows again. "Really? Yeah, I guess you have. Anyway, I think the police took the easy way out when they were offered it, and because nobody turned up to make a fuss and demand an investigation. Sad, really, when you think about it. Everyone should have somebody who cares." For an instant she actually sounded less like the hard face and more like someone with human instincts. She shook her head and looked at her watch. "I've got to go."

Riley nodded, deflated by the lack of information. "Thanks for coming."

"No problem. I'm sorry it doesn't help with your girl, but I don't think the circumstances are the same. She might turn up again one day. Some do, you know."

Riley considered the news Donald had given her about Katie Pyle. She took out the cutting about the dead woman and passed it across the table. "Actually, she won't. Katie's dead."

Nikki's eyes widened. "You're kidding. This was her?" She sat down again and read the cutting, then looked at Riley. "I can see why you're intrigued." She gave a grudging smile and seemed to relax. "And I can see why you weren't too quick to give away the bit about her being dead. I wouldn't have done, either, in your position."

To her surprise, Riley felt herself warming to the other woman. "You'd better go to your meeting."

Nikki sat back and waved her hand. "To hell with it – I can be a bit late. We're only sorting out a couple of minor contractual points." She chewed her lip and stared off into space. "Look, I don't know how I can help. People go missing all the time… mostly to get away from bad marriages or impossible debts. Some just discover they've had enough of the life they've got. They've run out of mental gas or something. The archives are stuffed full of people who went walkabout and never came back."

"But that's older people. Your reports are about kids." A kid like Katie, she wanted to say.

"Sure. But name a reason for running away and there's a kid out there to match it; abuse, neglect, bullying, alcoholism, fear of failure, broken hearts, drugs – even a row over the colour of the school uniform. It's a tough time - some just pick up and run without thinking. By the time they look at the issues clearly, it's often too late to go back. Too much water and all that." She looked at Riley with what could have been sympathy. "Is that the problem here?"

"How do you mean?"

"You obviously feel bad about this Katie Pyle. I can understand that, although I think you're nuts if you let it get to you. We've all had our Katie Pyle stories, believe me." She waved a hand, dispersing the cloud of smoke. "That's one issue. Then there's the question of timing. Things have changed hugely over the last ten years. Runaways now… they live differently. They're not into it for the adventure, not like some were years ago, packing a few things into a rucksack and heading off on the hippy trail to get stoned, drunk and laid. For these kids it's the only way of surviving. They take bigger risks because they have to; it's a much nastier world out there, and after living on the streets for a while they don't always care what happens to them. If they're lucky they get some help. Most don't want to know because they see it as another form of control."

"You mean from the agencies?"

"Sure. They want to be free of all that. It's very rare you get a kid leaving a good, safe, happy home. Most of them are rotten."

"But not all."

"No. Yes. Well, most of them - look at the statistics."

"Katie's wasn't." The thought made her wonder about Katie's parents. She would have to check to see if they were still around. It was a long shot but if anything made them resurface it would have been the discovery of their daughter's body. No doubt the police would have searched for the next of kin, and the press wouldn't be far behind. She would have to move quickly.

Nikki was staring off into space, ruminating. "Let me dig out what I can. To be honest, I think you'll find it's all to do with the home."

"It's still worth looking, though."

"If you say so. But so what? What if they trot to church every Sunday and Brownies on a Tuesday evening? Social position, class, religion - none of that guarantees a caring environment. Some of the stories I've covered among the so-called upper socio-economic groupings would make your eyes water. Like, if the four-wheel-drive and green wellie set love their kids so much, why do they send them to boarding school from the age of six? No wonder some of them are so fucking dysfunctional." The words came out with such venom, Riley wondered whether the reporter was quite as cold as she liked to pretend.

"I appreciate your help."

"Sure. But don't hold your breath." She glanced at her watch again. "Sorry – this time I'd better be off. I wouldn't want to push my luck. These telly people can be so temperamental, darling." She smiled and rolled her eyes.

"There's one other thing." Riley was acting on instinct. "Have you ever heard of the Church of Flowing Light?"

"It rings a bell. Is it important?"

"It could be, but I can't tell you why."

"Fair enough. I'll ask around."

As Riley walked outside, her phone buzzed. It was Palmer. "Are you busy?" he asked. "I need your womanly charms."

17

The Boothe-Davisons lived in a converted Regency town house just off Portland Place, midway between the BBC and Regent's Park. Riley spotted Palmer waiting for her in the doorway to a smart building, calmly ignoring the looks of disapproval from two elderly tenants keeping guard over a small Cairn terrier sniffing nervously at a nearby lamppost.

"Sorry to spring this on you," he said cheerfully, taking a last drag of a cigarette before flipping it into the gutter. "I blagged the address from Donald. I thought it might be useful to have a chat."

"Why do you need me?" asked Riley. "You think I have some sort of secret power over Air Commodores?"

"It's not him I'm worried about; it's his missus. She's a bit touchy. She didn't want to put me through at first until I mentioned I knew her husband from our time in the services. Said they didn't want to talk about their daughter, because it's all too unsettling." He shook his head. "Can you believe these people? Kid gone AWOL on the street and she doesn't want to talk about it."

"Could be she's strung up on something from her doctor. What do you want me to do – distract her while you talk to the husband?"

"If you can. I might get more out of him reminiscing on old times without her running interference." He turned and led the way through the front door and into a small lift, where they joined an elderly lady with pink hair and a tiny, aggressive dog with bug eyes and a fancy collar. Neither the lady nor the dog acknowledged Palmer, although the dog sniffed at Riley's shoes before backing away with a quiver of alarm and a show of teeth. Round one to the cat, thought Riley. Extra food for you tonight, puss.

The lift stopped and Palmer followed his nose along a carpeted and marble-lined corridor to an impressive, gleaming door with a small bell push. He thumbed the button and waited.

"Yes?" The door opened to reveal a tall, hawk-nosed man in his fifties, wearing a crisp shirt and cardigan. He was holding a small watering can. He stared out at Palmer with a look of suspicion, a trickle of water dribbling out of the can's spout on to the floor.

Riley stared in surprise, but managed to close her mouth in time. It was the man she had seen at the function at Broadcote Hall - the one with the sceptical expression and the dewy-eyed wife. She looked at Palmer to warn him, but couldn't catch his eye.

"Are you selling something?" the man snapped. Then he peered closer at Palmer. "I know you. You were army, weren't you?" He snapped his fingers, recognition and the beginnings of acceptance coming together. "Of course... you rang earlier. The chap from the Salisbury ranges."

Palmer nodded and confirmed that he had left the army and was now a private investigator. The former officer shook hands, but without any great show of enthusiasm.

"It's Angelina we've come to talk about," continued Palmer, and nodded towards Riley. "This is my colleague, Riley Gavin." He produced the poster, holding it up so the man could see the photo. "We're looking into other disappearances which might tie in with your daughter's."

"Really? How?"

"We're not sure yet. But she isn't the first, and if we

can establish a pattern, it might help us find out what happened."

"Who is it?" A thin, reedy voice echoed down the hallway behind the former Air Commodore, and he shook his head in irritation.

"It's that chap Palmer, dear," he muttered, giving Riley a brief nod without any sign of recognition. "And a colleague. You'd better come in." He turned and led the way through to a spacious living room decorated with military prints and a large, Constable-style landscape, and indicated two armchairs for the visitors. He put the watering can down on the floor and stood by the window with his back to a wrought-iron balcony overlooking a rear garden. "Sorry about the chilly reception. We've been plagued by sales bods recently. Slick buggers can talk their way inside an elephant's arse – oh, sorry, young lady."

"Well, who is it?" The owner of the voice swept into the room and stopped short, staring at Palmer and Riley as if they had materialised out of the carpet. She wore a plain but expensive dress and court shoes, and her hair was pulled back in a tight bun pierced through with a tortoise-shell slide. Riley instantly thought of women who lunch. It was the dewy-eyed wife from the function. "Oh."

"They've come about Angelina," the man explained flatly. "D'you want a drink?" He might have been unenthusiastic about their visit, but plainly wasn't about to overlook the common courtesies.

"Tea would be nice," said Palmer, smiling at Mrs Boothe-Davison and offering his hand. She took it with a look of surprise, and backed away out of the room. Seconds later they heard the sound of crockery being assembled. Riley tried not to smile. It was a neat move; get the woman out of the way so he could talk directly to the girl's father.

"You obviously haven't found any trace of her, then." Boothe-Davison stared hard at Palmer and wiped his nose on a chequered handkerchief, then turned towards Riley. "Sorry if I seem matter-of-fact about this, but we've had a rough time. All this waiting. Can't help being cynical, you see."

"About what?" said Riley. She had debated going into the kitchen with Mrs Boothe-Davison, but this line of talk looked far more productive. If the man became difficult, she could always take his wife outside on the balcony and threaten to throw her over.

"Where she is… what she's doing." He looked at Riley. "You ever had anybody go missing? It's not pretty, I promise you. Bad enough they walk away… without charlatans and that coming out of the woodwork to feed off your hopes."

"Charlatans?"

"People promising to find them." He blinked with a faint sign of recognition. "I've seen you before, young lady. You in the forces as well?"

"No," said Riley. "We almost met a few days ago. Broadcote Hall?" She waited while the name registered. When it did, he snapped her a second look, this one less friendly. "But I'm nothing to do with the Church," she added quickly, before he ordered her to leave. "I was look-ing for a friend of mine."

He nodded and subsided, then blinked at Palmer. "Will you find her, do you think?"

"I can't promise anything," said Palmer carefully. "I'll certainly try. I'll need a briefing first."

"Good man. Ah, here's the tea." He watched as his wife entered with a large tray. She poured tea, and everyone sat down. "All right, what do you want to know?"

"Why did Angelina leave?" Riley asked. She was looking at the woman as she spoke.

Mrs Boothe-Davison hesitated momentarily and glanced at her husband before answering. Riley guessed there had been a discussion before their arrival, and she had been snapped into line. "Arguments, mostly," she said. "About all sorts of silly things. Everything was a trial, you see, to be fought over. We wanted her to go to boarding school, but she wanted to stay on in London, at the local school. She wasn't getting on academically. We felt her school was allowing her to coast. She's always been a bit airy-fairy, unfortunately, keen on doing her own thing. There was also a bad element… into drugs and all that stuff. She seemed to gravitate towards them. We wanted to take her away from that."

"Kids that age are rebellious," her husband put in, his voice showing signs of softening. "They push the envelope… it's part of growing up. Not that we were allowed to in my day. But we – my wife and I – tried to move with the times and relax the reins a bit. It didn't seem to work. We had her late in life, you see, what with all the travelling. Foreign postings aren't the best places to bring up kids. Maybe that's part of the problem. We'd give anything to have her back." He looked at them with a faint mistiness in his eyes and shook his head. "Anything."

"What about the poster?" said Riley. "Who arranged that?"

Boothe-Davison looked at his wife and made a gesture. It was clearly something she had done, possibly without his agreement.

"A charity group was very kind," said his wife, sitting upright. "Some friends had heard of their work, and recommended them. We – I – called them and they said they might be able to help." The way she looked at her husband showed he had not been too keen on the idea.

"Did they say how?"

"Not at first. They said they had people on the ground, here in London, and that if she was still in the area, there was a chance they could find her. We were ready to try anything. We were going to hire some private detectives, but they suggested they could work faster because it was their speciality."

"So it was you who approached them," said Palmer.

"Yes. They were very good… they seemed to know about Angelina. Maybe our friends told them."

"Did they ask many questions?"

"Oh, yes. They wanted to know all about her… her likes and dislikes… friends… habits. Even things about us as a family. We told them everything they wanted to know. It seemed only reasonable."

"And you, sir?" Riley looked at her husband.

"Me?" He gave a short bark of a laugh. "I did what I always do – I went along with it. Answered all their impertinent questions, gave them more than I thought was necessary, to be honest. But what else could I do? We even went along to their blessed meeting the other day. No idea what that accomplished, save them getting a fat donation, although I suppose that's fair enough, someone has to. We are talking about our daughter. She's important to us, d'you see? Our Angel." He coughed and dried up.

"This donation," said Palmer after a few moments. "How much did you give them?"

They exchanged a look, then the husband said, "A thousand pounds. I said I'd double it if they found her."

"Who suggested that figure?"

"I can't remember. It... came up."

"It's a fairly specific figure, though."

"They told us they were hoping to set up a drop-in centre for the homeless here in London," said Mrs Boothe-Davison. "I thought it was a marvellous idea. Mr de Haan said they were planning to raise money for it by asking for fixed blocks of donations, but he was trying to come to a reasonable idea of the amount of each. He thought anywhere between five hundred to a thousand pounds would be acceptable, and my husband said we would contribute a thousand."

"That was very generous," said Riley. "And he accepted?"

"Damn near took my arm off," said Boothe-Davison sourly. "I don't mind the money, to be honest – it's not as if we can't afford it. But I'd like to see some action, that's all." He cleared his throat loudly and exchanged a look with his wife that was edged in pain. "I never thought I'd do such a thing... but you find yourself ready to do anything in this situation. We just want to know she's safe."

"Have they found anything?"

"So far? Nothing. I had a call yesterday, saying they had some promising news, but nothing concrete. There have been a few crank calls but that's not unusual, apparently. They said something about how these groups of kids move around a lot in the daytime to avoid the law, which makes them difficult to track down. Then some twaddle about belonging and fellowship and praying. Fat lot of good that'll do." He glared at his wife as if she might contradict him, but she remained silent. Riley wondered if her starry-eyed demeanour at Broadcote Hall had been because of de Haan's presence, and whether being away from it had allowed a cold dose of reality to creep in. Not, she thought, that it could have been all that far beneath the surface. Forces wives were generally made of stern stuff.

Palmer stood up. "Do you have a recent photo of her?"

Boothe-Davison nodded and turned to a burnished mahogany side table, where he opened a slim drawer. He took out a photo from a small stack and handed it to Palmer. "No need to bring it back," he said gruffly. "I had several done in case… " He shook his head and said nothing more.

"OK. Leave it with us." Palmer handed Boothe-Davison a business card. "My number, in case they call with any news. We'll see ourselves out."

"Wait." Boothe-Davison stepped forward, looking puzzled. "You're not asking for payment?"

"No." Palmer shook his head. "It's not an issue."

Outside on the street, he looked at Riley. "What do you think?"

"I think," said Riley, "they are two very vulnerable people who were carefully lined up and allowed themselves to be conned out of a thousand quid. Or am I being cynical?"

Palmer smiled coldly and set off along the pavement. "You and me both."

Riley stared after him. "Where are you going?"

"Things to do, places to be," he tossed back over his shoulder. "You wouldn't want to know." His tone suggested she wouldn't be welcome.

"Don't worry, Palmer," she muttered after him, startling another elderly passing local. "I've got some digging of my own to do."

18

The area where Katie Pyle had lived hadn't changed much over the years, and seeing it again brought back to Riley sharp memories of her visits here when she was covering the story. Situated close by Elstree Studios, where she remembered Katie's father, John, had been employed as a technician, it was a comfortable, middle-class area of semis and detached houses with large gardens, set in broad, well-kept roads. Although the M1 thundered north barely a mile away on the other side of a section of woodland, it was deeply rural by inner-city standards.

Riley called Donald on the way and asked him to confirm the address. He came back within minutes. "It's the only one I can find, but it's not recent." Then he asked bluntly: "Do we have a story?" Once he knew there was something solid on offer, he'd be chasing her non-stop for progress reports. But he'd also be an invaluable mine of information should she need it.

"We might," she told him cautiously, "but I'm not sure where it's going. It could be nothing, but I'm going to see if Katie's parents can tell me anything else… like whether they heard from her over the years. It's hard to believe she's been around all this time and didn't make contact."

"Well, stranger things, sweetie. Stranger things. Keep in touch." He rang off to answer another phone warbling in the background.

Riley found the street on her third try, misled at first by a new sports centre now masking the approach to the road. She parked and walked up a brick-paved path to the familiar double-fronted house. It sported vertical blinds instead of curtains and a revamped fascia and remodelled porch. The garden was different, too, with signs of recent landscaping including newly laid turfs and flowerbeds, and a small cherry tree with straggly branches.

The woman who came to the door was tall and slim, and several years younger than Mrs Pyle would have been. She had a mobile phone in one carefully manicured hand. Riley introduced herself and explained the purpose of her visit.

"Susan Pyle? She moved a few years ago," said the woman with a sigh. "As I've been telling a stream of police and other reporters. We bought the place from her after her husband died. She'd pretty much done nothing to it." She nodded towards the garden. "That was a jungle; you wouldn't believe the weeds we had to blast out. My husband hired one of those flame-thrower things – ghastly machine, it was – and that was just so he could *see* where the roots were. And the interior was simply Gothic... well, that's how I describe it, anyway. So much dark cloth and furniture... I'm amazed the poor dear wasn't blind with having to peer through the gloom all the time. And the smell!"

"Bad, was it?" said Riley with studied patience. She wondered if this woman had ever been through anything half as bad as Susan Pyle. Undoubtedly not, otherwise she'd have shown a bit more sympathy.

"It was so thick you could cut it. And I'm not surprised; after all those incense sticks she burned night and day, the ceiling was black with the smoke. You can still smell it when the house gets hot. I swear it's been absorbed into the brickwork." She shook her head and looked belatedly guilty. "I'm sorry - I'm not being very kind to her, am I? We heard about her daughter, what with the press and police still thinking she lived here. Poor woman must have had a terrible time." She turned away and picked up a slip of paper from a glass-topped side table inside the porch. "I'm afraid I don't know her new address, but this lady apparently does. I had my husband print them up because of all the callers. She's a friend from way back, I believe, and lives down the road, although she doesn't see callers. You'll have to ring. But I'm sure she'll be able to help you."

Riley thanked the woman and returned to her car. The piece of paper held a number and name. Gail Hunter. When she dialled the number it was picked up on the second ring.

"Miss Hunter?" said Riley. "I've been told you can help me contact Susan Pyle."

"Are you the press?" The woman's voice sounded tired but grudging, as if she had been fielding questions for days but didn't want to simply slam the phone down. "Only, when is this going to end? I really don't think –"

"Mrs Hunter, I know Susan already; I met her when Katie disappeared. I was one of the reporters assigned to it. I think I was the only one she spoke to." Riley let that sink in, then continued: "If you say Susan won't want to see me, that's fine. But would you ask her, please? I think it's important."

"Really? To whom?"

"I'd still like to find out what happened to Katie."

There was a long pause before Gail Hunter spoke. "Give me your name and number. If she wants to see you, I'll let you know." There was no room for negotiation in the voice and Riley knew instinctively that there was no point in pushing. As soon as she gave the woman the information, the call was disconnected.

On the way back to town, her phone rang. She expected

it to be Gail Hunter, calling to say there was no point to a meeting, but it was Nikki Bruce. Riley pulled into the side of the road and cut the engine.

"I haven't got the info about the other deaths yet, but I've just been on to a colleague who does social issues," said Nikki. "He says this Church of Flowing Light run soup vans around London, mostly into places the other agencies won't go. They sound a tough outfit. They don't use women and they don't take any crap. Sort of benevolence with an iron fist by the sounds of it."

"Oh."

"Yes. They dish out hot drinks and blankets to kids who have nowhere to sleep, but they don't make a big thing about it. He thinks they have a place out in the Cotswolds but he doesn't know where. That's it, I'm afraid. They sound pretty genuine."

"Thanks. You're probably right." Riley cursed inwardly. Soup vans. God, how emotive could a charity be? You didn't get more personal than doling out bowls of soup to the needy. And who would question their right to be anywhere, no matter what the time of day or night? "I'd better tell Frank."

"Frank?"

"Frank Palmer. He's the investigator friend I told you about. I wouldn't want him charging in without warning."

There was a silence for a few moments, then Nikki said, "That wouldn't be Frank Palmer, late of Her Majesty's Redcaps, would it? Tallish, thinnish, vague-ish – seems half asleep a lot of the time?"

Riley was surprised. There couldn't be two men with such similar descriptions. "You know Frank?"

"Yes. I met him when I was doing a piece about bullying in the army. A colleague gave me his name and he supplied some background about the Special Investigation Branch. He promised to call me afterwards." Her tone indicated that he hadn't.

"When was this?" said Riley. Putting Nikki Bruce and Frank Palmer together in her head was hard work; they were chalk and cheese, and she couldn't see Palmer putting up with a wannabe television performer, news or no news.

"Nearly three years ago. It's a good thing I'm not of a frail disposition; a girl could be quite insulted. Actually, Frank's all right – but if you tell him I said that, I'll report you to the Press Council."

"I wouldn't dream of it. Anyway, Frank never airs his laundry in public –" Riley stopped, an image springing out of nowhere into her mind. "God, I'm so stupid!" The words came out before she could stop them.

"What?" said Nikki. "Are you all right?"

"White vans and tinted windows." Riley was seeing a rolling flashback of images and remembered where she had seen the white van for the first time. *A* white van, anyway. It had been there, right at the beginning, only it hadn't registered at the time because she had been distracted with something more important. White vans are like black taxis – part of the scenery, invisible. And this one had been at Heathrow... right outside Henry's hotel. She remembered it now: it had been parked there when she'd arrived, next to the police car. Then, as she was leaving, a white van with tinted windows had pulled out of the hotel car park right in front of her. If it had penetrated her consciousness enough to make her question it at the time, she would probably have assumed it was a laundry van. After all, why else would a commercial vehicle be calling at a hotel at that time of day if it wasn't a service delivery? Only they weren't making a delivery... and the

package hadn't been bed linen.

"Riley?" Nikki's voice pulled her back to the present. "What is it?"

"Nothing. I've just remembered something. My problem is going to be proving it."

Back at the flat, she fed the cat and picked at her laptop while nuzzling a large glass of red wine. It was a moot point which would give her a headache first, but she needed the familiarity and the tannin. Between sips she updated what she had learned so far, along with random thoughts as they occurred. With a bit of hard work, it would eventually begin to distil down into the coherent outline of a story.

Tired with the keyboard and with too many gaps in the data that she had no way of filling, she switched off the laptop and slumped on to the sofa with her wine, hoping relaxation would generate some clear thinking. It would be some time before Nikki got back to her with details of the other deaths, so there was nothing to do but wait. Tomorrow she would bring Palmer up to date with what she had so far. When the cat oozed on to her lap and began purring, she was asleep within seconds.

It seemed only moments later that she was being dragged out of a fractured dream by the phone. She had a crick in her neck from the sofa's low back and a mouth made gummy by too much wine. The cat was nowhere to be seen, and the readout on the VCR told her it was five in the morning. Christ, this was becoming too much of a habit. She leaned across to the phone and snatched it up.

"Is that Riley Gavin?" The woman's voice was soft, with a faint rural burr, and her tone suggested she was deliberately keeping her voice low to avoid being overheard.

"Yes. How can I help?"

"I'm calling on behalf of Susan Pyle. Katie's mother."

Riley sat bolt upright. God that was quick. She stood up and made for the kitchen. She had a feeling she was going to need some coffee. "Can I see her?"

"Oh, yes. I'm sorry it's so early, but… she insisted. We heard you were looking for her, and she just woke up and said she didn't want to wait. Can you come here?"

"Of course. Where are you?"

"Near Dunwich in Suffolk. Minsmere Lodge. We're right on the coast." The woman gave brief instructions, as if the place was so well known it would be impossible to miss. "I'm Mrs Francis, by the way. I'll be waiting for you."

Riley grabbed a pen and notepad and scribbled down the address. "When can I come? Later this morning?"

"That would be best, I think. The earlier the better, in fact."

Something ominous in the woman's tone made Riley straighten up, hand poised above the notepad. "I don't understand."

"Forgive me. I hate to tell you this, Miss Gavin, but Susan's sick. Very sick." Her voice dropped further, as if weighed down by ineffable sadness. "She's not expected to live very long."

19

Minsmere Lodge was a squat Edwardian building sitting at the end of a narrow, sandy lane which appeared to have run out of tarmac within earshot of the sea. Other than the faint wash of a close tide and the occasional shriek of gulls dipping and swooping across the dunes, it wore a cloak of tranquillity beneath the thin morning sun, as if nothing here could possibly disturb its end-of-nowhere remoteness. The air was sharp with the tang of salt and a faint undertone of something not quite fresh.

Riley parked to one side of the gravelled drive, which was vacant save for a rotting old Rover parked to one side. Flat tyres, a cat curled up on the bonnet and a bicycle leaning against the side suggested that the vehicle wasn't about to go anywhere soon. She approached the house and touched a bell in the wall next to the front door, partially covered by a hanging growth of ivy. The original green paint was faded by the salt sea air, and around her feet the flagstones were all but covered in a layer of fine, wind-blown sand.

The door clicked open to reveal a small, neat woman in a starched blue overall. Riley guessed this was the woman who had called her.

"Miss Gavin," the woman said softly in confirmation, and stood to one side. She didn't offer to shake hands, but closed the door and led the way silently across the small reception hall into a cramped study. It was a masculine room, cluttered and stuffy and smelling faintly of old paper. All that was missing was the heavy tick of a grandfather clock. The woman indicated an armchair and said,

"I'm Mary Francis. I live in with Susan. Thank you for coming. Would you like some tea?" She smiled and disappeared before Riley could decline, closing the door softly behind her.

Riley took the opportunity to check her phone for messages. She had called Palmer's mobile before leaving, to tell him where she was going. Unless Mrs Francis possessed an unfortunate sense of the dramatic, her brief explanation had left little doubt that Susan Pyle wasn't long for this world.

"She might know something useful," Palmer had agreed. In spite of the early hour, he'd sounded surprisingly awake, and Riley thought she detected the noise of traffic in the background. Somehow the idea of a dawn jog round the park didn't quite fit her vision of Palmer, but she decided not to enquire. "What about the father?"

"He died some years ago." Riley went on to tell him about Nikki's call and what she had picked up about the Church of Flowing Light and their charitable activities. She also mentioned remembering the van she had seen outside the Scandair hotel.

"How sure are you?"

"It was there, but I don't know how significant it might be."

"Be handy if we could get confirmation – even if only to eliminate it."

"I was thinking I might ask my friendly hotel employee if he can help. It could be entirely innocent, of course."

Palmer was more pragmatic. "It was there, so worth checking. In the meantime I'll see if I can get a closer look at the two boys who've been following you. Remember to watch your back." He rang off, leaving Riley wondering what would happen if Palmer and the two men came too close. They might discover that he wasn't quite as laid-back as he liked people to think.

She wondered what she would find when she finally got to see Susan Pyle. The last time they had spoken had been some time after Katie's disappearance, when the most obvious mechanics of the search had begun to scale down. The posters had produced no response other than one or two crank calls, and, short-staffed and with no obvious evidence of foul play, the police had been obliged to move their attention to other cases. Even Riley had been forced to call it a day by then, and had called on the couple to explain her position. It had been a difficult meeting; John Pyle had been stiff and resentful, although his wife had seemed more understanding. Or maybe, thought Riley with hindsight, she had been too weighed down with grief and internalised sorrow at life's wickedness to put up much of a fight any more.

The atmosphere in the house had been heavy and sombre, not much helped, she now recalled, by the dark décor – especially in Katie's room – and the lingering smell of incense. It hadn't meant much at the time because of the circumstances, but now the new occupant of the house had reminded her, she found herself reliving those first impressions. Odd, really, because neither John nor Susan Pyle had seemed the sort of people to use incense, nor had they come across as naturally sombre in their every-day lives, in spite of the tragedy which had suddenly overshadowed them.

And now it looked as if it had called yet again, with the discovery of Katie's body.

"How long is it since you last saw Susan?" The study door had opened without a sound, and Mrs Francis's voice dragged Riley sharply back to the present. The older woman was already juggling cups and saucers on a side table, and she paused until Riley nodded, before adding milk to a cup.

"Nine years – maybe ten." Riley wondered to what extent Katie's mother would have changed in ten years.

"Susan's condition," Mrs Francis began carefully, as if reading her thoughts, "has not been good just recently. I know something of the history, but she has never been too keen to talk about the circumstances surrounding her daughter. I just wanted to clarify that."

"I understand. How long has she been here?"

"She bought the house about four years ago, following the death of her husband. I was taken on as a residential companion a year later." She looked at Riley over her cup and a flicker of distaste touched her face. "They prefer the term 'carer' these days. Such a horrible word in my view. It sounds so false. My role is – was – more companion than anything."

"You've done this before?"

"Oh, yes. I'm a qualified SRN, so it usually involves a degree of nursing as well as companionship. But some people are better served by having another person about the place."

"Like Susan, you mean?"

"Yes. She told me a little about Katie, but it was very difficult for her. It must have been a sad business… but I suppose you'd know more about that. In spite of that she's been happy here, Miss Gavin. Very happy… until recently. She has had cancer for some years, you see. We thought it was in remission, but then she went downhill very suddenly."

"I'm sorry."

"No need, my dear. It's part of life. I do know she never

got over losing Katie." She stared out of the window. "In a way, it was as if she tried walking away from the past instead, hiking along the coast day after day. I never knew anyone who could walk the way she did. I couldn't keep up, so I stopped going. After a while she seemed to take a better hold on things; she settled and seemed to find some peace. Then one day about three months back, she was out walking on the shore and got caught out in a storm. She fell and broke her ankle, but managed to make her way up the beach. She began to get well, then about four weeks ago something upset her terribly and she suddenly got worse."

"What happened?"

Mrs Francis took a sudden deep breath, and flicked an imaginary crumb from her overall before folding her hands into her lap. "She was home here, doing really well. Still weak, of course, but improving. The consultant at the hospital said she simply needed plenty of rest, although, to be honest, I think we all knew it couldn't go on indefinitely. Then, one day when I was out, two men arrived."

Riley felt a chill of apprehension. "What men?"

"Susan described one as thin, as if he didn't eat much. And very hard-faced. Dressed in dark clothing, like those characters in the movies. Like... what was it, *Matrix* or something. We watched it on video once. The other man stayed in the car."

"What did this man want?"

"He demanded to know where Katie was."

20

"Never seen her." The man in the stained army surplus coat shook his head at Palmer and turned away, eyes already slipping into half-focus. He was as thin as a slate and just as grey, with an unnatural pallor to his skin, and didn't react when Palmer slipped some coins into his hand. Yet another refusal in a long line of similar responses.

Palmer had been at it for two hours now, trawling the hidden corners and niches on the fringes of Oxford Street, and was fast running out of options. The rush hour was just building, and few of the street people who had surfaced this early had given the photo of Angelina a glance, shutting off further questions with a sour look or a shake of the head, whether out of indifference or ignorance it was hard to tell.

The older ones merely retreated behind blank faces, immune to involvement. They had their own problems. The young ones were quick to ask for money when he approached, but equally quick to melt away when he mentioned missing kids. Not their business; best not get involved.

Palmer continued on through the underpass, and wondered how Riley was getting on. He checked his watch. Wherever she was, it had to be more fragrant than this place. The rumble of traffic around Marble Arch sounded overhead and his footsteps echoed off the curved walls. He stepped over discarded sheets of stained cardboard, crumpled coffee mugs and a torn blanket that were the previous night's debris, and saw a needle glistening in the gloom. Close by, a square of scorched silver foil fluttered away on the wind, and he felt a deep sadness at the squalid conditions existing barely yards away from the prosperity of the shops above. The long tunnel smelled of damp, carrying with it the sharp tang of urine and hopelessness, and he found himself holding his breath as he approached the exit stairs to the west side of Park Lane.

On the pavement above, he breathed fresher air and hailed a taxi, giving directions for the embankment south of the river. One youth earlier, tempted by the promise of cash, had muttered a vague comment about the area behind Waterloo station. Before Palmer could press him for more details, another man had appeared and the youth had clammed up and moved away. Palmer had stored the information and left. He wasn't offended by their suspicions; few people wished them well, and it was no surprise if they believed that no one who came asking questions had the best of intentions.

He took Angel's photo from his pocket and studied it again, wondering if she was still at large or had found shelter of some kind. Her background would have ill-prepared her for the harshness and brutality of life on the streets, while her age, clothes and skin would have marked her out for special attention among the monsters prowling the shadows, always on the lookout for fresh meat.

There were hundreds of places where street kids congregated. Covering them all would take weeks, always assuming he could keep up with the ever-shifting population. But a hint was all he needed to pick up a trail – if it still existed. At least it would be somewhere to start, rather than wandering aimlessly in the hope of a chance sighting.

He had the taxi drop him off outside County Hall and

made his way on foot to the area east of the station, where the smells of the river were sharp and pungent on the breeze. He saw no signs of youths on the way; none of the customary shuffling figures and wary, pale faces turned towards him; no listless bundles squeezed into grubby corners. Perhaps they were busy up west, where the pickings were sometimes easier.

He reached the river and scanned the surrounding streets. It was as if the place had been evacuated, save for a couple of bemused Japanese tourists staring up at the buildings in wonderment. It was colder here, the early wind lifting off the water and bringing with it a bone-slicing chill that added nothing to the grey concrete and blank windows.

He turned away from the riverside and eventually entered a narrower street bordered by blocks of flats. It was quiet here, even normal. He was about to turn back when he caught the smell of cigarette smoke. Too fresh to be far away, it held an underlying sweet tang familiar from his time prowling back-street dives in Germany, where squaddies hung out and thought they were being cool by indulging in banned substances.

He rounded a corner and found a narrow alley with two large rubbish skips parked inside, taking up nearly all of the available space. A profusion of building rubble and domestic cast-offs were barely held in place by nylon netting, and a scattering of debris on the floor of the alley betrayed the visit of skip pirates searching for treasure.

A faint fog of smoke hung in the rear of the alley, and a slither of noise came from the shadows. Palmer stepped forward, deliberately scuffing his feet. The last thing he wanted was to panic anyone into coming out in a rush, weapon at the ready.

He stopped when he saw movement beyond the skips, and a tall, stocky youth stood facing him. He was dressed in an oversized black coat and dirty jeans, and a pair of new Timberland hiking boots. His face was broad and weathered, with a wisp of beard around the chin and a cluster of sores at the edges of his mouth. The youth's eyes were unnaturally bright, his whole manner tense with suspicion and aggression.

"What do you want?" he demanded, his accent betraying Tyneside origins.

Palmer put out a calming hand and stood still. Best not push it too far. "I'm looking for someone," he explained. "A kid. I've got a photo." He pointed at his coat pocket.

The youth said nothing. In the shadows behind him someone else stirred, and a whisper came fast and furious, followed by a giggle. Palmer got the feeling he'd interrupted some urgent business. He prayed it wasn't Angelina back there.

"She's too young for this," he said quietly. "The girl I'm looking for."

"Aren't we all?" muttered the youth with no sign of humour. He coughed and leaned forward, carefully dribbling a wad of yellow spit on to the floor in a show of indifference. When he looked up again he smiled, showing a discoloured front tooth. "Show us, then."

Palmer stepped forward and held out the photo. The youth put out a hand, then dropped it with a subtle shift of his shoulders. Palmer heard a metallic click and felt a twitch in his gut. When he looked down he saw a glint of metal in the youth's hand, just a few inches from his stomach.

Palmer tensed. He hated knives. He'd come across too many of them over the years, mostly in the hands of idiots.

They were as indiscriminate as bullets and just as likely to cut you by accident as on purpose. Either way they could hurt. Or kill.

"Put it away, sonny," he said softly, "or you'll be wearing it."

The youth blinked, as if unaccustomed to such cool indifference and unsure how to react. He hesitated a fraction too long. Palmer reached out and clamped a hand over his knife wrist, then pulled and twisted. It was no contest. The youth yelped and bent his knees to counteract the pain, which put him conveniently close to Palmer's other hand. There was a sound like a paddle on meat, and the youth fell in a heap, his weapon clattering to the ground.

While the youth collected his senses, Palmer bent and retrieved the knife. It was a cheap mass-market item with a well-worn blade and scarred, imitation bone handle. But still deadly in the hands of someone prepared to use it. He stuck the point in a crack in the wall and snapped it cleanly, then flipped the handle into the nearest rubbish skip.

"Bastard," the youth said sourly, sitting up and rubbing his wrist. Palmer wasn't sure whether he was annoyed at the pain or the broken knife.

He flapped the photo in front of the youth's face. "All I want is a yes or no. That's not too hard, is it? Now, let's try again. Have you seen her?" The words were slow and deliberate, the gritty tone behind Palmer's voice making the youth blink harder and shuffle urgently backwards on his rump until he bumped against the side of the skip.

"Might have." He glanced sideways towards the shadows, but got no help from that direction. He sighed. "Aye, all right. She was down here yesterday. Pretty lass. That's why I remember her. She was with us for a bit…

then someone came by and she left."

"Who did she leave with?"

The youth shrugged. "I don't know. Some bloke. It wasn't any of my business. He came, he spotted her and they went away. Maureen would know, though. Maureen knows everything." He looked up and smiled coldly. "That's if you can get her to talk. She doesn't like men much. You'd be best taking her a pressie. Know what I mean?"

"Tell me where I can find her," said Palmer. "But set me up or try to screw me, and I'll come back and haunt you."

21

It was too much of a coincidence. Two men, one of them thin and dressed in dark clothing, asking about Katie. It was as if a veil had suddenly been drawn over the windows, dimming the sunlight. "Did the man say why?"

"He wanted to know if she'd been in touch, and where she might be. Of course, Susan didn't know – she thought the poor girl was dead. She told him that, but he didn't believe her."

"You said Susan went downhill. Was it after these men called?"

"Oh, definitely. I don't mean he did anything… physical. He asked questions, then he went away again. But the shock affected Susan. It was like something had been stirred up inside her. Not hard to guess what it was." She shook her head with a look of distaste. "Then, when the police called a day or so ago to tell her… well, you know, it seemed to be the end. I think you'd best speak to her. She'll tell you what she needs to."

Riley followed Mrs Francis back out into the hallway and up a flight of broad stairs, past three doors to a room at the end, overlooking the front of the house. The view was of a line of low sand dunes, and beyond them the grey tint of the sea. Mrs Francis nodded wordlessly towards the door, then disappeared downstairs.

The room was large and elegantly decorated, but sparsely furnished. Susan Pyle looked tiny and lost, staring up at the ceiling from the middle of a vast double bed.

Riley stepped across the carpet. Up close, Susan looked as frail as spun sugar; her hands had the knobbly appearance of twigs, and the veins stood out across her knuckles and wrists like blue snakes on cold marble. Her hair was almost white, and impossibly thin and lifeless after the rich, dark colour Riley remembered from years ago.

"Hello, Miss Gavin," Susan said softly. The voice was the same, only weaker, less vibrant, as if all the goodness had been sucked out by the pain of the years. The eyes were different, too, lacking light, as if that too had been dimmed almost to extinction.

"Susan." Riley reached for the woman's hand. It was cold and stiff, the flesh unyielding, though the answering grip was surprisingly strong.

"Mary told you," she said. Her eyes searched Riley's for confirmation. "Mary Francis."

"Yes. I'm so sorry." It seemed a pointless thing to say, but Riley couldn't immediately think of anything else. She found a chair and sat down. "I was so sorry to hear about Katie –"

Susan shushed her. "No. Don't say it. There's no need." She swallowed with difficulty and took a deep breath. "What's done is done. It's time to accept things as they are... to let go." She sighed and looked down at her fingers, twisting the sheet in a knot. "I still can't believe she was alive, after all this time. They say mothers always know. But I didn't."

"She never made contact, then?"

"No. She never did. That wasn't normal, was it?" Susan stared at Riley with a look of intense pleading, as if confirmation of her daughter having been beyond helping herself in some way would confer a degree of mitigation for her lack of contact. "Could you get me some water, please?" She pointed towards a glass on the bedside table.

Riley held it out so she could sip from the straw on one side. She swallowed and sank back, nodding in gratitude. Even the few words spoken so far had plainly been an effort. The minutes ticked away, punctuated by Susan's shallow breathing and the noise of birds in the trees outside. In the distance a petrol engine sputtered into life, then faded to a buzz. Riley held on to the bony hand and wondered if she hadn't been wrong to come here.

"You look well," said Susan suddenly. Her voice was stronger, and her hand held Riley's with renewed vigour, as if the brief silence had recharged her depleted batteries. "I'm glad you came."

They talked for a while, exchanging pleasantries, with the sounds of Mrs Francis moving around downstairs. The talk centred mostly on life here, what Susan did, had done and planned yet to do. There was no mention of her illness. From what she said, life had not been easy and her move to the coast had not offered the escape she had been searching for. She asked Riley about herself, but her interest seemed to wane after a few minutes, and in spite of holding hands it was like talking to someone behind a screen.

After a brief lull in the conversation, Susan said, "There's something I have to tell you, Riley. About Katie."

Riley felt her stomach tense. Was there anything she didn't already know? Surely not.

"When Katie… when she went, there was something I didn't tell you. Didn't tell anyone. She and her father had been… on different sides for a long while. She was going through the difficult age and nothing was ever simple. She was a teenager; what can I say? Everything was black and white… no grey areas, and neither John nor I could say much without causing an argument. Poor man, he took the worst of it. Rows, sullen behaviour, furious sulks, throwing things, staying out all night... it was pretty unpleasant. Then, one day she came home and told me she was pregnant."

The surprise was total. *Katie pregnant?* Of all the things Riley might have expected to hear, this wasn't even anywhere near the list.

"By whom? Since when?"

"I didn't believe her at first. God knows, I didn't want to. She was so young... still at the beginning of her life. I had no idea she was already doing... that. But in the end I was forced to face up to it." She gave a weak cough, and Riley helped her to more water.

"Why didn't you tell anyone?" The words came out slightly sharper than Riley intended, but given the climate at the time, she was sure it would have made a difference to the attitude and response of the authorities.

Susan seemed to read her mind. "She was only two months gone," she said softly. "I wanted to tell the police – and you – but John... he would have been so upset. It would have destroyed him."

"You never told him?"

"I know – you'll think that was wrong. So do I, some-times. But I knew him, you see... knew how he thought. How much he loved Katie. Sad enough that his only daughter leaves home; think about how much worse it would have been if he'd learned about her expecting a child." She shook her head slowly, eyes closing. "He was a very moral man, you see. Much more so than I. His parents were very strict churchgoers, and he was ingrained from birth. The idea of an illegitimate baby would have been unthinkable. It was better he believed she had gone alone than because of..." She rolled her head on the pillow and opened her eyes again to look out of the window. "A few moments of careless fumblings and your whole life becomes a mess. That's all it was… carelessness. I know what he would have said. He would have closed his mind to the whole thing, shut it away like a sordid little secret in some deep part of his mind, never to be mentioned or talked of again."

"Would Katie have known that?"

"Oh, yes. She didn't hold with his views, you see. She thought he was narrow-minded and pious. Anal, I think she called him one day, when they argued. I didn't really know what it meant, but John was furious."

Riley felt her breathing beginning to tighten as an awful prospect began to take hold in her mind. Yet her instincts kicked against it. "Did they argue a lot?"

"A fair bit. Sniping, mostly, from Katie, once she knew how to get under his skin. He couldn't stand up to her when she began shouting." She paused and stared into the distance. "But inside he would have been dying. He loved her so much. You have no idea what this… this kind of thing can do to a family. One minute things were fine. Next our world seemed to be tearing itself apart."

"But you bore it." Alone, she almost said, trying to imagine the woman's torture.

"Not so well, as it turned out. I don't like saying it and may the Good Lord forgive me, but there were moments when… well, I actually hated Katie. Hated what she did to her father… what she did to us. And there was no reason for it. That's what I find so hard to understand. If it was simply the pregnancy, I would have helped her. I might even have found a way of convincing John. But once she'd gone, it was too late."

"Was there anything else it could have been – that made

her leave, I mean?" Riley squeezed the question out, dreading the reply.

"I honestly don't know. I don't think so, but…"

"But what?"

"Not long before she left, Katie became… secretive. As if she knew something the rest of us didn't. Something huge that we weren't in on and never would be. She used to get all starry-eyed and say odd things, about how much we didn't know or how we were unaware of things – especially her father. Yet she never told us what those things were. It was like she was laughing at us for being ignorant, when all the time she was the only one who knew what she was talking about. As if she had an invisible friend, urging her on."

Was that something they had all ignored back then, Riley wondered. The possibility of someone waiting in the background? But would that have been enough to pull Katie away, even given the atmosphere Susan had described?

Riley recalled Donald mentioning that the body by the Thames was wearing a crucifix. After what Susan had just told her, she was surprised Katie would have tolerated ever wearing a symbol of her father's faith. But people change. Maybe Katie had, too, over the years. "Well, she evidently believed in something," she said gently, rubbing Susan's hand. "Maybe in the end that's all she needed. Did the police say when they would send you her things?"

Susan's head rolled on the pillow, her eyes closing. "Things? Oh, there wasn't much. They said they had identified her by a bracelet. I'd like to have that… something to remind me."

"And the crucifix. You'll want that, too."

Susan's eyes flickered open, confused. "Crucifix? Oh, no

dear, that can't be right. Katie wouldn't have worn a crucifix. They must have made a mistake." She stared hard at Riley, shaking her head with insistence.

Riley leaned closer, feeling the older woman's breath on her face, sour and with a trace of mint. "I'm sorry. I don't follow. What do you mean?"

Susan gave Riley a dry smile, as if she was talking to a child. "Katie didn't believe in Christianity. Her father put her right off it. It's what most of their rows were about."

"Are you sure?"

"Oh, yes. You see, Katie found another path. It upset John dreadfully, of course, but he couldn't do anything about it."

"Another path?"

"Yes. For the last year we knew her, Katie rejected Christianity completely. She became a devout Buddhist."

22

"But that doesn't make sense. I mean… " Riley clamped her lips shut. Whatever Susan Pyle believed her daughter had been part of, now was not the time to shake those thoughts. "How devout was she?"

"Oh, very. She had posters in her room and a small prayer wheel, and she used to meditate a great deal. It was no passing fad - I could tell. Some girls her age go through that kind of thing, but not Katie. She was very serious about it. There was the incense, which stank the house out all the time. John hated it, but he could never have forbidden her to use it. Anyway," she smiled faintly with the memory, "I quite liked the smell – it certainly made a difference to John's awful pipe tobacco."

"I remember it now," said Riley, casting her mind back. It confirmed what the new owner of the Pyle's house had said. But she didn't recall the posters and prayer wheel.

Susan Pyle seemed to read her mind. "We moved them after she… she left. A friend said if the police thought she had joined one of those religious sects or got involved with some outlandish group, they wouldn't want to get involved. I said they weren't a sect – it was nothing like that. Well, Buddhism is an established religion, isn't it? Katie seemed to be so gentle whenever she talked about it… as if she were a different person. In the end, though, it seemed better to simply put the stuff away. But we never disposed of it completely."

Riley wondered if a belief in Buddhism would have contributed to Katie's leaving home. Certainly nothing she had heard about it suggested anyone would have persuaded her to go. On the other hand, maybe having to tell her new Buddhist friends that she was pregnant had been an obstacle too far. It might be worth talking to those friends. She decided to broach the subject of Susan's recent visitor. "Mrs Francis said a man came to see you a few weeks ago. What did he want?"

A shudder went through Susan and she shook her head. When she spoke, her voice was as flat as iron. "I don't want to talk about him. It was nothing. Just some nonsense."

Riley said nothing, but waited, watching the older woman intently. Something in her manner told Riley she would talk, given time.

The tactic worked. Susan glanced across at Riley, and decided that keeping secrets was no longer an option.

"He wanted to know if we'd heard from her," she said finally, her voice paper dry. "I couldn't believe he was asking me such a thing. Not after all these years. I mean... we assumed she was dead. Of course this was before the police called the other day... and told me what they had found."

"So this man knew Katie was still alive." Riley wondered how anyone could be so callous. The effect on the old lady must have been unbearable. But why was he looking for her now? Did it mean Katie knew something that somehow made her a threat?

"He wouldn't say any more. He just kept demanding to know where she was... as if I was hiding her. When I asked him who he was and how he knew about Katie and where I lived, all he would say was that they knew everything about me."

"Did he say who 'they' were?"

"No. When I told him that I hadn't heard from Katie since she first left, and that she was probably dead, he seemed surprised, as if the idea hadn't occurred to him. I thought that was the end of it. But then he became very unpleasant – almost desperate. He started shouting and making threats, saying he had to find her, and if she spoke to anyone she'd regret it. We all would." She looked up with sad, moist eyes, her expression one of hopelessness. Her breathing had become faster, causing her thin chest to rise and fall unevenly. She swallowed and continued sadly. "I had no idea what he meant. All I could think of was that my Katie was alive."

Riley stroked the woman's arm. "What happened then?"

"He said he knew why Katie had run away and how it was all going to come out. I told him to leave… I was very frightened by then and suddenly he was churning everything around. You have to understand, I had managed to shut out most of the past… about what could have made Katie leave… and what might have happened to her. Or I thought I had." She swallowed and wiped a tear from her cheek. "I still can't truly understand, even now. Then he said he would make sure everybody knew and it would cause such a scandal." She stared up at Riley, her look suddenly vulnerable, like a small child. "Can he do that, Miss Gavin?"

"No," Riley said firmly. "No, he can't." She took the mystery man's threats to be a last desperate effort to frighten an old lady. Who was there to harm? John Pyle was dead, and Susan was beyond being affected by long-forgotten secrets. There was no leverage in a purported scandal if the main participants or victims were no longer around to suffer. And who would be shocked these days by a teenager running away?

Susan seemed to relax momentarily. "Poor Katie. So young… but already in love. I suppose it wasn't really her fault… " Her voice trailed off, and for a second Riley thought she had misheard.

"What did you say?"

The older woman opened her eyes again. She looked very tired now, the added strain of talking for so long showing in her face. "I'm sorry?"

"You said Katie was in love? Who with?"

"Oh, that won't help now. He died. It was such a shame. She was very fond of him, anyway."

"I'd still like to know. It could be important."

"But why, dear?"

"Because I want to find out where Katie was all this time. And what happened to her. I think we owe her that."

Susan Pyle nodded at last, and told Riley the boy's name.

Riley left an hour later. After they had finished talking, Susan showed signs of weakening and Mrs Francis suggested it might be time for Riley to leave. She rang for a doctor, then walked with Riley to her car.

Riley shivered in the early spring sunlight and wondered if the Buddhists were right; that there was only impermanence.

23

Frank Palmer swore softly as he faced yet another feature-less south London street, and debated going back for a talk with the youth in the alleyway. He had tried three different streets now, each one vaguely similar to the one described by the youth, but none yielding anything concrete in the form of the mysterious Maureen. He decided to check this last one and call it a day. The kid would most likely have legged it by now, anyway.

No more than two or three cars had passed by as he'd been walking down the street, and he could easily have been in some remote rural backwater instead of close to the centre of London. A child squealed nearby, and a woman emerged from a side gate and eyed him with care before walking to a car by the kerb and slipping inside. She quickly closed the door behind her and snicked the lock.

He found a footpath bordering a small industrial unit, just like the youth had described. So maybe he'd been telling the truth. This, apparently, was one of Maureen's regular haunts. He stopped and scanned the area carefully. On one side of the path was a high brick wall. On the other, a chain-link fence separated the path from the factory, thick with wind-blown rubbish and crumpled drink cans. Grass grew thick and spiky along the base, adding to the sense of wilderness. Just the place for a set-up if that was what the youth had planned.

Fifty yards along the path stood a battered golf trolley and leather bag. The youth had said she pulled it everywhere, her complete world in place of golf clubs. Across from it was a heavily bundled figure eating from a polystyrene tray, feet splayed out across the path. Nearby sat three other bulky figures, passing round a bottle. The youth had warned him Maureen wouldn't talk while others were close, that he had to get her alone otherwise he'd be wasting his time.

A train rattled by. This was going to be hard enough, without the added barrier of having to shout to make himself heard. With the other three in close attendance, if what the youth had said was true it would be impossible.

He stepped on past the path and walked away. Now he knew where Maureen hung out, he could always try again later. Barging in right now, with the others close by, would only scare her off. And there was the added risk that setting up shockwaves in the area might cause Angelina to disappear further underground. In the meantime there was something else he needed to do.

It was close to lunchtime and Palmer was approaching his office when his phone rang. It was Riley, on her way back from Suffolk. He could hear the hubbub of voices and traffic in the background, and guessed she was calling from a filling station.

"Any news of Angelina?" Riley asked,

"Getting closer," he replied. "But nothing solid yet. She's moving around, probably with someone. But I did latch on to our two friends. They're good; they know some neat ways of throwing anyone off their trail. Anyone would think they had something to hide."

"How did you find them?"

"I got lucky; I picked them up near your place, then followed them down to the embankment and around the West End. Whatever they were doing, they were slick; the driver would slow to a crawl, the passenger would jump out and disappear, then be back by the time the van had gone fifty yards. I think they were checking contacts. Then they headed out to the M40." Palmer explained that he had followed them out through west London on to the M40 motorway, hanging back until the traffic had become too light to avoid being seen. He was fairly sure they hadn't spotted him, although they had taken a couple of unlikely detours which he was sure were meant to isolate anyone following. At that point he'd backed off. The M40 led out towards Oxford and the west. A big space in which to get lost. "How about you?"

Riley filled him in on her talk with Katie's mother and the girl's pregnancy. "At least I got a name – a boyfriend who may or may not have been the one to get her pregnant. His name was Nicholas Friedman. He was about seventeen. Katie mentioned him in such a way, her mother said it plain she was in love. I'll call Nikki Bruce in case she can turn up something from the archives. Failing that, there's always Katie's school. It might be a dead end, but it's the only lead we've got."

Palmer agreed. "Did you say he *was* seventeen?"

"He died. I'm not sure how."

"Oh. Anything else?"

"Susan Pyle got a visit from two men a few weeks ago. They sound like our two."

"What did they want?"

"Information about Katie. It sounds as if they knew she hadn't died all those years ago. They didn't pull their punches, either." Riley told Palmer about the threats. "I've no idea what they meant by a scandal."

"They were just trying to scare her. She OK?"

"No. Not really. She's very sick and unlikely to get better. If it was our two, it sounds as if they must have known where Katie was for at least some of the time." And probably, thought Riley, what had happened in her last few minutes down by the Thames.

"Assuming," said Palmer, "they were the same two men in the white van. But we still don't know who the other man is – the one who spoke to Henry."

"True enough." There was a pause, then Riley asked: "Are you still OK with this?" She meant was he still on board. Even over the phone Palmer was sharp enough to know what she was getting at.

"You kidding? You think I'm going to bail out just when the fun starts?"

"Just checking. You don't have to, you know."

"Forget it. Anyway, I need an adrenalin rush. Whereabouts are you?"

"Not far. Just approaching the M25 heading west. I'm thinking of having another chat with de Haan. See if I can push him into letting me see Henry this time."

"I wouldn't bet on it. Worth a try, though. You want company?"

"I was hoping you'd say that. Where shall we meet?"

Palmer pushed open the downstairs door to his office and climbed the stairs. After the morning he'd had, he needed a warm-up and a smoke before she arrived and began voicing her disapproval. "I'm at the office. Coffee's on me."

24

The iron gates to the headquarters of the Church of Flowing Light were wide open when Riley and Palmer arrived, and the lodge still looked deserted. Palmer lounged in the passenger seat, scanning the surrounding scenery.

"Open all hours," he commented. "Unusual, I'd have thought."

Riley nodded. "Maybe they've got nothing to hide."

"Nothing they mind anyone seeing, anyway."

He had said little since leaving the office at Uxbridge, and Riley guessed he was impatient to find out more about the identity of the two men who were following her. While they were on a long quiet stretch along the M40, he had made a couple of phone calls, one of them to an unnamed contact Riley guessed was in the Met, asking for details on Nicholas Friedman. The person on the other end had said something which left Palmer with a silly grin on his face.

"So," said Riley with studied lightness, after he'd switched off the phone. "Your snitch in the records office is a girl." She hadn't seen Palmer act this way before, and it made her want to laugh. She really didn't know much about his private life, but at least there were signs every now and then that he had one.

But Palmer wasn't playing. "She's just a friend, that's all." He stuffed his phone in his pocket and concentrated on the passing traffic, but Riley could see by the set of his jaw that he was still smiling.

"Of course. And the relationship is strictly professional.

Hah. Tell that to your mother. Incidentally, when you promise to call a girl, you should stick to it. Remember Nikki Bruce?" She recounted with relish what the reporter had told her, and Palmer seemed to sink in his seat.

"I wondered when that was going to come up. She's not my sort, that's all. She wanted bright lights and lots of attention. Not really my scene. Have you heard from John Mitcheson lately?"

The question was a deliberate curved ball to stop Riley asking more questions. When she didn't reply Palmer grinned knowingly and settled back with his eyes closed, the conversation over.

Unlike Riley's first visit, there were no signs of life beyond the chorus of birdsong in the trees surrounding the main house. And when she parked, there was no spooky appearance by Quine from the trees, demanding her car keys. There were no rows of other vehicles in evidence, either. Evidently things were a little slack on the meetings front today.

Riley had no specific plan in mind, and after chewing over the options with Palmer on the drive down, had decided to play it by ear. They still only had de Haan's earlier admission that Henry was with them: no real proof. All they could hope for was that he might let something slip about Henry's whereabouts.

The front door was ajar. She pushed it back and stepped inside. The reception area was deserted, although voices drifted in from the direction of the meeting room. Riley walked across to the connecting door de Haan had led her through the other morning. It opened easily and she stepped through, with Palmer close behind.

The room where the crowd of the other morning had gathered was now empty, and the chairs were stacked neatly against one wall to the side of the podium. The banner was gone, as were the microphone and lectern. Riley glanced at Palmer, who merely shrugged. They heard the voices again, one of them loud and accusing. Down at the far end of the room, standing in another doorway, was de Haan, in discussion with a man in overalls. The pastor was stabbing the air and pointing towards a radiator with a broken end of metal pipe leaking into a growing pool of water. He broke off when he heard their footsteps.

When he recognised Riley, his face dropped momentarily into a scowl before resuming the same genial expression he had adopted the first time they met. He flapped a hand at the man in overalls and scurried across the room towards them, his small feet carrying him with deceptive speed.

"Miss Gavin," he said expansively, his voice booming around the panelled walls. He was dressed in a suit today, the expensive fabric immaculately tailored over his bulk, and his shoes gleamed black under the mix of natural and overhead lighting. A crisp white shirt and silver tie completed the image of a successful and important man. He lifted one meaty hand in greeting, but looked anything but pleased to see her again. "I'm sorry – we're having trouble with the heating." His eyes ran over Palmer before coming back to Riley with a faint frown. "Did we have an appointment? Only I have to go out."

"This won't take long," said Riley.

"Good. Good. Let's go out into the reception area before that man begins banging again." He took her arm in a firm grip and ushered them both back through the door, pulling it shut behind him. Then he turned and looked at Palmer, who was studying the wood panelling as if it might yield up some long-held secrets. "And this is –?"

"Frank Palmer," the investigator replied. "Along for the

ride." He smiled pleasantly and took de Haan's hand. "Nice place you've got here. Peaceful."

The pastor shook his hand and gave a ghost of a smile, dropping into professional mode. "Thank you. How kind. We like to think it has a certain serene simplicity. Some say we should do it up, modernise, but – " He shrugged – "there are much better things on which we can spend our limited resources. Are you a practising churchgoer, Mr Palmer?"

Palmer shook his head. "No, not really. God gave up on me a long time ago."

De Haan looked almost shocked. "Oh, I doubt that, Mr Palmer. God never gives up on anyone. Perhaps you need to re-establish contact." He let go of Palmer's hand and turned to Riley. "So, what can I do for you?"

"I'd still like to see Henry," replied Riley. "How is he?"

"Oh, much better. But still not up to visitors, I'm afraid." Pastor de Haan gave a brief smile. "Perhaps in another day or two, when he's feeling stronger."

"Stronger?" This from Palmer.

"Yes. He's been through a traumatic time. It's taken its toll and he needs complete rest. I'm concerned that anything stressful will put him back completely. Do you suffer from stress, Mr Palmer?"

"Me? No. At least, only when I think I'm being given the run-around." He smiled enigmatically, his eyes never leaving de Haan's face. "That gets to me quite a bit."

"Oh." De Haan glanced at Riley with a flicker of nerves and she wondered if he was hoping for Quine to appear like a genie out of the aged woodwork and rescue him. But she had a feeling Quine wasn't around, otherwise he'd have been out here by now.

"I was talking to Henry's neighbour the other day," she

said chattily. "She's looking after Henry's cat and sends her regards, by the way. She said Henry showed her some snaps once, of a day out with some young people. I got the impression it was here."

"Quite possibly," de Haan murmured, with a faint frown. "We have held barbecues and functions here from time to time, but it's not something I encourage. The main thrust of our efforts lies in the cities. I suppose Henry might have taken some photos at one time." He brushed at a sudden hint of perspiration on his brow, his eyes shifting between Riley and Palmer.

"So he helps with the young people, then? I thought his efforts were purely on the admin side." Riley wondered why de Haan was so nervous. She started to turn away, then looked back at him. "I didn't realise he was so public-spirited. He's such a dark horse. Still, just like him to record everything."

De Haan looked as if he wanted to gag, and his face lost its colour. "How do you mean?"

"Oh, nothing. Just that Henry's a newsman through to his socks. And we tend to over-record everything. You never know when you might stumble on a story. Like these missing kids that are in the news at the moment."

De Haan's expression hardened, but he managed a brief nod. "A sad sign of the times, I fear."

Riley pulled out the folded flyer from the coffee house, showing Angelina Boothe-Davison's details and photograph. It was a spur of the moment thing; until they had entered the building, she'd forgotten all about it. "Like this girl. Is this one of your flyers?"

De Haan looked at it as though it might bite, then nodded. "We try to help when asked, yes. I remember this one vaguely. A tragic case." His expression softened as if to reflect his concern, as if the missing girl was a personal burden he had to bear alone. "Poor girl. She stepped off the path. We can only hope she can be persuaded to come back."

"So you haven't found her yet?"

"Not yet. Why do you need to know?"

Riley ignored the question. "But the parents asked for your help? Why would they do that?"

"I don't follow."

"How did they know to approach you? You're not exactly in Yellow Pages."

He studied her for a second, a pulse beating in his throat, and glanced at Palmer before answering. "Actually, it was a bit of both," he admitted carefully. "If I remember correctly, a friend of the family asked if we could intervene. I suggested they got the parents to call us." He shrugged with elaborate vagueness. "I don't recall the specifics. It seemed more important to get the notices out there so we could begin the search before it was too late. People have very short memories, Miss Gavin. Life moves so quickly, demanding our every spare moment. It's vital to get people to think before they forget what they have seen. Is this important to you – a family friend, perhaps? Because if you have any ideas about where she might be, you should tell me." His words sounded almost syrupy in their sincerity, but Riley thought she detected a sub-text which was more about suspicion. She was also certain he was lying about remembering how the Church became involved. She got the feeling de Haan was a man who forgot very little.

She folded the flyer away and shook her head. "I don't. But when we spoke last time, I got the impression you only took people in – and then only if they came to you for help. This sounds as if you actually go out looking for missing people on behalf of their families."

He inclined his head as if dealing with a persistent and not terribly quick child. "Well, we do that, too, of course. When we're asked. I'm sorry if I didn't make that clear before. But I fail to see why this should be of interest to you or –" He glanced at Palmer – "your friend, here. We have certain facilities and skills which allow us to perform that function. It would be wrong to waste them. Now, if you don't -"

"In exchange for a fee?"

He stiffened. "I'm sorry, but that's none of your business."

"I'm sorry, too. The grateful parents show their gratitude, is what I mean."

De Haan took several seconds to answer, as if willing himself under control. "Some do, of course. But it is not and never has been a condition of supplying our expertise. That would be little better than bounty-hunting." His mouth clamped shut on the words in evident distaste.

"And Mr Quine?"

De Haan frowned. "Mr Quine is a valuable asset. He has a great deal of experience in this area. I would be foolish if I denied anyone the opportunity to use his skills. I'm sorry, but what does this have to do with Henry Pearcy?"

"Where does he get them?" Palmer put in, taking the lead.

"Get what?" De Haan looked confused by the switch.

"His skills. Finding missing kids isn't something you get through the Open University or as an NVQ. What is he – ex-police?"

"I really have no idea. I seem to recall he may have once worked in your law enforcement field, now you mention it. As far as our work is involved, he has an understanding of the habits and networks in current use among the young, which is invaluable. As I said to you before, over the years we have built up some expertise at tracing runaways. It's not our main activity, but I'm proud to say we have an enviable record of success… when we're permitted to work freely, that is." He bit the words off with a snap, which Riley took as a sign that she was finally getting under his skin.

"Permitted?"

"Unhappily, not all those who are found wish to go home." He shrugged impatiently, wanting rid of the subject, and no doubt the two of them. "There's very little we can do to force them, under those circumstances. We do our best, but sometimes prior… events are against us."

"Such as?"

"Family matters. I'm sure I don't have to go into that. Adults, you see, usually find their own solutions, Miss Gavin. One way or another. The young do not have that luxury, and it is they who have most need of guidance when they feel the need to tread their own paths. But you probably know that already."

Riley felt the sudden force of de Haan's anger. From irritation at being questioned, he now looked as if he had stepped over an invisible line he had not intended to cross. Or was it the passion of the true believer? He ducked his head, his cheeks showing a sheen of perspiration, and Riley wondered if he was always this affected by his own rhetoric. "Please, forgive me," he added lamely. "It's simply that I feel… strongly about what we do here."

"I can tell. Thank you – you've been very helpful." She turned to go, then paused. "By the way, has Mr Quine been to the Suffolk coast recently?"

De Haan's eyes flared in surprise before he clamped

down on his reactions. "I'm sorry?"

"Suffolk. It's on the east coast. Has he been there?"

"I have absolutely no idea, Miss Gavin. You'll have to ask him, won't you?" His expression was suddenly ice cold, all attempts at geniality gone.

"Maybe I will."

Riley turned and walked out, leaving Palmer to follow. Her head was ringing with the echo of de Haan's words: *"But you probably know that already."*

She had deliberately not told de Haan about Katie, yet she was certain that he knew. Could Henry have told him about her? She wondered if it was the real explanation for his unease. Pastor de Haan had allowed his control to slip a fraction, letting Riley know that he knew more about Katie's past than he had any right to.

Back in the car, Riley glanced at Palmer. "What do you think?"

Palmer toyed with a cigarette, flicking it against his thumbnail. He wore a slight frown. "If I was a betting man," he said finally, "I'd say Pastor de Haan, along with his changeable accent, is as bent as a dead dog's dick."

"How quaint. Should we tell DS McKinley? He might be able to force them to produce Henry. At least then he might take me off his list of possible suspects."

Palmer shrugged and said nothing, so Riley stopped the car by the gates and took out the card the police officer had given her. He answered after three rings. "McKinley."

"You asked me to call if I heard anything about Henry Pearcy," Riley announced.

"Did I?" McKinley sounded tired. "Oh, yes. Sorry, that's no longer an investigation."

"What?" Riley was surprised. "But you said his disappearance was suspicious."

"So it was. But not any longer. Word came from on high; Mr Pearcy had some kind of breakdown. As a result of taking some anti-depressants, he had a fall in his hotel room. He's now staying with friends. There's nothing more I can do, I'm afraid. Now, if that's all, I have an urgent call."

"Breakdown? But that's crazy—" But the line was dead. McKinley had hung up.

Riley switched off her mobile and dropped it in her lap. "Do you believe that? What does that mean, word from on high?" She drove out of the gates, causing a spurt of gravel behind her.

Palmer pulled a face. "It means a senior person on the totem pole pulled rank. You don't argue with that if you value your pension. De Haan must have got to somebody."

"And that's it? That's all you're prepared to do?" She looked at him in exasperation. "Why don't you go ahead and light your cigarette; it might give you some inspiration."

"Well, if you wanted me to tie de Haan to a chair and beat him over the head with a rubber hose, you should have said. I said he's bent, but that doesn't mean he's involved in Katie Pyle's death. And if he's convinced the Met that Henry's safe, there's nothing we can do." He gave a wry smile and put the unlit cigarette back in the packet. "All the same, it might be interesting to go back and take a quiet look around."

Riley smiled with relief and put her foot down.

When they were close to Uxbridge, Palmer gave her directions to a small block of flats set in a leafy back road. He hesitated, then asked her if she wanted to come in.

"I don't know. Is it safe?"

"Perfectly. Why shouldn't it be?" He gave her a shark-like

smile. "If I'd wanted to tie you up and do unspeakable things to you, I'd have done it before now." He punished her by taking out a cigarette and lighting it, and blowing the smoke around the inside of the car.

Riley ignored the provocation and tried another tack. "Well, I wouldn't want to risk upsetting your girlfriend. Or doesn't she mind you inviting strange women into your lair?"

He gave her a sideways look. "God, you women are so transparent. Actually, my girlfriend, as you insist on calling her, doesn't mind. In any case, she's a lot stranger than you are." He opened the door and got out. "Tea, coffee or see you tomorrow?"

"Palmer, you've got a real way with women. Make it tea." She followed him into the two-storey block of apartments, where he led the way to the first floor. He unlocked the door and ushered her into a neat, well-ordered sitting room with a small kitchen. The furniture was good quality and comfortable, and the colour scheme pleasing if unspectacular. Riley was surprised by how tidy the place was, in spite of needing a dust.

Palmer noticed her look as he walked through to the kitchen. "I don't do dust. I prefer to wait for the local electricity sub-station to build up a bit of static." While he made tea, Riley nosed around, peering at bookshelves and out into the rear gardens. She decided against intruding into the bedroom.

Palmer returned, carrying two mugs of tea.

"You just don't get this, do you?" he said with a smile, handing her one of the mugs. "You'd have been happier if I'd turned out to be a slob with pizza boxes piled up on the table and empty beer bottles rolling around on the carpet."

Riley felt guilty. "Actually, I didn't know what to expect.

Something a little less… orderly, I suppose?"

He stirred his tea, licked the spoon and shrugged. "So, you reckon I've burned my bridges with Nikki Bruce, then?"

"Burned and dropped in the river. Unless you fancy a girlfriend in the broadcasting media."

"Forget it. Anyway, I prefer police uniforms to designer jackets." He tried to give what Riley guessed was a deliberately boyish snigger, but missed it by a mile. They talked a little about what they would do next, then Riley left him to it and drove home.

What she didn't expect to find was a stranger sitting on the front steps.

25

It was the man Mr Grobowski had seen hanging around. He was thin, wore glasses, and his clothes bore the crumpled and over-pressed look of constant wear and cleaning, like someone governed by upbringing and habit but constrained by a limited wardrobe. Riley guessed his age at anywhere between forty and sixty; it was hard to tell.

He stood up as she approached and brushed at the seat of his pants before stepping down on to the path. He was taller than she'd thought, and slightly stooped, like a spent reed. Then she realised she had seen his face before; he was the Nissan driver from outside the headquarters of the Church of Flowing Light. She stopped a cautious three paces away, and wondered if he was a friend of Quine's.

"Miss Gavin." If he was nervous he hid it well, and he plainly knew who she was. Riley wondered what had prevented him from making himself known before. She doubted it was shyness. "My name is Eric Friedman."

She kept her expression blank. *Friedman.* Another building block suddenly began to fall into place. "What do you want?"

"I'd like to talk to you. I think you know what it's about." His voice was well modulated, the words carefully pronounced, and Riley wondered what his profession might be.

She gave it a few seconds of deliberation, then mentally tossed a coin. "You'd better come in," she said, and led the way up the stairs. There was no sign of Mr Grobowski, so she guessed he was out. She picked up her mail on the way and unlocked the door to the flat. As she pushed it open, the air left her lungs in a rush.

The walls either side of the hallway were covered in red spray paint; vivid and garish, it was a hideous pattern of meaningless scrawl and foul words, a mish-mash of graffiti. A thick spray of the same colour ran down to the floor, across a small, semicircular antique table where Riley usually kept her keys and bits and pieces, and up again in a wild slash across a row of hooks holding a windcheater, scarf and spare jacket. A large, dripping cross, glittering with black paint, stood out starkly on one wall, with smaller ones on each door.

As Riley stepped inside, her feet crunched through pieces of broken crockery. Plates, saucers... her teapot – even an unused butter dish. It must have been kicked or thrown from the kitchen. As she stepped over the shards she heard Friedman take in a deep breath and mutter softly behind her. It might almost have been a prayer.

The hallway was merely a taster of what lay ahead. As she entered the living room, she recoiled with the shock. More crosses and more spray paint. A lot more. They were daubed across every surface, soaked into fabrics, ghosted across the ceilings and walls in a mad, obscene frenzy, a venomous mix of crazy art exhibition crossed with inner-city underpass. Nothing had been spared.

The other rooms were the same, with food from the fridge trampled into the carpets alongside broken glassware and slashed chairs. Cans of beans and tomatoes had been opened and sprayed around, and the vivid slash of orange juice arced across the floor and up one wall like a grotesque smile. A jagged hole pierced the television screen, exposing its electronic guts, and her laptop lay on its side, mangled beyond repair. In the bedroom, the mattress had been opened up like a dissected corpse and the duvet was a tangled frenzy of scarred fabric, gaping holes and feathers mixed with faeces and urine. The human smell hung heavy in the air, choking and vile, and deeply personal. Riley backed out and closed the door, too stunned even to feel sick.

Eric Friedman stood in the centre of the devastation that had been the living room, watching her. He looked greyer than he had a few minutes before, but somehow resigned, as if this was nothing new. His first words since speaking outside confirmed it.

"I'm so sorry," he said. "I've seen this before. It's… appalling."

"Christ! When?" She'd seen vandalism like it, too. But never this close and never directed at her.

"Somebody crossed them once before." He looked around and shook his head. "But that wasn't as bad as this. Not as… extreme. They must feel very threatened."

"They? You mean you know who did this?"

"I can guess."

With a guilty start she remembered the flat's other occasional inhabitant. She ran through to the bedroom, peering beneath the bed and behind overturned furniture, looking for any space small enough for a cat to hide in. "Cat? Where are you, Cat?" But there was nowhere left that hadn't been trashed. She went back out to the hallway, convincing herself that he'd have taken one look at intruders and bolted for safety.

She led Eric Friedman back out of the flat and locked the door behind her. The thought of dealing with what lay inside was beyond her at the moment; she'd come back and pick up a few things later. She doubted, however, the vandals had left much to salvage; she would probably have to start again – get a team in here to clean up, and leave it to the insurers. Right now she was too upset to think clearly.

She went back downstairs and stopped at Mr Grobowski's flat. This time she could hear him singing inside, accompanied by the rattle of pots and pans. She leaned on his bell until the singing stopped and he threw open the door.

"Hello, miss," he greeted her enthusiastically, the smell of cooking wafting around him. If he had heard any noise from above, he evidently wasn't going to complain about it. Then he noticed Eric Friedman in the background. "Ah. So your friend he has come in. Good. What can I do for you, miss?"

"Mr Grobowski, have you seen my cat?" she asked.

He nodded and gestured with a large thumb. "You bet, yes. He is in my kitchens, eating. First time he comes in, I promise. You not feeding hims, maybe?"

Riley sighed with relief. "It's a long story, I'm afraid. You haven't heard any noise from my flat, have you?"

"Not a things, no. I been out a lot, busy with some stuff. Lots of peoples, they want my times. Why? You had a party, huh?" He grinned and rolled his eyes as if he could give her a few hints about partying. "Is why your cat he move homes?"

"No, no party, I promise. Look, I might have to be away for a couple of days. Could you look after the cat for a while, please? Feed him some of your fabulous cooking?"

"Sure, miss. Of course. He good cat. Like Polish recipe. Don't you worry."

Riley thanked the old man and led Friedman to the coffee shop where she had seen the poster of Angelina Boothe-Davison. In spite of feelings of shock and nausea, she wondered if the girl had been found yet… and if the

Angelina who came back would be the same one who'd gone missing.

She asked Friedman to order two coffees and went to find a corner well away from the nearest customers. As soon as she sat down, she had to clamp her hands between her knees to still a sudden violent fit of trembling. She closed her eyes, instantly seeing flashes of the destruction to her flat, and opened them again before her stomach gave way and she threw up. Friedman set down two cups on the table but said nothing, stirring his coffee and waiting, his eyes on her. His hands were bony and red, with fingernails bitten to the quick and the skin of his first two fingers stained with nicotine. In the intrusive glare of the overhead lights he looked worn and stripped of energy, like an old car with too many miles on the clock. Only his eyes retained any spark.

"You said you know who did it," said Riley softly, finally getting the shivers under control.

Friedman nodded. "So do you." He looked at her steadily, then reached into his jacket and took out a three-by-four coloured snapshot in a worn plastic sleeve. It was of a teenage boy, smiling and fresh-faced in a school uniform jacket with a shield on the breast pocket. He had a ghosting of adolescent hair across his top lip and a few spots on his chin, and could have been any teenage boy anywhere. But the resemblance between the man and the boy was obvious.

"His name is Nicholas," he said softly, and let the photo rest on the table between them. "He's my son. He left home ten years ago, saying he wanted some space." Friedman shook his head with a bitter expression. "Space. It was the thing everybody was after at the time. Space to do, space to be. Space to… anyway, Nick had been having a tough time at school; bullies and exams and… other things. It was all piling in on him. In the end it got too much. We tried talking to him… drawing him out. But he wouldn't tell us. Then one morning he said he couldn't take any more, and announced he was thinking of going away. Just for a few days, to clear his head." He played with his cup, twirling it round in the saucer, slopping some of the contents on to his hand. If it hurt he seemed not to notice. "We tried to talk him out of it – he was only seventeen, for heaven's sake, no age to be wandering off. Whatever problems he had – thought he had – we could help him through. I thought we'd managed it, too. But he waited until we were at work one day, then bunked off school and disappeared. Cleared out his savings account of a hundred pounds or so and took off. Just like that."

"What happened?"

"We looked for him, of course, but it was like he'd left the planet. Not a trace. Well, you know what that's like. I went over his tracks immediately afterwards, and a hundred times since." He looked at Riley, and in that drawn face she saw failure, loss and impotence. "We used to be close, Nicholas and I. We did things together all the time… football matches, cricket – that kind of thing. I thought I knew him." He trembled like a man with a high fever. "Eventually I pieced together a picture, of sorts. On the day he left home he met up with a girl he knew. They stayed in a friend's parents' caravan on the south coast for a few days."

"Friend?"

"Just a friend. Maybe his only one." He stopped and sipped his drink, wincing as if the coffee was too bitter.

Riley was holding her breath, dreading what he would say next.

"Who was the girl?"

"The one everyone's been looking for," he said finally, looking her in the eye. "Katie Pyle."

They left the coffee shop and walked. Friedman suggested some fresh air would do her good, but she wasn't sure which of them was in more need of it. He seemed very fragile, as if he was holding on by willpower alone, and she wondered how long it had been since he'd eaten properly. She allowed him to dictate the direction, along quiet streets, through occasional pockets of green and past rows of houses and parked cars, skirting the occasional burst of activity yet crossing busy roads with unerring ease. The pity was, she had a feeling he was never going to be able to walk fast enough or far enough to get away from what hounded him. It would follow him always.

They found a small park and a children's playground, with a few battered playthings and a worn patch of stubby grass. A bench sat amid a scattering of litter, close by a pair of watchful mothers with a clutch of small, shrill children. It wasn't a restful place and there was a coolness in the air with a threat of rain, but she could see that Friedman needed to talk.

"I'm a lawyer," Friedman told her, after a few minutes of silence. "Was, anyway… before Nicholas left. I used to work for the Ministry of Defence, producing and vetting contracts, checking agreements, writing tenders, that sort of thing. It wasn't the most interesting work in the world. Nicholas always said I was one of the 'grey men'… like something out of *Yes, Minister* only not as colourful. Or exciting." He smiled to himself, a brief flicker of the lips as a memory reeled by. "He had a great sense of fun. Infectious. Lively. He could light up a room just by being there."

"Where did he go?"

"We found out later that he moved on from the caravan and joined a church. Not the established church... an independent group called the Church of Flowing Light." He looked up at her. "But you know them already, don't you?"

"Yes."

"He wasn't religious or anything – none of us was, to be honest. Why he joined them is still a mystery. But then so was his leaving. A total puzzle."

"Was it?"

"Pardon?"

She watched him for reaction, then said, "Did you know that when Katie Pyle joined Nicholas, she was pregnant?"

If she was expecting him to show surprise, she was disappointed. The news had little effect other than mild interest; no shock, no associated guilt, nothing. Yet Riley was pretty sure the revelation was new to him. "I didn't, no. Who was the father?" The question sounded normal, with no hint of guile, and she stared at him. If he was acting, he was very good at it.

"Well, I thought... your son."

But Friedman shook his head slowly, with enormous sadness. "No. It wasn't. I wish it could have been."

"What do you mean?"

He stared at his hands for a moment. "Because the 'other things' I spoke of earlier – the fears torturing him – were the facts of his sexuality, Miss Gavin. My son was gay."

Even as Riley took in what he was saying, she saw his eyes shift momentarily past her, scanning the area beyond her shoulder. He froze, his body stiffening and his eyes taking on the look of a hunted beast. His mouth worked helplessly. "I... I must go."

"What is it?" said Riley. She turned but couldn't see anything apart from the children and their mothers, and a few birds diving for scraps on the ground. When she turned back, Friedman was on his feet but hunched down, scrabbling in the pocket of his jacket. He produced a piece of white card and thrust it into her hand.

"Here," he whispered. "Take this and call me. I can't stay." Then he was hurrying away, thin shoulders bent and head down, a Lowry figure desperate not to be noticed.

When Riley turned to look again behind her, she caught a brief glimpse of a white van turning a corner a hundred yards away. She could have sworn there was a builder's logo on the side, but when she turned back to tell Friedman, he was nowhere in sight.

26

Riley tried Palmer's number , but the automatic voice told her the number was unavailable. She wondered what he was up to and dialled Nikki Bruce. While she waited to be put through, she studied the card Friedman had given her. It bore the name and number of a hotel, and a mobile number. She'd never heard of the place but saw by the number that it was central London and, she guessed, somewhere cheap. She thought about what he'd said. If Nicholas Friedman had been gay, it shot down any theory about him being responsible for Katie's pregnancy. Unless…

"I thought you'd left me high and dry." The *Post* reporter's voice drew her back. "What's new?"

Riley told her about Susan Pyle, and her revelation of Katie's condition. "At least we now have a reason for her leaving home. According to Susan Pyle, her husband wasn't the sort to take that kind of news well… at least, not at first. It makes me wonder if there isn't a child out there somewhere, waiting for its mother to come back."

"We could find out," said Nikki. "I know a friendly DCI who owes me a huge favour. What else?"

Riley related her meeting with Eric Friedman. She left out his hotel and phone number, principally because she didn't think he would be up to a sudden and all-engulfing press interest if Nikki happened to let slip his number to a colleague on the *Post.*

"That's unbelievable," said Nikki. "What did you say his job was?"

Riley hesitated. Given the resources available to the

press, it wouldn't take long to trace the department Friedman had worked in. On the other hand, given the rate of turnover in most government offices, getting anything up-to-date was no easy task. "He used to be a lawyer with the MOD," she said finally. "Years back. He'd have been an ideal target because he wouldn't have wanted anything broadcast which could have threatened his job. At least, that's what they thought."

"But it all went wrong. Poor man. And he just took off?"

"Yes. He got spooked by something. How about you?"

Nikki sounded a bit tense. "Look, why don't we meet up? I think there are a few things we can share. How about your place? I'm up that way later, anyway."

"I've got the decorators in," Riley lied. Telling Nikki about the state of her flat on the phone would be like trumpeting it to the world, something she wasn't sure would help at the moment. Instead, she suggested a pub off Kensington Church Street which kept strange hours. Neutral territory.

"I know it," Nikki agreed, and hung up.

Riley sat thinking about how much she had told Nikki, and what the results might be. Well, it was too late now. She rang Palmer but got the unavailable message again. Maybe he was in a bad reception area. She tried Friedman's hotel but the receptionist said he was out. At least it confirmed he was registered there.

She arrived in the pub early and watched customers come and go. Among the suits of both sexes who followed her in, she saw nobody who looked as if they might be Nikki Bruce's press colleagues. It wasn't that she didn't trust Nikki, but she wasn't taking any chances. While she waited, she tried Palmer again. Still not available.

Eventually, the *Post* reporter walked in. She wore slacks

and a thick polo jumper under a leather jacket, an unself-conscious display of expensive yet practical chic. If she noticed heads turning, she seemed to take it in her stride. Riley guessed that she was already benefiting from an enhanced sense of confidence about her new job.

Nikki smiled with a lift of one eyebrow. "Did I overstep the line, suggesting your place? I didn't put you down as the territorial sort."

"I'm not," said Riley. "It's just that I had visitors. They rearranged my furniture – amongst other things. Now the place needs fumigating."

Nikki's smile faded. "Burglars?"

"If they were, they didn't steal anything." Riley glossed over the extent of the damage. "I think it was a warning to back off."

"But that's awful."

"I know. I also think I know who did it." She raised a hand to cut short any further questions. It wouldn't help with what she needed to know. "So, what's the latest?"

Nikki gave her a funny look. "You haven't seen the *Post*?"

"No. I've been out of town."

"Oh. Right." Nikki fished out her notebook and began to read, then put it aside. "What am I doing? I know all the details back to front. Another kid's been found dead."

Riley experienced a feeling of dread and saw a sullen face on a poster. "Was her name Angelina?"

Nikki frowned. "No. That's a new one. This one was a rough sleeper – a girl named Delphine Wishman, daughter of a senior executive in the aviation industry, would you believe? That's more military than civil, although I wasn't allowed to put it in the report. He's got juice and had the reference to his own position pulled under the Official Secrets Act. Could be more to do with family embarrassment than his place at the boardroom table."

"Why?"

Nikki glanced down at her notebook. "From what I've picked up so far, it seems like the same old story: Delphine was an only child. She was spoiled rotten, sent to boarding school to get her out of the way, then rebelled and got in with the wrong crowd. A few arrests for minor drugs use, one charge of soliciting which was thrown out for lack of evidence – the aggrieved punter decided not to pursue it, probably when he found out how young she was – then Daddy kicked her out and washed his hands of her. Common story."

"You really don't like them, do you?"

"Huh?"

"Middle class parents whose kids go off the tracks."

"No, I suppose not. But I do understand them." She frowned and went back to her notebook. "Along the way, and so far unsubstantiated, there were allegations that the father abused her when she was younger."

"Who was the source?"

"Delphine. She was one angry kid. She retracted it later, but the damage was already done. The father said he'd never forgive her."

"Was it justified?"

"He claimed his reputation was ruined, that he was being shunned in the business world because of what his daughter had said and had even been asked to resign by his fellow directors. Frankly, I think it's hogwash."

"Why? You don't believe in kids going against the grain for no other reason than the sheer hell of it?"

Nikki looked surprised and chewed her lip. "Sure. I suppose."

"What about the mother – what was her story?"

Nikki had the good grace to look pained. "The mother came down on the father's side and said it was all rubbish… that he'd never laid a finger on her because the dates the girl quoted didn't match, and she could prove it from his diary. He was out of the country a lot, apparently."

"So the girl had perceived memories?"

"More like a load of rancid bitterness. The social workers got involved and tried to get to the daughter to press charges, but in the end she wouldn't co-operate. They had to let it go for lack of proof. But mud sticks. None of this made the papers, by the way. Then she ran off again."

"How did she die?"

"Overdose. Sent her into shock. She never recovered. They found her on some waste ground near a known crack den."

Riley sat back and tried to see where this connected with Henry or Katie. On the surface it was just another girl who had taken a tragically wrong turn.

Nikki was still talking. "But get this: according to the mother, after she ran off the second time, Delphine rang her mother to say she was fine and was in good hands. She didn't give much detail, but from what little she said, the mother swore the girl had gone and got religion."

"Don't tell me."

"She couldn't be certain, but when I mentioned your Church of Flowing Light she said it sounded vaguely familiar. Apparently Delphine said something about being introduced to a charity church group by a boy she knew."

Riley felt a slow burn of anger. Why on earth could they be led so easily in some ways and not others? She wondered who the boy had been and what had happened to him afterwards. "Why do they fall for it?"

Nikki looked up from her notebook, her face suddenly set. "Have you seen how these kids live?"

"Yes."

"Really? I'm not just talking about doorways and benches, where they're simply bundles for people to ignore. I mean the alleys and subways and underpasses, where people throw their rubbish – and worse."

"I've seen it," Riley repeated. During her search for Katie, she'd seen far too much of it; she'd trodden through litter-strewn streets, into darkened, filthy underpasses puddled with stagnant, urine-stained water; she'd ducked under construction site barriers and through barbed wire fencing, and forced her way through wooden hoardings that did little to keep out the truly desperate looking for shelter. In the firelight from make-do braziers she'd seen rats scurrying over sleeping bodies; she'd heard the screams of nightmares in the shadows, and faced the frozen expressions of those who didn't want her around unless she put her hand in her pocket – and sometimes not even then.

Nikki nodded. "Then you'll know that there's a point where they're easy to get at. Where they'll do anything to get away – except go back home."

"Yes."

Nikki shrugged. "I've been in this business for a long time, Riley, so I'm the last person to think there's a conspiracy behind every story. If I thought that, I'd go mental. But with this one…" She shook her head.

"Go on."

"Well, I asked some questions about the Church of Flowing Light. I got a mixed reception."

"How so?"

"Well, a couple of my contacts said the Church has a reputation among kids for helping out. Food where needed, blankets, that sort of thing. Even somewhere to stay if the kids are clean of drugs. They're pretty much into the God thing, too, but they don't shove it down anyone's throat."

Riley could feel a *but* coming, loud and clear.

"One of my colleagues said he'd heard something else. An outreach worker in Kennington reported them for assaulting a kid one night. She was doing her rounds among a group of homeless ex-servicemen and walked in on two men holding this kid down on a piece of waste ground. She asked what they were doing and they said the kid had attacked them, probably after a bad drug reaction, so they'd had to subdue him. She thought something didn't look right, so she got the kid out of there and took him to hospital. It was lucky she did."

"What was wrong with him?"

"What shocked the medics was that he had signs of severe scalding on the inside of his mouth and throat, and fresh bruising around the lips and nose area. There was also a large amount of bruising on his chest, like somebody had been kneeling on him."

"So he'd been in a fight. It happens."

"Not this one. They said the injuries were consistent with someone pouring hot liquid down his throat, then holding him down so he couldn't spit it out."

"Christ. What did the victim say?"

"Not much. He was able to communicate that it was a disagreement over a squat which got out of hand. He discharged himself the next day and disappeared."

Riley digested the idea for a moment. The thought that someone could actually try to kill someone by drowning them in scalding water was appalling, if unlikely. Then Nikki dashed that notion.

"I had a trawl through the files, looking for anything similar. There was another one. It was the boy they found dead the other morning off Piccadilly."

"This last one?"

"Yes. I've only got some brief notes, but the preliminary examination concluded that he died due to choking on his own vomit. It's not unknown for heavy drug users or drunks, especially if they've also picked up respiratory problems. Their system just can't cope and they don't have the strength to resist it, especially after a big hit."

"But this one?"

"He had no history of heavy drink or drugs use, and no signs of injecting. In fact, he hadn't been on the streets more than a month. What they did find was an area of bruising on the upper chest, and what might have been finger marks around the nose and mouth. But that's not what killed him."

"So what did?"

"Suffocation. More bluntly, according to a mate in the police, he drowned in hot tomato soup."

27

Nikki referred again to her notepad. "It set me going through the files for details of some of the other cases of dead street kids. These are the easy ones, in reverse date order, starting with two weeks ago. Peter Casey, seventeen; father an industrialist, manufacturing electronics, primarily for use in radar systems. Paulette Devington, sixteen; father a scientist and director of a research facility, at the time working on a big project for the Royal Navy. James Van de Meuve, sixteen; parents on the board of a Dutch-owned engineering firm, specialising in submersibles for deep-sea salvage but building what is thought to be a drone tractor for the navy. And then I looked up the one you mentioned, which goes back even further: Nicholas Friedman, seventeen…"

"… Father a lawyer with the MOD," Riley finished off.

Nikki nodded. "There were quite a few more, though; the survivors. Most of them didn't make the news – they simply went back home and got on with their lives."

"How many?" Riley was beginning to feel the heat of excitement under her skin, pulsing away like a drum. "Dead ones and survivors?"

"Roughly? I haven't covered all of them. Once I got the idea I just went for the obvious ones."

"As many as you have."

"Twenty, approximately. Covering both groups."

They sat and stared at each other for a while, and Riley found herself wondering where Nikki bought her jewellery; a part of her didn't want to speculate on what had been happening. All those kids. The parents. The loss.

The pain.

"There's a clincher," Nikki said finally.

"What?"

"With only two exceptions, who turned out to be groupies, all of the survivors were tracked down and sent home by the Church of Flowing Light. I must be blind – I just never saw the significance."

Riley decided to play devil's advocate, although she felt reluctant. But objectivity at this stage was necessary if she didn't want to make mistakes. "Fair enough. But don't forget it's what they do: they track down missing kids."

"Sure. But what are the odds of all those parents knowing that? The Church of Flowing Light is hardly *Ghostbusters*. I've been reporting on this stuff for a while, but I only heard of them through colleagues. Not once have I ever picked up on the grapevine that the place to call when your kid goes missing is The Church of Flowing Light. In fact, I'd be surprised if more than a couple of the parents involved had stepped inside any kind of church in decades. They'd more likely go to the Sally Army."

"So the Church must have approached the parents."

"Mostly, yes. But how would the Church know about them?"

Riley said nothing. A good question. There were the inevitable posters people put up, and enquiries on the street were apt to spread quickly among its inhabitants, which was probably where the Church picked up most of its information about potential targets.

Nikki flapped the notes with her fingertips. "And looking at this list, we're talking about one hell of a success rate. Do you know how few missing kids get traced *and returned* even by experts? It's so small it doesn't even show up. Most is down to coincidence, the kids' desire to get back home to mummy or a chance sighting by someone who calls in and gets the parents or the police to make a pick-up. But there's something else." She sounded excited and Riley let her continue. "Most of these kids came from wealthy homes. Nearly all of them, in fact. I'm not a statistician, but the likelihood of this number of runaways from good backgrounds, all showing up on the radar in connection with the same organisation, is pretty low. In fact, it wouldn't happen, not unless Debretts started running a tracing organisation for runaway Guys, Sarahs and Deborahs."

Riley had a pretty good idea that this was where the soup vans came in.

"What about money changing hands when the runaways were returned?"

Nikki blinked. "You mean a bounty?"

"You've got a charity group relying on donations who track down missing kids and return them to the fold. Most of the parents are frantic with grief and fearing the worst. Nearly all of them have money and position. With maybe one or two exceptions, they'd do almost anything to get their kids back in one piece. And most of them would hope to do it as quietly as possible, to avoid any scandal. I doubt the Church does this for fun."

As the implications of what Riley was suggesting sank home, Nikki looked stunned. "Christ, am I glad to be getting out from this side of the business. Isn't that a form of extortion?"

"Why? They perform a service. If the grateful parents wish to make a donation to show their appreciation, where's the harm?"

"But these parents are all rich. It's a bit obvious, isn't it?"

"Not really. They know their market and target it, like

any other service provider."

Nikki frowned as though Riley was deliberately finding obstacles. "Are you defending them?"

"I'm simply saying how it would look to an investigation. I bet they can hold up their hands and prove beyond doubt that they've never asked for anything of the parents or the children." Riley recalled the way the Boothe-Davisons described their encounter with the Church, and the function she'd walked in on at Broadcote Hall. How many among that crowd were other parents whose wayward kids had gone walkabout and who, magically, had been contacted by the Church of Flowing Light with good news? And if they showed their gratitude then, it probably went on being carefully drawn on for a long time afterwards, like an emotional bank account. Generosity born of gratitude doesn't always have a time limit.

Nikki looked at her notes. "But look at the jobs these parents have: MOD, army, navy, defence contractors, industrialists... are you saying they're using blackmail, too?"

Riley shrugged and decided she needed another talk with Friedman. He could fill in some of the gaps – especially about the potential for extortion. Personally, after hearing about the kind of parents involved, and their closeness to authority, she had doubts. "I'm not sure they need to go that far. Why risk it? All they need is to target runaways from good homes. And these particular good homes are probably easy to read: high-flying parents, good jobs, newsworthy, they move around a lot and leave lots of footprints. The kids become disaffected through all the upset, being placed in boarding schools, lack of care, time, etc. Chuck in military or public school backgrounds and you get parents who are tough on their kids and have high expectations which can't always be met. Add pressured jobs and positions open to scrutiny and the press, and the same parents have a hell of a lot to lose if their kids run off and end up begging for handouts or exchanging money for sex in some grotty underpass. If it is blackmail, it's very subtle."

As Riley left Nikki Bruce in the pub and hailed a taxi, Quine watched from the passenger seat of the white van along the street. He was toying with a spray can of black paint, a tinny rattle indicating it was empty. The atmosphere inside the vehicle was pungent with the smell of cellulose, and he sniffed appreciatively.

"We should see who she was with," said Meaker, and made to open the door. But Quine put out a hand and stopped him.

"Forget it. We know who it isn't, that's the important thing. Let's see where she's going."

28

The Puttnam Hotel had seen better days, and had the tired air of a stately home worn down by the passage of too many visitors. The carpets were dull and lifeless, the woodwork scarred by wear, and what had once been an elegant if gloomy structure for well-heeled out-of-towners was now simply a stop-off point for economy travellers seeking a cheap but convenient place to lay their rucksacks and holdalls.

Riley approached the front desk, where a young Asian girl was arranging brochures in a wooden rack, and asked for Eric Friedman's room. The girl checked the key-board, saw number eighteen was empty, and rang the room. "Sorry," she said, flicking back her long hair and tapping glossy, dagger-like fingernails on the phone cord. "He must have taken his keys with him. Do you want to leave a message?"

"Thanks," said Riley. "I'll come back." She took a quick tour of the ground floor, checking there was no second entrance, then went outside and waited in a café across the street. If Friedman was still spooked from their meeting, he'd most likely head for somewhere he considered safe. She guessed that might be here.

Twenty minutes passed before she glimpsed a familiar figure ghosting along the pavement. Friedman was scanning the street with nervous darts of his head. She watched him disappear into the Puttnam, then gave it two minutes before following him inside.

Friedman answered the house phone with caution. His sigh of relief when he recognised her voice was audible.

"I'll come down," he said. "The room's a bit of a mess, I'm afraid." He hung up and Riley waited for him to appear on the stairs. When he did, he looked even more tired and drawn, his appearance not helped by the dull interior lighting.

Riley suggested a nearby pub where they could melt into the background. When they were seated with drinks, he gave her a look of apology.

"I'm sorry about before," he said quietly. "I get a bit jumpy. Thought I saw a familiar face." He took a sip of beer and pulled a face. "You must think I'm a bit of a sad case."

"No," said Riley frankly, "I don't. You've been through a horrible ordeal." She decided to steer the conversation back to Nicholas. Tragic as it was, at least it seemed to make Friedman appear more comfortable. She could always introduce the subject of who or what he was scared of later. "You were telling me about your son."

He nodded and twirled the glass on the beer mat. "His being gay was the root of his problems at school. Nicholas had known for some time. He'd tried to fight it, but the older he became the more certain he was." Friedman looked up at her. "We couldn't believe it, either. But in the end it seemed simpler to try and help him come to terms with it, rather than put up barriers. Unfortunately, some of the other boys found out. They wouldn't let go. You know what children are like – they pick on the weakest and exploit their fears and failings. He tried to deny it, but they didn't believe him."

"Is there any likelihood he tried to prove it?"

"And Katie became pregnant by mistake? I don't think so. Nicholas didn't want to change. He was highly intelligent, and in spite of the... problems, he wasn't ashamed of what he was. It was others who made living with it so difficult." He sat back with a sigh. "I was very proud of him for that. It took guts. I'm sorry, that's not what you wanted to hear, is it?"

"Not really." So she was back to square one. If Eric Friedman was right, then all it did was raise the spectre of someone else in Katie's life; another person who knew what had happened to her. But who? She took a deep breath. "Did the Church of Flowing Light initiate the contact?"

Friedman flinched. She'd obviously struck a nerve. "What do you mean?"

"Did the Church approach you or did you contact them?" She already knew the answer, but she needed to hear it from him.

"They rang me." He wasn't looking at her now. It was as if he was retreating into himself, having used up a storehouse of energy coming this far and finally running out of steam. "I'd put out posters wherever I thought it would do some good; on walls, lamp-posts, trees – anywhere I thought he might see one. One day they rang with offers to help. They said they might be able to intercede on my behalf… to talk to Nicholas."

"So he was with them?"

"Yes. But he wouldn't come home. They were kind… understanding… considerate – the way you'd expect. Not at all judgmental. They spent hours talking to him, trying to get him to call us. But it was no use."

"How do you know?"

"I'm sorry?"

"How do you know they spent hours talking to him?"

He didn't answer right away, but stared right through her. It was almost unnerving, and Riley wondered if the question had ever occurred to him before. Eventually he nodded and gave a flinty smile. "You're right. I don't. I suppose I took it on trust. Not that I was the first."

"Why do you say that?"

"The Church of Flowing Light," he replied, taking a deep breath which made him tremble, "is a scam. They operate as a charity, dishing out soup to the homeless, shelter for the needy and tracking down missing children. You've been to their headquarters; you'll know the man who runs it is a self-styled pastor called Paul de Haan. He's clever, articulate, charming and dedicated to helping the homeless." The expression on Friedman's face belied his words.

"I've met him."

"His real name is Paulie James Deane and he was born in Fort Worth, Texas, one of six children. His father was a convicted rapist and petty burglar and his mother was a prostitute whenever she could crawl out of her trailer and find herself a fix of smack so she could stand upright. Amazingly, given that background, Deane aspired to a different lifestyle."

Riley didn't say anything; she was too stunned – not least by the sudden strength of passion in Friedman's voice.

"Deane started out as a petty con-artist, duping old people out of cash in return for worthless medicines and faith treatments. Then he got more ambitious. He's now wanted in the States on several charges of embezzlement and using criminal means to take money from gullible and desperate people. Three of his so-called churches have been closed down because of tax fraud and alleged money-laundering, and attempts at getting him extradited from the UK have failed because of poor paperwork by the

FBI and the skill of de Haan's lawyers." Friedman took a deep draught of his beer and Riley guessed he had been waiting a long time to get this off his chest. It must have been as stressful as it was cathartic.

"How do you know all this?"

"Because I've spent a long time looking into Deane and his enterprises. Too much time, as it happens. That's what I was doing when you saw me outside the gates. Over the years, it cost me my job and my marriage."

"I'm sorry. What put you on to him?"

He looked down at the table and twisted his hands together. "When de Haan told me Nicholas didn't want to... to come home, I didn't believe him. I couldn't, I suppose – it was too much to take in. I told you we were close... and in spite of him running away, it was true. But to suddenly cut us off like that... " He shook his head again.

"Go on."

"We decided to be patient and wait. It seemed the sensible thing at the time, because the Church was talking to him. But every time we rang them they said pretty much the same thing: that it was delicate, that Nicholas was fine but needed some time to come round. He was fairly happy, they said, but it was best to wait." He shrugged. "They seemed to know what they were doing, so we did as they suggested."

"How do you know they actually had him?"

"I thought of that. I demanded proof that he was in their care or I'd get the police involved. Every now and then they let us have something... a comment or something that could have only come from Nicholas. Something about himself or school or a friend, things like that." He toyed with a beer mat, the ghosts of the memories in his face. "It was when they told me he'd talked about being gay that I knew for sure. It wasn't something we'd made public, you see. How else could they have known? It was quite wicked, what they did. It was as if they'd kidnapped him. I think they worked on him, his insecurities and his… fears, until he couldn't distinguish between what was real or false."

"Brainwashing?"

"No. They're too clever for that. They don't want acolytes, or groups of disciples going around preaching their philosophies – they don't need them. They're far more interested in money."

"And the parents' undying gratitude," Riley added. It confirmed what she'd thought. It was a neat scheme. What parents wouldn't be grateful to the group responsible for returning a lost son or daughter – and with no hint of a threat or a demand. She wondered if Katie Pyle had always worn her crucifix, or if it had been put in place in the final few minutes. "But how do they get them to come in? Most kids these days are too streetwise."

"They use Sirens."

Riley stared at him. "Come again?"

"Sirens. It's a term they use taken from Greek mythology. They find a connection to the target – a friend, someone they can work on to draw them in. If they can't find a close contact they make one – usually a person of the opposite sex. Once the target is drawn in, the Siren's work is done."

Nikki's words about Delphine Wishman being introduced to the Church by a boy she knew came floating back. "What happens to the Siren afterwards?"

"Unless they can use them again, they push them away. It's not hard; these kids are accustomed to rejection – what's another along the way? As I said, it's all about money, Miss Gavin. Profit. Don't confuse that with compassion."

"What else?"

He shrugged. "People in the States said Deane had a reputation for fast living and grandiose schemes. That's how he ran into trouble; investors in his church schemes discovered there was no payback other than the gratitude of The Lord. They didn't want to wait that long. When the complaints became public, he shut up shop and moved over here. Since then his priorities have changed. He still likes money but now he's developed a taste for power and influence, mixing with so-called society. Same game, different style."

"And they fall for it."

"Evidently. And in the meantime he keeps gathering more new targets and grateful parents." It was a frightening thought that if cultivated carefully, de Haan/Deane's scheme could continue indefinitely, boosted every year by a new intake of relieved and beholden families.

"But surely there must be some who tell him to get lost?"

"Of course. If he can, he applies more pressure – especially if there's anything unsavoury in the background. Don't forget he has these kids for weeks, talking them round, prying into every deep, dark corner of their minds. Some are bound to come complete with secrets the parents would rather remained hidden."

"Child abuse?"

"Yes. If they can be coerced, he applies subtle pressure. A word here, a hint there. But never anything direct. He's too smart for that. If they still don't pay, he cuts his losses. No fee means no return – in the financial sense. Deane is a very practical businessman. He doesn't need to make enemies."

"It makes sense." Riley chewed her lip for a while. She'd been putting off the obvious question, but decided it couldn't wait any longer. "But you didn't get Nicholas back."

The expression on Friedman's face almost made her wish she hadn't asked. Yet she needed to know the answer, because what had affected him through his son had also struck at the heart of Katie's family. And others.

"About six months before Nicholas left," Friedman said softly, "I and a couple of friends had set up a small company offering legal advice on the Internet. In the beginning, we restricted ourselves to things like family law, contracts, property and dealing with the police, courts and so on. The first signs were good. Better than good. We were a discount shop for people wanting cheap, reliable advice before they ran up big fees with their own solicitors." He paused and Riley could feel the awful dread of what was coming. "We became victims of our own success. We took on a couple of tax experts, and to justify the extra costs, encouraged them to broaden the field into the corporate market. It seemed a sure-fire winner. We began to advertise, and set up the company headquarters here in London. We had to borrow heavily, but the potential was enormous. Then one of the tax people was asked to advise a small group of offshore companies operating out of Gibraltar. It was simple stuff to begin with; setting up shell corporations, tax planning, building investment funds and so on. Plenty of others were doing it, but we were cheaper. Gradually we all became involved, to share the load."

"What happened?"

"Some of the advice given was flawed. Deeply so. The clients went ahead with an investment scheme on the basis of what we'd told them, and lost everything. Unfortunately, they hadn't told us everything, and ended up dragging a lot of other people down with them." He stared down into his glass. "We hadn't done our homework properly. It was awful."

"But you had professional indemnity, surely?"

"Yes. But when your other clients suddenly lose confidence and melt away, and the banks get nervous, professional indemnity isn't much good." The creases in his face deepened with bitterness. "The whole fabric collapsed around us. It was staggering. We paid off a lot of the debts but it wasn't enough. I was suspended from my job at the MOD."

"And Deane found out?"

He nodded. "That's when I discovered what he was really like… when he realised I had nothing to give. He began making vague comments about how the news of our son being gay might become public knowledge. I thought it was my imagination: they were a charity and a church, surely they couldn't be making threats like that? He began ignoring my calls, so I went to see him. Deane has two men working with him who do all the legwork. They also operate the soup vans, although that's just a cover for finding these kids, of course. They wouldn't let me in. Not long afterwards they delivered a message."

"What sort of message?"

"The same as the one they just sent you. They destroyed my home."

"Is one of these men called Quine?"

"Yes. The other is Meaker – an American. He and Quine are like twins, although I think it's a look they cultivated to intimidate people. The three of them *are* the Church of Flowing Light. They are all very dangerous; you shouldn't underestimate them."

"I don't. Did you report them?"

"More than once. The last time was after they visited my house. I went to the police but they couldn't find any evidence it was them. They said it looked more like kids trying to score money for drugs, and it got out of hand." He shook his head. "By then things between my wife and me were at rock bottom. The distress had got to both of us, but I suppose I'd neglected her. It proved the last straw and she left. Not that I blame her. Then my financial problems became public knowledge, and there were rumours about an insurance scam. I kept a low profile after that, although I'm pretty sure Quine and Meaker would like to meet me in a dark alley somewhere." He gave her a grim look. "Pastor de Haan is not a man who forgets those who cross him."

"I'll keep that in mind."

"Not long afterwards I met a couple who'd been cut off by Deane in the same way. Oh, he was very careful in the way he did it. But the method was the same: no money meant no help. And if pressure didn't – or couldn't – work, then all contact ceased."

"What about Nicholas?"

"I heard from him once afterwards. He'd left the Church and was trying to get work. I think he was ashamed of what he'd done... of the pain he'd caused. I tried to talk him round, but it was like talking with a stranger. I thought brainwashing at first. Then I realised the Church had done the worst thing possible... they'd convinced him that I'd refused to have him back. They hadn't mentioned the financial problems or the lengths I'd gone to to find him. He was devastated." He stared into the distance. "I begged him to come back... tried to convince him he'd been used. The last thing he said to me was that he could never trust me again." His eyes swivelled round to Riley and his voice broke. "He was a confused and unhappy boy, Miss Gavin. He didn't deserve that."

"What happened?"

"They found him in the river two days later. By Putney Bridge."

29

Riley held her breath, not wanting to break the silence.

Friedman seemed frozen for a moment, before continuing doggedly. "The police said he might have fallen in while under the influence. He'd been drinking, they said. There was also some... damage to the body. They thought a boat or something."

"But you think he was murdered."

"Yes. I think they panicked. The same way they've done with others. They let things get out of control and finally there's only one solution. Mostly I think it's Quine's doing. He's the coldest human being I've ever met."

"What about Katie?" Riley's throat was dry and her voice came out sounding like somebody else.

"She was the one they used to draw Nicholas in. His Siren."

"I figured."

"I looked into her family background. It wasn't difficult. Her father couldn't have been de Haan's target – he didn't have the position or money. In any case, John Pyle was too devout; he would never have fallen for de Haan's brand of doctrine. That meant they were after me... and whatever I could be milked for. The fact is I believe they had somehow stumbled on Nicholas – maybe through another boy – found out about my job and looked at his background to see how it could be handled. In doing that they chanced upon Katie. She was his only friend: the ideal Siren. They drew her in first and used her to attract him – most likely with promises to help with the pregnancy." He paused, then continued, "They work on people very skilfully. They don't fill their heads with mantras or psycho-babble about good works and religion; in fact they concentrate on what they call de-cluttering – clearing their minds of anything to do with the past. Some call it dissociation. It's during this process that they look for weaknesses or family secrets and exploit them in any way they can. Lies, distortion, suggestion – anything. Remember, these are troubled kids we're talking about. For the most part they're going through some kind of trauma in their lives."

"Like an unexpected pregnancy," said Riley, "and an unforgiving father."

"Exactly. They're desperate enough to believe anything. And if someone sympathetic comes along and supplies a good enough reason for leaving home… well, why not?"

"But what if they decide to go back? Isn't there a risk they will talk and reveal everything?"

"Reveal what? That the Church took them in and gave them support? Fed them, clothed them… gave them a friend when they needed one? Deane is very careful; he doesn't tell the kids anything they don't need to know. Who would believe otherwise? The parents are usually so relieved to have them back, they'll sweep the whole episode under the carpet. Same with the kids, especially after what they've been through. And all courtesy of the Church of Flowing Light."

"But if the Church discovers a juicy secret along the way, they profit from that, too."

Friedman nodded.

"How did you meet Henry Pearcy?"

"The first time was about eight years ago. I'd gone to speak to Deane directly. I'd had no luck by phone so I decided to try a personal approach. There was nobody in.

As I was walking across the car park, Henry arrived and asked if he could help. I don't think he knew about me or… Nicholas… he was simply being kind."

"Did he say what he was doing there?"

"Helping out. I got the impression he was a casual volunteer. He seemed a gentle soul, but he couldn't help, so I left."

"When did you see him again?"

"He rang me out of the blue about two weeks ago. He said he'd kept track of me but hadn't told anyone. He said he was still part of the Church but… he had things to tell me. He sounded upset. I didn't trust him at first – I'd had one or two close brushes over the years with Quine and Meaker – but we arranged to meet one day in a pub not far from here. He insisted we sit in a corner, near a fire exit. He told me that as well as being a volunteer for the Church, he'd been asked to run their database."

"What sort of database?"

"About the runaways and their parents; names, addresses, employers – anything the Church asked for. I asked him why he did this and he said it cut some corners to help bring families together. The more information they had, he said, the easier it was to make a judgement on how to deal with each case. He explained that he had access to extensive data through his press job, and the Church paid for him to access other databases where needed. Some of the information was highly confidential, but in a way it all sounded logical and practical, if a little unethical." He pulled a face. "The fact is, when your child goes missing, ethics go out of the window."

Riley was stunned. "So Henry could build a dossier on every family from scratch." It explained how he'd known about her connection with Katie Pyle; he must have stumbled on her name while trawling through some press archives. No doubt finding where Susan Pyle had moved to would have been no problem. It also explained why Henry had such a large collection of business directories in his study. All tools of his adopted trade.

"That's right. He knew things about me I'd almost forgotten: my schools, job details, colleagues, career path – even my wife's family. The detail was frightening. I didn't know our lives were so open."

"How did he explain that?"

"As far as he knew they were exactly what they seemed to be: a charitable organisation helping the disadvantaged. He wasn't really on the inside, and knew nothing about the Church's previous history in the States. All he was doing was providing a resource for them to use in their work. For a while, that was enough."

"And you believed that?"

"Sure. Why not? I think Henry had suffered tragedy in his own life, and belonging to the Church made him feel wanted, which is their speciality. Then, not long ago, he stumbled on something which revealed what they were doing with runaway kids."

"Did he say what?"

"It was a bank transaction slip. He recognised the name and realised that all the time they'd been telling the parents they were still searching for the runaway, they'd got the child hidden away in a room at Broadcote. He thought he'd confused the dates, but his suspicions grew when he overheard Quine and Meaker talking about getting rid of somebody."

"The runaway?"

"No. Me. By then I'd long been a thorn in their sides, constantly asking questions." He gave a bitter smile.

"I suppose I was pretty relentless over the years. I was lucky they decided to leave me alone for most of that time. Careful, too. Anyway, Henry started digging back in the files. When he began comparing dates with the time Nicholas left home, it all became clear. He found the entire edifice, far from being charitable, was actually based on something deeply sinister. I think the whole idea destroyed him. It was one shock too many. I haven't been able to contact him since. I think Quine and Meaker may have taken him."

Riley thought about the Henry she had known. In spite of his news background, in a vulnerable state he would have been easy meat. "Why did he give you my name?"

"He said you'd been involved on the Katie Pyle story – and he'd always admired you, I think." Friedman smiled faintly. "He described you as tenacious and said he'd been following your career over the years. It seemed a natural idea to get you involved."

"But why has it taken so long for you to find me?"

"Over the years, after I found out what was happening, I became ill. These things creep up on you; the twin evils of obsession and ill health, I suppose. My wife couldn't cope – she claimed afterwards that she'd first lost Nicholas, then me. The marriage failed and I became very sick. I was out of action for a long time, some of which was in a private nursing home. It was very expensive." He smiled dryly, as if relishing a private joke. "Although ironically it may have saved me from the careful ministrations of Quine and Meaker; unwittingly, I'd put myself beyond their reach."

"But Henry knew where you were."

"Yes. He kept track on the quiet, and caught up with me during one of my spells outside. I had to go back in very recently, for checks."

"Checks?" Riley held her breath; she didn't like the sound of what was coming.

"I have cancer."

"Oh." The word sat between them like a loathsome lead weight, a sentence of death with no repeal. The irony of his sharing Susan Pyle's fate was almost too cruel. There was nothing else Riley could say.

"Now I just want to finish things. Before it's too late."

"What happened to Katie?" The question was out before she could stop it, the subconscious mind's way of filling the gap. If Katie had been the Siren to draw in Nicholas, what had happened to her afterwards?

Friedman took a while to answer. "I don't know. Nicholas never mentioned her again. She simply disappeared. My guess is, after the abortion, she couldn't face going back and started a new life."

Riley's mobile rang. She excused herself and looked at the screen. It was Palmer.

He didn't waste time on small talk. "I need your help right away. Can you come to Waterloo station?" Then he hung up.

"Sorry," Riley said to Friedman. She felt guilty at having to leave him, but guessed Palmer must have tracked down Angelina. "I have to go. I'll call you later."

Eric Friedman sat for a few minutes after Riley had gone, letting his thoughts settle. Talking about Nicholas always left him unnerved, even after all these years, and he had long ago ceased trying to pretend that he was in any way left normal by the experience. He wondered yet again how other people coped.

Outside the pub the chilly air made him shiver. He

hurried back to the Puttnam Hotel, glad to have found somewhere he felt safe, away from prying eyes and side-long glances. It wasn't much, but it was all he needed.

As he ducked through the entrance and walked upstairs, he failed to notice the thin man in the long, dark coat following in his wake.

Moments after reaching his room, there was a soft knock at the door. He guessed it was Riley Gavin. She must have forgotten something. He smiled, relieved at finally having found someone he could talk to about what had happened. Someone who understood. It had been a long time.

He threw open the door.

30

Riley bagged a passing taxi and told the driver where to go, then sat back and tried to think about what Friedman had told her. She was beginning to feel overwhelmed by the speed of events, and saddened by his shock news. It seemed so unfair after all he had been through.

She curled up in the corner of her seat, exhausted by the day's events. In spite of the coffee and alcohol, but lulled by the warmth of the cab, she fell asleep.

The driver woke her outside Waterloo station. She paid him off and took a few deep breaths of cold air to shake off the cobwebs, then turned and hurried up the steps on to the station concourse. The Eurostar terminal was to her right and the main departure and arrival boards to her left. She veered left and slowed her pace. Palmer hadn't said where to meet, but she had a feeling he would find her.

She was passing the W H Smith stand in the centre of the concourse when he suddenly materialised at her side and told her to keep walking. She tried hard not to stare at his messy hair and growth of stubble; he looked as if he'd been up all night.

"Christ, Palmer, you look a sight."

He hustled her to the far end of the concourse before answering, occasionally looking over his shoulder. Riley went along with him, allowing him to dictate the pace. They ducked through a narrow entrance and he stopped and turned to her. "I've got a line on Angelina. But I need your help."

"Of course. Where is she? Is she OK?"

"I don't know yet." He turned and led her outside the station. They walked hard at first, moving away from the main thoroughfares and winding through narrow streets where there were few pedestrians. At first they ran parallel to the river, then he veered away towards an area Riley thought was somewhere on the borders of Southwark and Newington. Cutting down narrow streets flanked by the sombre outlines of old warehouses, Palmer seemed to have the ability to skirt round darkening clutches of shadow where the whisper of movement was suddenly stilled and voices stopped speaking. A thin crackle of flame echoed in the depths of a half-demolished building, revealing a circle of faces gathered over the fire, silent and brooding. The group watched them go by with unblinking stares, then turned back to the fire. It was much colder here, the sharp wind coming off the water gathering an icy venom as it sliced through the dark canyons, sending up a flurry of paper scraps and stinging grit into their faces. Riley wished she had put on an extra layer of clothing. It was raw and desolate and there was a rank smell of stale water in the air. Even the street lights seemed to have a weaker glow.

Palmer turned a corner into a deserted yard and stopped. A large bundle was sitting against a graffiti-covered wall under an overhanging slab of concrete. A weak light beneath the overhang washed over a clutch of rubbish skips, their edges dripping an overdose of refuse. Alongside the bundle was an old golf trolley loaded with string-bound packages wrapped in grimy polythene sheeting. Out on the river, the sound of a boat chugged past.

"Her name's Maureen," Palmer said softly. "She won't talk to me. Hates men, apparently. I've been keeping track of her. She moves in an area roughly half a mile square and knows everyone and everything. All she would say was she'd only talk to a woman. I think she knows where Angelina is. I'll lead the way and you chip in whenever you think necessary."

Palmer walked up to the bundle and hunkered down carefully to one side, scanning the surrounding area as he did so to make sure they were unobserved. He waved Riley to the other side. In the thin light, Riley saw the old woman's head was wrapped in layers of cloth, with just a small hole to reveal a dark, weather-burned face. Her legs stuck out in front of her like two sticks, encased in heavy woollen stockings and a pair of surprisingly stylish boots on her feet.

"This is the friend I told you about, Maureen," Palmer said softly. "Her name's Riley." He pulled a half-bottle of whisky from his coat pocket and handed it to the woman. She took it without comment and snapped off the cap with easy skill, then swallowed a generous mouthful. Nodding in approval, she took several small sips in quick succession, allowing the liquid to seep down her throat in controlled doses as if savouring each one. She gripped the bottle tightly throughout as if Palmer might snatch it back at any moment.

Palmer looked across at Riley while the old woman was drinking. "I showed Angelina's photo around, concentrating on the younger kids at first because they hang out together. Nothing doing. Then I was put on to Maureen, here. She's the local bush telegraph."

"That's me, dearie," Maureen piped up suddenly, looking directly at Riley. "Regular neighbourhood watch, I am. Everyone knows me but nobody notices. The girl was with a couple of Dukes." She took another swallow from the bottle.

"Dukes?"

"There's a pecking order down here," explained Palmer. "The Dukes are the top dogs. They feed off the cardboard cities by allocating the best places to sleep. If you don't get permission from them, you sleep somewhere else. It's as simple as that. They also offer protection to those who want it. But they don't do it for free and you can guess what they ask for in return." Especially, his tone implied grimly, if you happen to be a young girl.

"What about people like Maureen?"

"They don't bother me." The words came out of the bundle with a burst of defiance and a fine spray of whisky-soaked breath. "You can ask me direct, you know – I'm not deaf. I'm not mental, neither. Not like some." She belched softly and sighed.

"Sorry," Riley said. "Go on."

"They don't touch me because I ain't got nothing to give them," Maureen continued matter-of-factly. "Men. I'm too old for all that. And I ain't got nothing else, have I?" She took another sip from the bottle, then held it up. "Except this. They'd take this, though, if they could. Just to show they can. Men are bastards, in my experience." She peered at Palmer and surprised him by winking. "He's not so bad, though."

"Nice people," said Riley.

"Right," said Palmer. "And they're not pushovers. Anyone crosses them, tries to muscle in, they're likely to end up floating in the river. They're hard as nails and they've got nothing to lose."

Riley looked at the old woman. "How long has Angelina been with them?"

"Is that her name? Nice. I wish I'd been called Angelina.

Sounds like a doll, doesn't it? I used to have dolls – lots of them. She's been with 'em a couple of days, no more. She's pretty. Just like you, dear." She smiled up at Riley. "They'll be sure to hang on to her, I bet."

"Do you know if they've touched her?" asked Palmer. His voice was unnaturally calm and Riley stared at him through the gloom.

Maureen shook her head, evidently regarding Palmer as acceptable. "Not yet they haven't. They're very careful about underage girls. DNA, you see."

Riley's surprise must have shown because the old woman cackled and crossed her arms with a sudden, almost childish show of pleasure, kicking her feet out in front of her at the same time. "See, I know about things like that. Told you I wasn't stupid. If they do anything to her and she gets away and goes to the police, they'll test her for DNA. Then the Dukes're in big trouble."

Riley guessed the Dukes must have a record, and their DNA was on a database. Any allegations of rape would activate that database automatically. "What will they do with her?"

"If they can, they'll sell her back," said Palmer briefly. "Get her to go home in return for a finder's fee." He shrugged beneath his old coat. "The Church didn't invent the concept."

"And if she won't go?" Or, Riley thought cynically, if she was unlucky enough to have the sort of parents who refused to pay.

"Then they're fair game to sell on. There are others who won't be so cautious." The way his face clamped down said it all, and Riley decided she wouldn't want to be a Duke if he discovered they had done anything to Angelina. By the sound of it, they didn't have much time before she was moved on somewhere else.

"OK. Where do we go?"

"Maureen?" Palmer gently nudged the old woman. The whisky appeared to be having the effect of making her retreat further inside her cloth bundle, away from the cold outside. She gave a start as though surprised they were still there and gestured with a grimy thumb towards a jungle of buildings away from the river. "Try the arches," she muttered, her voice beginning to slur. "Down below the Causeway."

Palmer patted her on the shoulder, but it was unlikely that she felt it through the layers of clothing and the effects of the alcohol.

31

Palmer led Riley at a brisk pace through the streets, heading south and sticking to the shadows. He seemed to know precisely where to go and rarely seemed to check his bearings. Riley was hard pushed to keep up, but made no protest; this was Palmer's turf and whatever he felt necessary was fine by her.

Eventually, they rounded a corner and saw a row of railway arches huddled together beneath an ancient viaduct. A railway line ran overhead, the embankment below covered in debris and litter, the old fencing torn and rusted. Even the lack of light couldn't conceal the aura of sad neglect in the rotting brickwork, defaced concrete and wind-bunched litter. Where there would once have been signs of life and industry, there were now heavy metal barriers and marine-ply screens festooned with warning notices.

Palmer ducked into the doorway of an abandoned shop across the way and squatted down, pulling Riley in behind him. The recess was a harbour for litter and dead leaves and God knew what other debris Riley tried not to think about. The smell was enough to choke an elephant but if Palmer noticed he gave no indication. The letterbox of the shop door was jammed tight with junk leaflets, and Palmer turned and pulled a wad of the papers free and dropped them on the floor for her to sit on. Riley stared at him in surprise.

"Do this a lot, do you?"

He shrugged. "A few, here and there. This is a good one, as doorways go." He nodded towards the arches. "I just want to check the lie of the land." He took a small metal flask from his coat and passed it across. "Try this. Coffee with a bit of something added. It might be a long wait." Then he handed her a woollen ski hat. "You'll need this, too."

The something added was brandy. The welcoming heat spread through her stomach. She hadn't realised how cold she was. It made her appreciate Maureen's eagerness for the contents of the bottle Palmer had given her, although she doubted the local social workers would see it the same way. She returned the flask and pulled on the ski hat, tugging it down over her ears. It wasn't the first thing in style, and smelled of mothballs, but frankly, she didn't give a damn.

The minutes ticked by, then Riley said, "I got a message from Mitcheson." Even as she spoke, she wasn't sure if Palmer would be impressed. He wasn't.

"Uh-huh."

"He's in Florida. On a job."

She sensed his head turning towards her. "Florida. What, you thought sharing that with me right now," he murmured wryly, "would make this easier?"

In spite of herself, Riley smiled. "Well, It gives us something else to think about, doesn't it? Sun, sea, spare ribs."

"If you say so. What else have you been up to?"

She brought him up to date on her talks with Eric Friedman and Nikki Bruce, and briefly told him about the flat. It made her realise that she was temporarily homeless. Palmer said nothing throughout, rarely taking his eyes off the arches across the road. But she knew he was taking it all in and storing it away. When she finally fell silent, he nodded and passed her the flask for another drink.

"You've been busy," he said. "Whoever did it means

business."

"Eric Friedman thinks it was Quine. They did the same to his place."

"It was a warning. Next time they might wait for you to be home. Best not be there." He sounded matter-of-fact, as if this kind of thing happened every day, and Riley wondered how he'd got so used to it. If indeed he ever had. He sipped from the flask, tipping his head back to let the liquid trickle down his throat the way Maureen had done. "Nikki Bruce has been very helpful. You sure she won't steal your story?"

"No. She's too hell bent on getting out of hard news into television; taking up this story would keep her mired in the world of the *Post*. She's interested enough to help me, but not enough to hang about."

They fell silent, feeling the cold seep out of the ground and into their bones, leaving them numb and shivering. They sipped the coffee sparingly. As the light faded further and what little pedestrian traffic there had been diminished to a trickle, lights began to come on in houses further along the street, beyond the fenced-off area. A few cars and vans nosed their way past and disappeared in a fog of exhaust fumes, leaving a growing feeling of desolation hanging in the air. In a small, scrubby play area nearby, a plastic carrier bag was tossed into the air by the wind, before catching on the upraised snout of a broken see-saw, where it flapped ineffectually like a trapped bird.

Riley dozed intermittently, brought awake by faint night noises from the shadows around them; a clatter of a pigeon taking off in panic from a nearby rooftop; a scurrying sound of something furtive along the outer wall of the building they were sheltering in; a burst of tinny music from somewhere above their heads. It was hardly what anyone would have called rest, and was too draining and uncomfortable to be anything but ultimately exhausting.

The sound of her mobile buzzing against her hip sounded frighteningly loud in the silence. It was Nikki Bruce.

"There's been a development. The *Post* ran a photo of Katie Pyle. It was seen by a couple in Chesham who rented out a flat for the past seven years to a special needs teacher named Jennifer Bush. Either it's Katie or she's got a double. Jennifer disappeared a few days ago, early one morning, which they say was completely out of character. The woman says she thought she heard a car door slam. And this Jennifer was into Buddhism."

"It must be her. But why Chesham?"

"Who knows? Close to home, perhaps? From what you said, it's only about twenty miles from where she used to live. Maybe it was as near as she could get. We'll never know. The police got both sets of medical records and made a match. And guess what: Jennifer Bush had an abortion a couple of months after the date Katie Pyle disappeared."

"Christ, poor kid," whispered Riley. "Another reason she never went back." It hadn't been enough that Katie had felt compelled to leave home, she'd endured the mental agonies of an abortion alone and even changed her name. She thought about Susan Pyle's description of her husband's intransigently religious nature, and wondered how such attitudes could become set in stone. Yet all it would have taken was for Katie to go home. At least then she would have known for sure how they felt; perhaps they could have worked it out somehow. Still, easy for Riley to say. She had never been in that situation. "Wait a minute –

why did the police bother looking up Katie's medical records if she died of choking?"

"That's what they first thought. Then they took another look. They found suspicious bruising around her throat. Katie's death is now a murder enquiry."

32

Riley felt Palmer's hand on her arm. A scraping sound echoed softly in the dark, coming from the direction of the arches. She whispered to Nikki to read out Jennifer Bush's address, then switched off her phone, praying she hadn't been heard.

The shadows moved and a man emerged from a wooden door, back-lit by a faint yellow light from inside the ancient brick structure. He was tall and broad-shouldered, and stood for a moment, nosing the wind like a gun-dog, scanning the area around him before glancing at his wrist.

"He's expecting someone," Riley whispered.

Palmer nodded but made no move to stand up. "And soon, by the looks of it." He looked at Riley. "The call. Bad news?"

"Katie's death is now a murder enquiry. They've also found out where she's been all these years." She told him briefly about the discoveries and the revelation of Katie Pyle's second life.

At the end of the street there was a flicker of movement and the man outside the arches turned his head to watch. An elderly man wrapped in an old coat and a balaclava rolled into view, mumbling as he moved along the street. His course was erratic, alternating between the gutter and the buildings as if looking for something. Then he wandered into the play area and began digging in a rubbish bin, scattering the contents indiscriminately and muttering a fluid stream of obscenities.

The man near the arches watched for a minute or two, then lost interest. After another impatient look along the street, he turned and went back inside, pulling the door closed behind him.

The minutes trickled by as silence descended again, the cold seeping even further into their bodies now they were back to staring at the dark. A siren sounded somewhere towards the river, followed by an answering hoot further off. Both Riley and Palmer were desperate to see what lay behind the wooden doors, but getting caught wouldn't do the missing Angelina any good. And if there were others arriving soon, their chances of getting in and out unscathed would be zero.

A white van turned the corner and moved slowly towards them, the headlights washing the walls with light. It had darkened windows. The tramp at the rubbish bin ignored the new arrival, absorbed in his task. Over at the arch, the door opened again and the man they had seen before stepped outside. He was holding a mobile phone to his ear and talking. When he saw the van he waved before moving back to stand in the doorway.

Palmer stirred carefully, steadying his feet beneath him and flexing his arms. Riley did the same, moving awkwardly as pins and needles invaded her legs with the renewed blood flow. The moment the van stopped in front of the arches, Palmer was up and dragging Riley by the sleeve to follow him across the street and into the doorway of a disused launderette, giving them a better view across the street.

Two men climbed out of the van and approached the man with the mobile. There was a brief exchange before they shook hands and followed him inside. Even though the light was faint, it was enough to make out long, dark coats and the sheen of short-cropped hair on bony skulls. One man in particular was easily recognisable.

Quine.

Palmer inhaled deeply, and Riley felt the tension radiating off him like a hunter about to go after big game.

"If they take the girl, we're too late," he said softly, as if to himself.

"But we know where they'll be going." It would be to the Church's headquarters or home to her parents. Unless they were playing games and had somewhere else in mind. Riley preferred not to think about that. If they lost sight of the girl it could end in tragedy. She thought about calling up a taxi. Moving around this area on foot at night with a traumatised girl would substantially increase the risks of getting caught once they made their move. On the other hand, what could she say to a cab firm's controller? 'Hang around while we snatch a kidnap victim – we'll only be a few minutes'?

Palmer settled back down into a squatting position, ready for action.

Suddenly the door opened again and one of the new arrivals walked out, shaking his head. It was Quine. Raised voices came from inside before the other man followed, shoving the door further open with an angry thrust of his arm. Behind him, the man who had emerged earlier held up a hand and flashed his open fingers twice, before closing the door again. Quine and his companion climbed back into the van and drove away with a squeal of tyres.

"Interesting," murmured Palmer. "Thieves falling out, do you reckon?"

"Ten minutes," said Riley. "Is that what he meant? Come back in ten minutes… or he would follow in ten?"

"Could be the price they're asking. Ten grand gets her back with all her fingers and toes."

"They might ask it of the parents, but I can't see the

Church paying that."

He nodded. "Yeah, you're right. Either way, they're negotiating for her. Let's get in there. You ready?" When she nodded, he stood up and walked across the street, Riley following close behind. She was glad to be on the move again, but her legs still felt unsteady after having been confined to one position for so long. As they reached the outside of the metal barrier around the arches, Riley heard a click and looked down. In the dim glow from a street light, she saw that Palmer was holding a retractable police baton by his side.

Riley bent down and scooped up a length of wooden fence post lying in the gutter. She wasn't sure how effective she could be, but given her anger at what these men were doing, and the cold and filth she had been sitting in, she wasn't about to stand and watch Palmer have all the fun.

She followed as he eased carefully up to the doors and listened. A rumble of voices came from inside but without more surveillance time, it was impossible to tell how many were standing the other side of the thin wooden structure. And time was something Angelina, if she was still inside, simply didn't have.

Riley could now see that the door nearest to her was sagging weakly on its hinges. It was one half of a double set, big enough to allow a car to drive in and no doubt once used as a garage or lock-up. There was an unpleasant smell of mould and damp in the air, and she reached out and ran her hand across the rough and peeling surface. It trembled slightly, betraying the decay in the wood, and she guessed it wouldn't take much to bring the whole structure down.

Palmer was evidently thinking the same thing. With a sweep of his hand, he signalled for Riley to step back.

33

The condition of the door was worse than it looked. Palmer's kick demolished one half, which fell away, dragging the rest like old cardboard, showering him with fragments of damp and rotted wood.

Two men were standing in the centre of what had once been a workshop, their backs to the entrance. The walls were rough brick, covered in a thin screed of plaster that did little to hide the dilapidated structure. A single neon tube hung from the ceiling by two thin chains, throwing a sickly yellow light over the squalid interior.

Some attempts had been made to add a degree of comfort by the addition of a couple of greasy armchairs, two camp beds and a small, battered table covered with tea and coffee-making paraphernalia. A gas heater hissed nearby, casting a ghostly light up to the curved brick ceiling and adding to the depressing atmosphere soured by the smell of damp, dust and petroleum waste.

The two men were solidly built, with dark hair curling out from under woollen caps. Both were dressed in nondescript ski jackets, jeans and boots. Outside, nobody would have given them a second look. Towards the rear of the workshop, stretched out on one of the camp beds, lay the slim figure of a young girl, her head thrown back on a stained pillow. She looked fragile and wan in the yellow light, but still seemed to be breathing. *Angelina.*

The two men spun round, their faces registering shock at the intrusion. Neither looked unduly alarmed when they saw Riley and Palmer, but the one on the left instantly reached inside his jacket and produced a large hunting knife.

Palmer moved towards him without hesitation. The directness of his approach caught the other by surprise. He slashed wildly with the weapon, displaying more aggression than skill, his breathing harsh and animal-like in the enclosed space. Palmer stayed carefully out of reach, but moved forward relentlessly, crowding the other man back. When he reversed into one of the workbenches with a grunt of surprise, Palmer flicked the baton across his face. The man's head went back with a grunt, the knife falling from his hand and clattering to the concrete floor. Palmer gave him no time to recover. Taking a long step past his opponent, he swept the baton across and down, aiming at the side of the man's knee. His opponent crashed to the floor with a cry of agony, his leg useless.

The second man was even less technical. Ignoring Riley as any kind of threat, he grabbed the kettle from the table and made to throw it at Palmer. The move left him wide open and gave Riley all the opportunity she needed. Grasping the post like a short lance, she lunged forward and jabbed him hard in the centre of his body. He gave an agonised squeal and dropped the kettle as the point sank into the soft part of his stomach. Turning the post in her hands like a windmill, Riley followed up with a side-swipe which sat him back in one of the armchairs, his eyes wide open as he gasped for air, no longer able to put up any fight.

Palmer walked across and inspected Angelina. She groaned faintly and turned as he touched her shoulder. But it was soon apparent that she couldn't move, as her hands had been tied to the bed frame with nylon rope.

"It's all right," he said soothingly, as the girl struggled to pull away from him, eyes flaring in terror. "We've come to take you home." He signalled to Riley, who scooped up the hunting knife and brought it over to him. While he began to saw at the ropes, she knelt down so the terrified girl could see her face. Seconds later the girl was free and Palmer was able to slide his hands beneath her, lifting her without effort. "Time to go, kiddo," he said easily, and looked at Riley. "They were definitely expecting company."

Riley nodded and led the way past the two men, who were still groaning in pain, and peered through the open door. Satisfied the way was clear, she jogged down the street with Palmer padding along behind her, carrying Angelina.

Minutes later, they were on a broader street and spotted a taxi dropping off passengers outside a pub. Riley whistled and seconds later they were in the back and on their way, explaining to the driver that the girl had food poisoning. As they turned on to a main road leading towards the river, a white van going the other way drove past at speed, the street lights reflected in its darkened windows.

"Surprise, surprise," murmured Palmer, looking back. "Are they going to be pissed."

The van skidded to a halt just as one of the men staggered from the arches, angrily kicking aside the remains of the door. He stared left and right, then swore viciously at the night sky.

Quine stepped down and faced the man, head cocked to one side. "Please don't tell me we have a problem." His voice was unnaturally calm, and the other man seemed to shrink in reply.

"They took her away!" he said defensively, gesturing into the dark. "You must have been followed here. Yeah, that's it – how else would they have got here? We want our money."

"I don't think so." Quine's voice was coldly emphatic. "You paraded her around, didn't you? Allowed her to be seen." He loomed over the other man like a menacing shadow. "You should be the one paying. Know what I mean?"

34

The girl remained silent all the way to Portland Place. Huddled into one corner of the cab, she stared resolutely at the floor, shivering and tense. She had made no attempt to get away from them, and Riley guessed she was in shock. If she recovered enough to start thinking about what was happening, she might panic that she was being moved on somewhere else and start screaming her head off. Riley gradually eased closer, trying to establish contact as a reassuring presence.

"She OK?" the driver asked, peering over his shoulder. "She ain't gonna be sick, is she?"

"Just drive," Palmer said quietly, and the man turned back to the road. Palmer took out his mobile and dialled the Boothe-Davisons' number.

"Will they try to get her back, do you think?" said Riley softly. She was wondering how much value the Dukes or Quine and his companion placed on Angelina, and whether it might be sufficient to compel them to recover their investment. If they did, then the genteel and open surroundings of the building off Portland Place wouldn't be the safest place to leave her.

"I doubt it. But they might not let this go without some kind of response." He gave a slight start to indicate the phone had been answered.

"Great," murmured Riley. "Maybe this time they'll tidy my place up again."

Palmer calmly informed whoever had answered the phone that they were twenty minutes away. From his succinct manner, Riley guessed he was speaking to the former Air Commodore. "She's fine," he concluded reassuringly. "But you might want a doctor there to check her over, just in case." He clicked off and sat back, and Riley wondered if he was as calm as he seemed. She had seen Palmer in action before, and she was under no illusions about how effective he must have been in the military police. He would remain single-minded and controlled until this thing was over – or at least, until Angelina was back with her parents. After that, well, time would tell. She just hoped that when the reaction to her own part in the arches set in, which it surely would, she wouldn't fall apart like an old wardrobe.

He seemed to sense what she was thinking, and turned to look at her. "You OK, Riley? You did well back there." He so rarely used her name, it sounded odd. Then he smiled with casual indifference, a welcome trace of the normal laid-back Frank Palmer. "Of course, I would have taken the other bloke, too. You just got there first."

Riley patted his hand in the exaggerated manner of a concerned big sister and gave him a patient look. "Of course you would, Palmer. I know that. But you wouldn't deny a girl some fun, would you?" She sat back, wondering if she hadn't just seen another chink in the armour of the Palmer façade: a glimpse of guilt at having dragged Riley into a situation where things could have gone dramatically wrong.

The cab dropped them outside the front entrance to the building. The street was quiet, with only a few vehicles and very little pedestrian traffic. If anyone had followed them, they had used a stealth craft. With Palmer hovering close by, Riley ushered Angelina across the pavement and through the front door, gently murmuring to her that everything was going to be fine. She had no idea what was going through the girl's mind, but she guessed she was probably dreading stepping back into her parents' lives after whatever drama had compelled her to leave.

Mrs Boothe-Davison was waiting at the front door to the flat, and rushed forward to greet her daughter, arms open. Gone was the restraint of their last visit, and amid tears and murmured apologies, they disappeared into a bedroom, followed by a youthful man carrying a black leather briefcase. That left Riley and Palmer with the Air Commodore, who handed them each an enormous whisky in crystal glasses. His whole body was tensed with worry and he nodded gratefully to them in turn before downing his own drink in one hit. The shudder which ran through him afterwards said it all.

"Don't know how to thank you," he muttered finally. His voice caught on the words, but Riley couldn't tell if it was the emotion of the moment or the belt of whisky on the back of his throat that caused it. "I'm so relieved I can't explain." He sniffed and shook his head, and poured himself another drink. When he came back, he seemed calmer, and it was plain he was exerting a massive amount of self-control. "Where did you find her?"

Palmer gave the details in crisp report fashion, as if he was attending a de-briefing session after a military exercise. "As far as we know," he said carefully, "they didn't harm her. There wouldn't have been any value in it. But the experience will stay with her for some time. She may need specialist help to see her through – but I'm no expert." He drained his whisky and placed the glass on a coffee table. "I think you should take her away for a few days. Both of you. Give her time to recover."

Boothe-Davison nodded. "Of course. Good idea." He was no fool, and seemed to consider what Palmer had said, before asking the same question that Riley had earlier. "You think these men may try to get her back?"

"Seriously? No. They must know who you are – that you've got connections with the MOD. They'll know if they push it too far and identify themselves, you could call down a lot of firepower on them. They won't want that. My guess is they've already cut their losses and gone. I can give you the address where she was held, but I doubt you'll find anything. It was a hole they used, that's all. They'll have others."

Riley noticed Palmer said nothing about Quine or the Church of Flowing Light, and wondered why. She decided to go along with him and leave out the presence of de Haan's sinister colleagues.

Mrs Boothe-Davison intercepted them as they were leaving and took Riley's arm. Her eyes were red-rimmed and she looked deathly pale, but managed a tight smile. Riley guessed she was tougher than she looked and would be the mainstay in getting Angelina through the next few days and weeks. "Thank you so much," the older lady said softly. She gestured towards the bedroom where a man's voice could be heard speaking in a low murmur. "The doctor says she's fine. A bit bruised here and there, and dirty, of course, but… I'm so grateful to you both."

"Hey, don't mention it," said Riley airily, suddenly keen to escape. They needed time alone, the three of them. Mending fences. "It was Palmer who got all hairy-chested, not me." She took the older woman's hand and squeezed it tight. "Give her time."

They left the family to begin the course of recovery and stood for a moment on the pavement, allowing the night air to flow around them. Palmer lit a cigarette, inhaled, then sent it spinning away into the gutter with a sigh.

"I smoke too much. It's the stress of being around you that does it."

"Did you mean what you said back there?" asked Riley. "We can't just let it go; there could be other kids like Angelina."

"I'm not going to. I'll feed him the address in a day or two when he's feeling calmer... and when they're not expecting it. Any sooner and he'd send in the troops all guns blazing and get nothing." He turned to Riley. "Anyway, you're writing the story, aren't you? That'll set the hounds running. I just don't want them tramping all over us in the meantime. We need to finish this."

Riley took his arm and they began to walk towards Portland Place, where they could pick up a cab. "We need to find Henry. He'll fill in the blanks."

"If he's still alive." Then Palmer stopped dead, snapping his fingers. "Christ, I must be getting slow. Henry's car – didn't you say it was missing from his garage?"

"That's right."

"So how did he get to the Scandair, if not by car?"

Riley saw where he was going and shook her head at her lack of foresight. Find Henry's car and it might give up a clue they could use. "It must still be at the hotel. But wouldn't the police have thought of that? The first thing they'd do would be to check the register. Unless... " She paused, thinking back to something Henry had said on the phone.

"What?"

"I've just remembered. When I spoke to Henry the other morning, he sounded rattled. He'd switched off his mobile at one point, and when I finally got him back, he wanted me to meet him at the Scandair rather than talk over the phone. He said something about meeting me, but that he couldn't get to his car… get to it easily, or some-thing like that. I forget the exact words."

"He must have been on foot." Palmer stared at the pavement. "If he didn't have it at the hotel, he'd parked it somewhere else. What did you say it was?"

"An old Rover. Running boards, crank handle, the lot."

"There's your answer. A classic – and easily identifiable. Anyone looking for him would only have to find the car to know he wasn't far away."

"But the Church must have tracked him down by some other means."

"Unless they were already watching him. If they found out he'd been talking to Eric Friedman, it would be more than enough reason to want to shut him down. It explains why they got heavy-handed at the hotel."

"But would Henry have been thinking clearly enough to hide it? He's hardly the ready-made secret agent type. The more I think about it, the more I get the impression he was simply running. All he wanted from me was… well, I can only guess." She thought about what Friedman had told her. If Henry really had been suffering acute pangs of conscience at what he'd discovered, he would have wanted to unload the information he had on to someone he knew could do something with it. And that would be reason enough for Quine to be after him. Given what Henry had been doing, according to Friedman, he probably had enough information in his possession to surround Broadcote Hall with blue lights for weeks.

"Thinking straight or not, he'd still have enough sense to keep the car handy. He'd have needed it for the following morning, to get to the airport. You said he was flying out somewhere."

"But he was already at the airport. And the Scandair is

served by a shuttle bus like all the others."

Palmer pulled a face. "You're right. But the parking around Heathrow is vast. There's the official long-term and short-term car parks, the off-site private parking companies – they're spread out all over the place – and God knows how many smaller firms. It could take weeks."

Riley gripped Palmer's arm. "What about the hotels? Some of them have parking arrangements. At least, the ones I've used do. The fees are a bit steep, but at least the car doesn't get dumped miles from anywhere in a gravel pit and forgotten for two weeks."

"That narrows it down. But which one? There are dozens."

Riley smiled triumphantly, mentally crossing her fingers. "I don't know. But I know a man who might. And there's something else I want to ask him, too. Remember the white van I saw the night Henry disappeared? I bet he saw it, too."

"Good thinking, Batwoman. Let's hope his memory's still good."

She dug out her mobile and dialled the Scandair. After a brief chat, she switched off and nodded to Palmer. "He's in tomorrow morning." She yawned. "I could do with a bath and bed. Where's the nearest hotel?"

"Forget it. You can doss down at my place as long as you don't mind the settee."

"No, I couldn't. Anyway, I need to pick up the car then arrange for the flat to be cleaned and redecorated." She shuddered. "I can't face it. I'll be fine eventually, but I can't go back there until it's spotless again."

Palmer nodded. "I know someone who'll do that for you. I'll call him tomorrow. In the meantime, we can pick up the car on the way to my place. I'll even throw in coffee and toast for breakfast at no extra charge."

"Are you sure?"

"Yes. But if you snore, I'll kick you out."

Riley looked at him and blinked, then slapped him on the shoulder. "Palmer, stop it," she said, her voice breaking. "Christ, you'll have me sobbing any minute." She took a deep breath, then added, "OK, deal. Have you got a shower? I prefer showers to baths. And how about some shampoo for colour-treated hair… and conditioner? I do like my conditioner."

Palmer sighed theatrically. "I knew I shouldn't have bothered."

35

Palmer hailed a taxi and directed the driver to Riley's flat. He walked by and checked the area carefully before allowing her inside to speak to Mr Grobowski about the cat. Palmer himself drifted upstairs for a brief look. He came back grim-faced, then went outside to make a quick check of her Golf.

Riley found him standing by the car, staring into the night. His stance radiated suppressed anger.

"You all right, Palmer?" she asked. She was surprised, and wondered how many facets there were to this man's character. He appeared to take so many things in his stride, yet here was one instance when he had not.

He nodded and opened the door before she could produce the key, proving he hadn't lost all of his humour. "The cat all right?"

"The cat's getting fat and learning Polish," she said. "And Mr Grobowski wants to call him Lipinski, after a violinist."

"Better that than Paderewski."

In spite of everything, Riley slept surprisingly well, and at eight in the morning, they drove out to the Scandair, where the reception area was busy with a group of late arrivals, fighting over a tangle of luggage. Palmer spotted a woman pushing a cleaning trolley along a corridor and dodged after her, beckoning Riley to follow.

"Is Andy around?" he said heavily, flashing his wallet. His manner said routine cop asking routine questions and don't be awkward.

The woman looked too tired to care, brushing away a

strand of greying hair that made her look older than her years. She pointed up at the ceiling. "He's on the first floor, fixing a leak."

Riley thanked her and followed Palmer up the first flight of stairs, hoping the policeman she'd seen before wasn't waiting round the corner. They pushed through a connecting door and walked along the corridor listening for sounds of maintenance work. As they passed an open door someone swore fluently and there was the sound of metal clattering on a tiled floor.

Andy was crouched under a sink unit with the guts of the piping exposed. A liberal layer of hotel towels was soaking up a spreading pool of water, and all the signs were that he was losing the battle as a steady drip-drip of water fell to the floor.

Riley tapped him on the shoulder and he ducked out with a start, his head narrowly missing the sink. "Yeah? Is that Mario –?" When he saw who it was, he pulled a face. "Oh, it's you. I thought you were the plumber. He was supposed to be here forty minutes ago." He stood up and waved a dismissive hand. "Sod it – there's nothing more I can do. Bloody thing's knackered." He eyed Palmer with a wary look, then wiped his hands on a spare towel. "What do you want?"

"You had visitors the other night," said Riley. "The night of the fracas. They weren't guests but they were allowed upstairs. When they left, they were carrying a parcel."

Andy looked between them, eyes shifting nervously. "I wouldn't know. I told you, I didn't come on until later." He glanced at the gap between Palmer and the door as if judging his chances of escape. Palmer smiled and moved to block the way .

"That's right," Riley agreed. She could feel Andy's tension

and wondered what he was worried about. "So you did. But your colleague told you about the visitors, didn't he? And you decided not to say anything to the police."

Andy sighed and shrugged. "They were only Holy Joes, you know? What was the harm? They said they were covering the whole strip, replacing stocks, like."

"They?" Palmer asked.

"Two blokes, he said."

"Is that normal, replacing bibles?"

"It happens. People nick anything these days. The night manager said they wanted to do the empty rooms while it was quiet, to avoid getting in the way."

"I bet," muttered Riley. "And he let them?"

"Yeah. He said it was OK as long as they went up the back stairs." He looked worried, as if realising he had broken another, deeper confidence and was going to regret it. "You won't say nothing, will you? He's not supposed to let anyone in who isn't a registered guest. But like I said, they were only replacing bibles."

"Do you know what these men looked like?" Riley asked.

Andy hesitated, then said: "I can do better than that. I can show you the tape."

Riley gave Palmer a surprised look. "Tape?"

"Yeah. The CCTV tape – from the front of the hotel."

"Didn't the police take it?" Palmer asked.

"No. They checked the system, but it wasn't working, so they assumed it was bust then, too." He gave a sly smile. "So bleedin' clever, aren't they?"

"Let's see the tape," said Riley.

"Sure." He shrugged and led them back downstairs to a small office containing a desk, two chairs, a filing cabinet and a video player. He hit some buttons and watched as the screen flickered, then walked over to the door. "I'm going for a fag. I narrowed it down to the one you want, to save time. You got two minutes."

They watched the screen. The picture was poor quality but clear enough to make out details of vehicles in the car park outside. A shuttle bus passed silently to one side, heading away from the front entrance, leaving a man and a luggage trolley in the background. As he moved out of shot a white van nosed into view and stopped against a shrubbery. The van was unmarked and had dark windows. Two men got out and walked round to the rear of the van, then came back, one of them carrying a cardboard box. Both men wore long dark coats and had short-cropped hair.

"Bibles," said Riley. She pointed to the man with his hands free, a glint of light showing off the lenses of his spectacles. "That's Quine. The other must be Meaker."

The two men walked out of shot. Palmer hit FAST FORWARD and they watched as other vehicles and pedestrians came and went in double time. When they saw a movement near the white van, Palmer hit PLAY again. The film slowed to show Quine's colleague helping another man, holding him by the arm. This man was dressed in a jacket and trousers, and seemed unsteady on his feet. Then Quine came into view, looking briefly over his shoulder.

"They must have come out of a side door," said Palmer. "Quick and neat."

The door opened behind them and Andy's head appeared. "Seen enough?"

Riley nodded. "Plenty." She knew he must have already watched the tape to stop it in the right place, and had drawn his own conclusions about what was happening to the third man. "So did you. And you haven't told the police?"

He shrugged. "I couldn't, could I? We'd all be in the shit." He appeared to reflect on what had happened. "He's OK, isn't he? I mean, they definitely left some bibles around, so they must have been on the level, right?"

Palmer switched off the video and slipped the cassette into his jacket pocket. "Where would a guest park a car they didn't want left in the normal car parks? This one's an old Rover – a bit like an old gangster car from the thirties."

"If they didn't use a private place, there's a small pound behind the Sheraton along the road. We use it, so do other hotels." Andy's eyes glinted with interest. "Does the car belong to the bloke who disappeared?"

"It might. Don't worry – we're not going to steal it. We just want to take a look inside."

"Give me some dosh and I'll even tell you the number of the bay it's parked in."

Palmer stepped forward and stared at him. The youth backed off with a sickly grin. "OK – no need to get heavy. You'll have to drop my mate something, though. He's the security guard on the pound." He picked up the phone and made a brief call, then replaced the receiver and gave them directions. "The guard will be waiting at the gate. He'll give you five minutes. Much more and someone might start asking questions. Bay fourteen."

The Rover was a dark, glossy burgundy, and although it had evidently seen better days, was still eye-catching among the other modern cars in the pound. The security guard, a young, brooding Jamaican, showed them through the gate, then stood waiting, solid and sombre in a maroon-and-grey uniform and heavy boots.

"You'll have to be quick," he warned them. He'd already pointed out the security cameras on poles. "People don't normally come and look round the inside of cars unless they plan on boosting the CD player." He handed them the keys. "If anyone asks, you forgot your credit cards or something, yeh?"

Riley thanked him and walked across to the car. When she pulled open the door, it emitted a strong smell of old leather, which reminded her of her Uncle Ray's car, an old Riley. He'd had it for years, according to her mother, and was where her name had originated. She thanked God Uncle Ray hadn't driven a Mini. "I always wanted a car with real leather seats," she said, sliding behind the wheel and taking a deep breath. It made her old Golf seem like a shoebox in comparison.

Palmer walked round to the passenger side and climbed in. He flipped open the glove box and checked beneath the floor mat, but all he found was a service manual and an old map book. He got out to check the boot, leaving Riley to scour the rest of the interior. She leaned over and slid her hands down the sides of the rear seats and under the rear carpets. These were modern additions with strips of Velcro to keep them in place, and made a loud ripping noise when she pulled them up. There were a few dried leaves and bits of gravel, but nothing else.

She went over it again from back to front, aware the security guard was watching impatiently. She concluded with the sun visors. Uncle Ray always used the visors to hold his revolving parking disk, she recalled, back when they used such things.

The floppy diskette was held on the back of the visor by a rubber band. She slipped it out and checked the label. There was no title, but she had a feeling that didn't matter.

She pocketed the diskette and climbed out and locked the car doors.

"Time to go, Palmer," she said quietly, giving him a quick smile of triumph. "And you the big search expert, too."

"Yeah, well, you got lucky, that's all," Palmer said dryly, and closed the boot. He led the way out of the compound and back to the Golf, handing the security guard a note on the way.

Back in his office, Palmer switched on his PC and indicated the tower underneath. "While you're checking the disk, I'll get on to Dave about your flat."

Riley looked at him, her mind half on the diskette and what secrets it might hold. "Dave? Oh, your friend. He must be a good one, to ask him that."

Palmer nodded. "He is. But don't worry – he's seen worse."

Riley slid into his chair and inserted the diskette. Her heart was thumping and she wondered if she wasn't getting her hopes up just a little prematurely. This could be nothing but a bunch of recipes for Indian cuisine for all they knew. Not that she thought Henry was into cuisine in a big way.

36

The machine whirred and clicked, and suddenly Riley was staring at a database of names, addresses and figures. At first glance it appeared to be a basic system, devoid of any fancy drop-down menus or graphics other than a series of generic headings. But on closer examination she noticed a number of highlighted boxes which she guessed were hypertext links to other parts of the original database. When she clicked on them, which should have instantly taken her elsewhere in the data, nothing happened. She tried a few more, but with the same results. It was as if part of the puzzle was missing. Or had been left out.

She scrolled down and recognised one of the names: James Van de Meuve. It was one of the victims Nikki had mentioned. In the next box was a host of family data recording parents, ages, names, income and other personal details including the de Meuves' positions on the board of at least three Dutch companies. The final box in the section made Riley go cold. Against James's name was the single word: DECEASED.

"Palmer, look at this." Riley hit EDIT and FIND, and entered Angelina's name. It came up with a mass of Boothe-Davison data, complete with the Air Commodore's service history, postings, courses and professional connections. No information about what might have happened to her, though. Next she entered Katie Pyle's name. A split second later she was staring at Susan and John Pyle's names, address and a mass of other family details. At the end of her file was another highlighted box, but no indication of what her fate had been. It came as no surprise that a cell had been inserted with Susan Pyle's current address in Dunwich.

She sat back feeling numbed. The amount of stuff in this small section alone was amazing; the entire database would have been stunning. They must have scoured an enormous number of sources for this level of detail.

Palmer whistled. "How big is that file?"

Riley shrugged. "It's only a 1.4 megabyte diskette, so this is probably a fraction of what they have. There are cells linked to other stuff – probably databases or other files – but they don't go anywhere. It's as if Henry lifted sufficient to hand over without all the other material. But there's probably enough on here to create a solid case against the Church and get an investigation started." She watched as the screen scrolled upwards, each batch of text and figures summarising the details of a family's life, a twisted balance sheet in an annual report of criminal behaviour.

"If nothing else, it proves they were gathering personal information. But that by itself might not be enough." He stared hard at one section of the screen. "Interesting. One of the parents is a senior officer in the Met." He took out a pen and notebook and began scribbling down phone numbers while Riley scrolled down the list. "I want to check something. Give me a few minutes."

"Fine. Where's your email connection?"

Palmer pointed to an icon on the screen, and Riley clicked on it to begin the dial-up. Seconds later a copy of the file was on its way to Donald Brask and another copy to her own email. "Just in case we get separated from the diskette," she explained neutrally. She would have to get a new laptop to access it, but the insurance company would have to take care of that.

Palmer was talking softly on the phone and making

occasional notes. Twenty minutes later he dropped the phone on to its cradle. "That's just six of the names of parents I've managed to contact. Every one of them said the Church of Flowing Light contacted *them* after their kids went walkabout, not the other way round. None had even heard of the Church before."

It confirmed what Nikki Bruce and Eric Friedman had said. "Which means the Church not only trawled for business…"

Palmer nodded and finished the sentence. "…they could have engineered it – or had a strong hand in drawing the runners in, anyway. Then they set about draining them of information or gossip – or both. Heads we win, tails you lose. Neat."

"What about the policeman?"

"He wouldn't talk. Just said his daughter was home and they wanted to forget it. I mentioned DS McKinley and he told me to forget it or he'd slap a harassment charge against me. End of conversation."

"So now we know where McKinley's instructions to drop it came from."

Palmer nodded. "Must be. Like I said, totem pole –" There was a squeal of brakes outside and Palmer went across to the window. "We've got visitors. Leave that – it's time to go."

Riley joined him. The white van was parked at an angle to the kerb and the black-coated figures of Quine and Meaker were already crossing the pavement. Two other men were climbing from a large BMW and following them. It was the men from the arches.

Palmer snatched the diskette from the tower beneath the desk and stepped over to the office door, pushing Riley ahead of him. "Turn right and go through the cupboard door," he urged quietly. "Don't look back."

Riley ducked through the door and found the cupboard was actually a narrow flight of bare wooden steps leading up to the roof. There was just enough room for one person, and she began to climb as Palmer closed the door behind him, shutting out the light.

Riley felt around at the top and found a trapdoor. She turned a handle and stumbled out on to a roof space overlooking the back of the building and a series of other rooftops stretching away into the distance. A large, peeling flagpole stood squarely in the centre of the roof space, which explained the original purpose of the steps. Now it was unused, a short strand of rotting hemp flapping uselessly from the pulley at the top.

The roof surface was laid with a thin screed of loose gravel on a waterproof membrane and cluttered with a series of vents pointing at the sky. Somebody had attempted to start a small garden on a trestle table. Most of the pots were dried to a crust, the remnants of plants withered and black.

Palmer closed the trapdoor and led Riley across the roof towards the rear of the adjacent building. Stepping over a series of cables and guttering, he used a key to open another trapdoor set at an angle in a slated roof, and ushered Riley inside. Another set of steps disappeared down into the gloom.

"How long have you had this bolt-hole?" Riley asked him, as he followed her and closed the door.

"Ever since that time I got my office rearranged with baseball bats," said Palmer pointedly, referring to when two former marines were ordered to warn him and Riley off an investigation. "It put me off having only one way out."

Minutes later they were walking down an alleyway between two office blocks and into a small car park, where Palmer kept his Saab. He opened the door and climbed in. "I'm a genius," he said, turning the key. "Now all we've got to do is get away without being seen."

He nosed out of the car park and turned away from the main street, circling the block to bring them up a hundred yards away from his office. Riley kept one eye on their rear while Palmer studied the side streets, ready to take off. There was no sign of the BMW.

"Is that it?" she asked. "You lost them just like that?"

Palmer looked at her. "What did you expect – a re-run of Bullitt? This is Uxbridge, not San Francisco."

He had spoken too soon. "Palmer!" Riley yelled. A flash of movement behind them indicated that the BMW had shot into view from a side road. The men from the arches must have decided to circle round and cover the rear of the property.

"Got it." Palmer nodded calmly and put his foot down, making the Saab engine howl. A horn sounded behind them as the BMW narrowly missed broadsiding a small Fiat nosing out of a driveway, and a flash of lights came from another car as the larger car swerved across the road.

The streets blurred as Palmer increased speed, and Riley decided it was better not to look at the speedometer. Palmer knew what he was doing. She looked back momentarily and was horrified to see the other car gaining on them.

They took a mini roundabout with barely a swerve, the suspension thumping briefly over the low-profile circle. Down a long gradual slope with cars on one side and a high kerb on the other, and round a sharp curve with the faintest hint of tyre squeal.

"Where are you taking us?" Riley asked. She figured Palmer had some kind of plan in mind, and would have computed the eventuality of a chase some time ago. It was the kind of thing she had come to expect of him, given his training in the military police and his current line of work. "Or is the plan top secret?"

He glanced across at her with a studiously blank look. "Plan? What plan? I'm just driving. I was hoping you were going to get the A-Z out of the glove box and navigate us out of here."

"Palmer!" Riley nearly hit him. She dived into the glove box. No A-Z. "Where do you keep it?" She turned and peered over the back seat, but the rear of the car was as clean and tidy as the rest of the vehicle. She turned to face the front again as Palmer steered them round a corner with a gentle hint of a slide, correcting the drift with an easy nudge of the wheel. She didn't know this part of the world, and had no idea where they could go to lose the men following them.

"What are you doing?" Suddenly Palmer was slowing down, allowing the other car to get closer. After the heavily built-up area near his office, they were now driving along an open road with playing fields on one side and large, detached properties on the other, set back off the road.

"Buckle up tight," said Palmer. "And keep your head away from the window."

"Why? What are you going to do?" Riley didn't like the sound of this. When Palmer went quiet, it was a bad sign.

"See the end of the road?" he said, and nodded to a line of trees barely two hundred yards away. Behind the trees was a short expanse of green, then a stretch of heavy metal fencing. The road they were on took a sharp right, but was hard to see with the rolling movement of the car.

"I see it." Riley felt sick. She suddenly knew what he was planning.

Palmer hit the accelerator. The Saab jumped forward and caught the BMW by surprise. For a few brief moments they surged away, leaving the other car behind. Then the bigger engine brought it rapidly closer again, and Riley could see the driver's face quite clearly. It was the knife man from the arches, grim and intent, with the other man mouthing something at him. She turned back to the front and was horrified to see the trees suddenly right in front of them.

"Now!" Palmer hit the brakes at the very last second and hauled the car round to the right. Riley just had time to brace herself and avoid slamming into the door as the energy of the turn tugged at her body. The Saab tyres squealed and the car drifted across the road and began to bite into the edge of the verge; a volley of grass, dust and gravel hammered against the car body. In the wing mirror, Riley caught a glimpse of the other car trying to follow and failing. The cruel scream of rubber seemed to go on for a long time before the BMW hit the grass. Then came a crash, followed by a grinding noise of twisting metal and glass.

Palmer was already changing down and braking, with one eye on the mirror. "You all right?" he said to Riley without breaking his concentration.

She nodded and kept her eyes to the front, wondering if he was going to turn back. But he showed no signs of stopping. "What about them? Shouldn't we check?"

Palmer shook his head. "Nobody else was involved – they went through the fence into an abandoned site. They took their chances." His voice was calm and cold. Then he added softly, "Don't forget they had Angelina… and God knows how many kids before her."

Riley had nothing to say. She knew he was right.

37

The house where Madge and George Beckett lived was a large Victorian villa situated in a quiet *cul de sac* half a mile from Chesham town centre. Various owners had added to the building over the decades, giving the place the haphazard appearance of a giant Lego structure. It was screened from the road by a jungle of mature trees and towering rhododendron, and whoever was responsible for the gardens had an obvious laissez-faire attitude to mowing, planting or pruning. The overall effect was dated, yet oddly attractive.

"Stone me," said Palmer. "Very Agatha Christie. Margaret Rutherford could potter out at any moment."

Riley stared at him. "Margaret who?"

"An actress my mother used to talk about."

As they climbed from the car, Riley felt the tension of the chase beginning to fade. It had been Palmer's idea to come straight here, partly, he said, to have something to do, partly to stay out of the way of Quine and his friends. Riley had agreed willingly, although she was anxious to see where Katie Pyle had been hiding herself all these years.

She pressed the lower button marked Beckett, and waited. Eventually, a large, comfortable shape appeared at the front door and a man looked out at them with raised eyebrows. "Not more of you – haven't you finished?"

"We're not police, Mr Beckett," said Riley. She explained who they were and why they were here. "We think it's possible that the woman you knew as Jennifer used to be known as Katie Pyle. Can we come in?"

Beckett led them along the hall to a conservatory at the

rear, where a grey-haired woman with fleshy arms was folding some laundry. The room was light and airy and furnished with cane chairs, and it was evident from the books and magazines scattered around that they spent a lot of their time here.

This time Riley explained fully her connection with the missing teenager, Katie Pyle, and that they were looking for some confirmation that she and Jennifer Bush were one and the same. The Becketts stared at her throughout, evidently stunned by the idea that their tenant had been leading a second life.

"We can only tell you what we told the police," said George, fiddling with a pair of reading spectacles. "She arrived here one day in answer to our advert in the local paper. We liked the look of her, she agreed to the rent... and here she's been ever since. To us she was Jennifer Bush."

"She never mentioned anything about where she came from?" asked Riley. "No mention of family... no names of friends?"

"Not a word," said Madge. "Anyway, it wasn't our business to ask, was it? She was a lovely girl, very polite, but quiet. She taught some autistic kids, she said, although we never found out where. There's a couple of places in the area - one over near Rickmansworth – which do that sort of thing." She shrugged. "To tell the truth, when you get a tenant like Jennifer, it's like having a good neighbour: you don't ask questions. It's like the Barnhams next door."

"Is it?"

"Yes. They've lived there as long as we have. But do we know anything about them? Not a thing. They're friendly, and cheerful enough, but that's as far as it goes." She squeezed out a smile at Palmer. "It's the British way, isn't it?"

"So in all the time she was here," said Palmer, "she never had visitors?"

"Not one," said George. "Quiet as the proverbial. Apart from the music."

"Loud?"

"Far from it. Sitar… guitar… whatever. Eastern music. I didn't hear it too clearly, but most days you could pick up a faint tone in the distance." He looked upwards. "Good walls in this place. Keep out most of the noise. Didn't do much for the smell, though."

"Oh, stop it," said Madge, glaring at him. "Honestly, he's such a moaner. Jennifer – well, you know her as Katie, I suppose – liked to burn incense in her room. It was all part of her thing, I suppose – although that's speaking with hindsight."

"What do you mean?"

"Well, we never saw it until the other day, when we went to her room, but one of the policewomen explained it was to do with Buddhism. She had a couple of pictures on the wall, and some incense sticks that she burned in a pot with sand in it, and a couple of other bits and pieces. The WPC said she must have been quite serious about it." She stopped and looked at George. "I thought they shaved their heads and wore yellow."

"Saffron," said George. "They call it saffron. And it's only the monks who shave. And a few western supporters." He glanced at Palmer and shook his head with a feigned air of patience. "I've tried to educate her in the ways of the world, but what can you do, eh?"

"No tea for you tonight," Madge muttered, but by the look she gave her husband, it was plain she was teasing him back. Riley wondered what it took for two people to have such a close and loving friendship after so many years.

"Could we see inside the flat?" asked Palmer.

The Becketts exchanged a look. "Why would you want to?" asked George. "The police already did that."

"Just to get a feel of the place," interjected Riley, looking at Madge Beckett. She had a feeling the woman would understand. "We'd like to know what happened to her. There might be a clue which will help her family."

"Oh. Of course." Madge nodded immediately. "Those poor people – they must be distraught." She bustled George out of the way and led Riley and Palmer upstairs, and opened the flat. Then she left them to it, clearly not willing to go inside until she had to.

"Toss the place?" said Riley, closing the door softly.

Palmer stood in the centre of the beige carpet, looking round at the walls and furniture. "The police will have already done it," he said. "If there's anything hidden here, it won't be easy to find without going into the fabric. And we don't have the time or justification for that."

Riley nodded in agreement. This room was so ordinary and uncomplicated. And it was so obviously a home – or had been. Yet it revealed so very little about its former occupant. Whatever had driven Katie Pyle to become Jennifer Bush, it must have gradually possessed her, until she probably no longer knew what her former life had been. If there was anything of Katie left in her, it had been buried very deep. Maybe it was the only way she could handle it. The only exception would have been the bracelet found on her body, bearing her original name. The final link taking her back to the beginning.

Riley stared up at a large, colourful poster on one wall, showing a stylised portrait of a woman – or was it a man, it was hard to tell – sitting with legs crossed and dressed in elaborate swathes of cloth and ornate jewellery. It was obviously a deity, although Riley didn't know which one. And on a bedside table was a heavy square frame with a picture of Buddha. Serene, gentle, smiling out at them. She wondered if the Buddha's smile was enigmatic or whether his followers would prefer to think of him as all-seeing and wise.

Palmer picked up an object from a small cabinet and twirled it between finger and thumb. "A prayer wheel," he said. "Well-used." He put it down and rubbed a half-burnt incense stick. "But no sign of a bible. So why the crucifix on her body?"

"De Haan's final sign of control? Or is that too petty?"

He nodded. "It would fit. If they knew she was a Buddhist, it could have been a last turn of the screw for her parents." He frowned.

"You're frowning."

"I know. I've seen some ordinary places in my time, but never one as plain as this. Apart from the Buddhist stuff, there's nothing personal here. Not a trace. But there's no sign of the place having been sanitised. It's just… ordinary – and the Becketts obviously didn't notice anything unusual. I bet we could tear this place apart and not find a thing."

Back downstairs, they thanked the Becketts for their time. As they were leaving, Palmer looked at Madge Beckett. "Did Jennifer ever wear any jewellery?" he asked casually.

Madge shook her head without hesitation. "No, dear. Just a bracelet, that's all. She was very… well, plain in that way. Didn't seem interested. A pity, really, because she was quite pretty – especially when she smiled."

They left and climbed back in the car, where Riley

looked at Palmer. "It's hard to believe anyone could leave a life without a ripple like that."

"Is it?" Palmer shrugged. "I've seen professionals who lived that way because they had to. No history, no footprints. Maybe that's how Katie Pyle decided it should be."

He started the car and headed back into London. While he drove, Riley tried Friedman's number again. There was no reply. She chewed her lip, feeling a frisson of apprehension. Eric Friedman hadn't seemed the sort to leave his phone unattended, not after all the years spent searching for answers about his son's death. And after his meeting with Riley, he would surely have been even more attentive, not less. She told Palmer to put his foot down.

38

There was no reply from Friedman's room, and the receptionist shook her head. "I haven't seen him, sorry."

"Thanks," said Riley. "I'll wait for a while."

With the receptionist engaged, Frank Palmer slipped away and found room eighteen on the first floor. The hum of a vacuum cleaner sounded from the level above, but there was no sign of movement anywhere close. As he knocked on the door he also checked for security cameras, but there were none in evidence. He counted to ten and knocked again, then tried the door handle. Locked.

The fabric of the hotel was old and worn, and had probably remained pretty well unchanged for decades, other than perhaps reducing room sizes by adding internal partitions, if the way in which a moulding in the ceiling suddenly disappeared into one wall was any indication. The doors were solid but old-fashioned, and had been painted over enough times for the panels to have almost merged with the frames. The Yale locks were yellowed and scratched from years of careless guests stabbing with their keys. He checked both ways again, then leaned against the door. There was a lot of give, especially at the top and bottom of the door, and the lock rattled when he pulled back, showing that wear and tear had reduced the effectiveness of the mechanism to near zero.

Palmer had passed a twin-drummed shoe-polishing machine at the top of the stairs. He walked back to it and prodded the START button. After a second or two it began to revolve, building to a clanking whine like a small but very sick jet engine. Then he returned to room eighteen where he set his weight against the lock and pushed hard.

The lock snapped out of its slot with barely a sound. Palmer quickly stepped inside and closed the door again, listening for sounds of alarm from the rooms on either side. Nothing. Maybe they were accustomed to people breaking the place up in the middle of the day.

When he turned towards the bed, he saw the man Riley had described as Eric Friedman lying across the mattress. He looked asleep, with his face on the pillow and his arms outstretched. But there was something too still about his body. Palmer knew he was dead, but he checked all the same, touching his fingers to the man's throat. Cold skin, beginning to harden.

He pulled out his mobile and dialled Riley's number. When she answered, he told her what he had discovered. "I'll go through the room but I wouldn't bet on finding anything."

"Why?" Riley was obviously trying to sound casual for the receptionist's benefit, but finding it hard. "I'll give it another five minutes, then I'll come back to the office. I'm sure Mr Friedman will be in touch – he's probably just gone sight-seeing."

It took barely a minute to find that, other than Friedman's body on the bed, the room had been sanitised; no clothes, no paper and no luggage. Palmer had seen it all before. When professionals knew the authorities were going to come calling, they removed anything which could leave a trail.

He left Friedman where he was. It wouldn't be pleasant for them, but the safest thing to do would be to let the hotel staff find him. That was unlikely to be before morning, which meant there would be nothing to connect

Riley's visit to the dead man in eighteen the day before. He stepped out of the room, pulling the door shut behind him and wiping the handle. Then he turned and followed the signs for the fire escape stairs. Thirty seconds later he was back on the street waiting for Riley to emerge.

"What happened?" she asked, as they returned to the car. She looked pale beneath her make-up and Palmer guessed she had taken a liking to Eric Friedman and sympathised with his plight. Dying of cancer or not, it was a miserable end for a man who had already suffered so much.

"At a guess," he replied grimly, "I'd say he was smothered. It didn't look as if he put up much of a fight, either. There was no disturbance in the room."

"He was ill – he wouldn't have been able to, poor man." She turned to him in shock as an awful thought occurred to her. "They must have followed me here."

But Palmer shook his head with absolute certainty. "Don't even consider it. You don't know that. They could have been watching him for days. He was on borrowed time, even without the illness."

"But why kill him now?"

"There's only one reason; they're cleaning up behind them."

39

Unlike on Riley and Palmer's previous visit to the Church of Flowing Light's headquarters, the gates to Broadcote Hall were fastened by a heavy steel chain and padlock. There were no signs of activity among the trees screening the mansion, and no sounds emanating from the direction of the house.

Riley fingered the padlock but it was too solid. That did away with the idea of using a hairpin, she thought sourly. Where was a decent hacksaw when a girl needed one?

"I could give you a lift over the top if you like," Palmer offered, leaning against the wall and lighting a cigarette.

"Dream on," said Riley, studying the railings either side of the gate. "Anyway, I bet I can climb better than you."

"I bet you can."

Riley looked at him but Palmer was keeping a perfectly straight face. "This place will be clean, too, take my word."

"Of course, there's no way," she said cuttingly, "that you could be wrong?"

"Hardly, let's be honest."

"But it's still worth a look."

"You betcha." He flicked the cigarette away and went for a stroll along the verge, casually kicking at tufts of grass and studying the wall. Two minutes later he was back. "Cheapskates," he said critically. "The wall only runs for a hundred yards, then it's iron fencing. My old granny could jump it."

"Pity she's not here, then," said Riley, following him back towards the end of the wall. "We might need her help if de Haan and his mates turn up."

The wall ended suddenly, as if the original owners had run out of funds to build more or had given up on the effort. A simple fence of rusting iron posts joined by simple square section iron rods now took over. Natural vegetation formed the main barrier, consisting of a thick layer of blackthorn. The ground on the other side was a tangle of dried grass and decaying deadwood.

Palmer found a stretch where the blackthorn had thinned out. Grasping the metal upright, he vaulted over. Not to be outdone, Riley followed, giving him a triumphant look before pushing past him and leading the way through the trees towards the mansion.

The thick grass formed a protective carpet underfoot, and by avoiding the branches and deadwood littering the ground, they were able to reach the trees bordering the parking area in front of the house with minimal sound. At the first flash of reflected light from the windows, Palmer tapped Riley on the arm and motioned her to stop.

"I know," she whispered. "Study the lie of the land. I was in the Girl Guides, you know."

"Jeepers." Palmer made a yuk-yuk sound and slid away, hunkering down behind a large cypress to watch the house, while Riley hid behind a laurel and peered between the branches. There were no lights in evidence from the building, and no cars in the parking area. The main doors were closed, too, something she had not seen on her two previous visits. Was that a good sign, or a trap waiting to be sprung on the unwary?

"It's too quiet," Palmer said softly. "Not even the birds are singing."

"Haven't you heard?" said Riley. "They're an endangered species. Anyway, we've come clumping along disturbing everything – what do you expect?"

Palmer nodded but said nothing, leaving Riley to reflect that he was right; it was too quiet.

"Thanks, by the way," Riley commented after a few minutes.

"What for?"

"For sorting out the flat. I appreciate it." She'd heard him on the phone in his office, arranging for the work to be completed within a week. She hadn't had a chance to thank him until now.

"No bother. I'd feel the same if it was me. Come on." He stood up and walked across the car park and tried the front doors. Locked tight and too solid to force. He turned right, eyeing the ground and first floor windows in turn.

Riley decided to go left, looking for a second door or a set of French windows. If Broadcote Hall was like most large houses, there had to be one somewhere. Finding a door left open was a slim chance, but depending on whether de Haan and his men had planned on ever coming back, they may have been a touch casual in their departure.

She was on the opposite side of the house, where the windows overlooked a large expanse of lawns and flowerbeds, when she sensed someone close by. Expecting to see Palmer coming up behind her, she turned in time to catch a blur of movement; somebody charged out of the treeline and bore down on her. Before she could react, a stunning blow on her shoulder sent her spinning against the wall of the house, her head smacking into the brickwork.

Riley felt nauseous, and her head pounded from the blow. She was vaguely aware of a dark form standing over her, and of a man's heavy breathing. Whoever it was wore a long dark coat. Quine? No, the outline was too broad.

Meaker, then. His mate. The unknown quantity. She waited, wondering what he was going to do. If she tried to get up now, he'd simply slap her down. She scrabbled with one hand for some gravel off the path, the only weapon available to her.

Suddenly Meaker turned and was gone.

Riley climbed shakily to her feet, puzzled but relieved at his sudden departure. The gravel thing only worked in corny films, anyway. Maybe he'd been spooked by Palmer moving around on the other side of the house. She was about to retrace her steps to warn Palmer that the American was on the loose when she heard a distinct noise from inside the building. She turned and continued her search for an entry. Palmer would have to look after himself.

She hurried along past more windows, and was on the point of giving up hope of finding a way in when she came across a single glass door set into a recess. Peering through the small panes, she saw it opened into a small room fitted out with rows of books and a large desk. The door was locked tight.

She cast around and spotted a piece of rockery the size of a football, which had rolled loose from the edge of a border. She debated the wisdom of what she was about to do for about three seconds, then muttered, "Oh, what the hell." Head still pounding, and with a swift prayer to the god of all ethical burglars, she picked up the boulder and heaved it through the glass close to the handle.

The noise was spectacular, and shards of glass and splinters of broken framework showered the carpet inside. She groped around for the handle, and with a quick twist, felt the retaining rods slip free of their moorings at the top and bottom of the door. With a push she was inside.

The air was musty and heavy, like an overheated room left too long undisturbed. She listened, straining for a telltale sound and trying to ignore the heavy-metal beat of her heart. This was a bad idea. She should have waited for Palmer.

She stepped out of the study and walked down the centre of a corridor, dark with heavy panelling. The carpet underfoot deadened any sound she might have made save for her breathing. On her left was the meeting room where she had first seen de Haan. She peered round the door, but the room was deserted, save for a few cardboard boxes with bibles and literature spilling from them, and a roll of parcel tape. It looked like someone had been interrupted in the middle of packing. The chairs were still stacked against the wall as they had been before, except for one in the centre of the room, lying on its side. She felt her pulse quicken, and the bruise on the side of her head began to throb with a vengeance. Attached to the chair back was a length of frayed blue nylon string, bizarre and out of place.

She heard a noise from overhead, muffled and distant. Riley swallowed, wondering why her throat had chosen this moment to dry up, and wishing she had some water. That and a couple of painkillers and a nice cup of tea…

Whatever the noise had been, it clearly meant someone – or something – was in the building in spite of the locked gates, doors and windows. A cat maybe? An opportunist thief? But waiting down here wasn't going to answer the question.

In the empty reception area there were more boxes. The stairs were to her right and she climbed them two at a time, the effort making her head even worse; she pulled out her mobile on the way, intending to ring Palmer when she got to the top. Failing that, she could always throw it at whoever was up there.

As she reached the top step, she heard what sounded like a cry of pain from a corridor to her right. She followed the noise to a door that was slightly ajar, allowing a shaft of light to cut through the gloom of the corridor, followed by the sound of… *someone humming?*

Riley was ready to run, feeling all kinds of nameless horrors lining up in her imagination. Whatever was on the other side of the door was no cat. It had to be human.

She pushed the door and stepped into the room.

It was about fifteen feet square and virtually devoid of furniture, apart from a single bed and cabinet against one wall. On the floor lay a heavy glass decanter on its side, near a ceramic bowl and a syringe, all no doubt knocked off the cabinet: the crash she'd heard earlier.

On the bed a body moved and an arm flopped over the edge, pale, thin and clutching at air. Riley started forward, her stomach tense. Then, from the edge of her vision, a dark figure swam into view from behind the door. She was unable to turn away in time, and her mobile was knocked from her hand and sent skittering away across the bare boards.

40

Palmer barely heard the first noise from the inside of the house. Then he heard footsteps, heavy and obviously running – too heavy for Riley – followed by the crash of breaking glass. He swore fervently and set off at a sprint, abandoning caution. If it was Riley, the noise she had just made would have been heard in the next county. Seconds later he skidded along the back of the house and found the smashed window, but there was no sign of Riley apart from a set of muddy footprints across the carpet inside.

Instinct and training made him stop and hold his breath. One of his first instructors had a mantra: two seconds of listening is worth thirty seconds of useless action. More importantly, he recalled the man saying, it might also save a careless Redcap from having his head bashed in. Palmer took a deep breath and stepped across the study and out into a corridor, trying to get his bearings. The house was a warren.

He heard a faint scuff of noise from upstairs. Footsteps? Then a shuddering moan which stirred the hairs on the back of his neck. He pushed through a half-open door and found himself in the large room where he had last seen de Haan. He noted the chair in the centre, and recognised its purpose. A door to his right was open, and the room beyond looked familiar. The reception area. The main stairway. He ran through the door and heard a creaking of floorboards from above his head. Taking the stairs at a run, he reached the landing with a main corridor leading off either side. He hesitated. Left or right?

More sounds: an object hitting the floor with a clatter,

then a scrabble of movement, fast and violent. "Riley!" he yelled.

"*Palmer!*" Riley's voice, from somewhere down to his right. He sprinted along the corridor in the direction of her voice until he saw an open door. He stopped, taking in a snapshot of the scene beyond.

Riley. She was kneeling on the floor by a single bed, hunched over in a tight curl, her hair hanging down over her face. Other than a bedside cabinet, the room was bare, little more than a prison or a holding cell. He took in the bed, with a huddled shape dressed in pyjamas, the material soiled and crumpled.

"Riley?"

She didn't respond. She was breathing heavily, holding herself across the middle, her shoulders shuddering as if in pain. Hurt or winded? Her mobile lay nearby, the back of the casing several inches away. Palmer tried to make sense of it as he stepped through the door. Had she fallen? Tripped? Was the decanter on the floor significant? Then another shape floated into view and stood before him, dark and still, and his questions were answered.

Quine.

Palmer breathed softly, allowing the tension to ease away. Whatever was about to happen here required concentration and fluidity.

There was a click and Palmer saw the glint of a knife in Quine's hand. Bugger. This man was a whole different box of tricks from the youth in the alley near Waterloo. He was fitter, looked far stronger and had the added motivation of needing to get past Palmer without stopping.

Quine seemed to do an odd shuffle dance on the bare boards, a deadly Astaire caught in the sunlight through the window, the knife blade flicking back and forth like a lizard's tongue. He still wore his long black coat and rimless glasses, and his soft boots seemed to move a millimetre above the floor, a deadly figure almost without substance.

Palmer stepped towards him, making the man dance backwards, light as a drift of smoke. He glanced down at the blade to see if there was any blood on it. Riley's blood. But it looked clean. He shook his head. He needed to stay focused. Instead, he edged sideways, putting himself between Quine and Riley. Whatever happened now, Quine wouldn't get past. Not unless he was very, very good.

Then Palmer realised Quine had engineered the move, planning on Palmer's protective instincts to out-manoeuvre him. With a brief smile, the man stepped over to the door, the knife held at head level in front of him, daring Palmer to approach.

"Sorry, Palmer." Quine's voice held a note almost of regret, and Palmer was surprised by how soft it was. There was none of the aggression he had expected, no taunting, no vicious undertone. This man could have just stepped out of a pulpit or a radio studio. But for the knife. "I'd stay and chat, but I have an appointment." He flicked his eyes over to Riley on the floor. "She's not hurt... well, nothing but her pride, anyway."

"Why? Are you saying you don't kill women?" said Palmer. "Or is it just girls?"

Quine's face gave nothing away. On the other hand, who was going to prove he had killed anybody? If the man was as clinical in his habits as he was in his dress and manner, he would have covered his tracks very carefully. To have killed Riley here and now would have been too open. Too obvious.

"Who's that on the bed?" said Palmer. He would feel a

lot happier about Riley when he saw for himself how she was. He stepped towards Quine, closing the space between them. But Quine mirrored the movement and stepped into the doorway. His way was now clear to flee.

"A nobody," said Quine. "Don't worry about him. I doubt he's going to be as lucky."

"Henry Pearcy."

"You got it." Quine looked at the knife and his hand seemed to drop as though suddenly tired. "I should have slotted him at the outset." He smiled, his thin face creasing like a mask. "I bet you know that word, don't you, with your background? Poor old Henry gets slotted for – what? Straying beyond the lines of his responsibilities, shall we say? Not the loyal trooper we thought he was, I'm afraid. It wasn't me who did him, though." His eyes glittered behind the glass lenses, and Palmer decided the statement wasn't as casual as it might have sounded. Quine evidently wasn't stupid enough to go for the classic stand-off confession. He knew better. Things could always go wrong. The laws of inevitability.

It made him wonder about Quine's background. Slotted was a military term, slang for dead. Killed. Shot. It figured. It would have taken someone with a military sense of duty to have performed the tasks Quine and Meaker had undertaken. A clean-up squad. If it moved, slot it; if it didn't, paint it.

A phone trilled somewhere close. Quine looked down at his pocket and shrugged. "Oops. Sorry – business calls. Things to do, places to be."

"Why Friedman? He get in your way too often?"

"Who? Never heard of him." Quine chuckled. Then, like a phantom, he was gone, and all Palmer could hear was his footsteps jogging unhurriedly along the corridor and down the stairs.

He turned and hurried over to Riley, ignoring the figure on the bed. From what Quine had said, Pearcy was most likely beyond help. He placed a gentle hand on Riley's arm, and felt a weight shift from his shoulders when her head moved and she looked up at him. One eye was badly bruised and the skin of her cheek was grazed. She was still short of breath but looked fine.

"What bloody... kept you, Palmer?" she muttered between gasps. "Christ, I'm going to have to sign up someone younger and fitter. You're over the hill."

He looked down at her, feeling suddenly more cheerful. Riley on the offensive was a good sign. Better than good. "Can you run, dear?" he murmured pithily. "Or are you going to sit here bleating all day?"

She shook her head and tried to get up, clutching her stomach. The movement seemed to bring about a burst of pain and she grimaced. "Bastard," she murmured. "It's all right – I'm winded, that's all. You go. I'll follow in a minute."

"I'm not leaving you here alone."

Riley forced herself upright and looked towards the bed. "Forget it, Sir Galahad. I'm fine. I promise I'll lock the door behind you. Anyway, I've got him to look after. Go on... you can't let them get away. *Go!*"

Palmer left.

41

Hearing Palmer's footsteps fading away down the stairs and leaving her alone in that bare, deathly room made Riley feel horribly vulnerable. She resisted the temptation to call after him, but knew she'd never forgive herself. Anyway, she doubted he would stop; Palmer didn't do droopy females, and while he was always ready to step in when the occasion called, he would expect her to get on with things. She wondered where Meaker had got to and whether he was now stalking Palmer in turn. And what of de Haan? To hell with the fat boy, she thought. If he comes near me I'll rip his throat out.

On the bed, Henry groaned and struggled to move. He was still alive! She gulped in a lungful of air. Come on, girl, she told herself. Time to get back into the game. Then she'd better start praying she could get help here in time before Henry weakened further — and before Palmer began killing people.

She stared at Henry, now on his back, eyes closed. He looked awful; thin as a reed and sallow in colour, his skin was damp with perspiration and almost translucent. She leaned close and could hear the faint hiss of breathing from between his lips. With it came a sour, acidic smell, overlaid by the aroma of soiled bedclothes. Whatever else de Haan and his people had been doing with Henry for the past few days, caring for him as a former Church member hadn't been top of their agenda.

She turned and scooped up the decanter from the floor. It still held a cupful of water, the majority having drained away through the cracks in the boards; she sniffed it briefly before tipping her head back for a taste. In her eagerness a rush of tepid liquid surged around her mouth and nose, making her cough. Plain water. At least she wasn't about to poison him on top of his other troubles.

She dribbled a few drops between his lips, which were chapped and flaking and rimmed with a white crust. His throat, covered in white stubble, began working instinctively, and his eyes fluttered weakly before he suddenly gagged and coughed, his head rising off the pillow. He was badly dehydrated. Maybe they'd kept him in a drug-induced stupor to keep him quiet, and he'd knocked over the decanter while reaching for a drink. Or trying to attract some attention.

She put the decanter back on the floor and sat back and studied him. He needed medical attention, and fast. She'd have to get an ambulance here. But what about the front gates? She cast around for her mobile. If she warned them, they'd have to bring bolt cutters. Must be plenty of times when they had to force their way into places to attend to emergencies.

Her mobile phone had split open on impact with the floor, revealing some wiring and the battery half out of its mounting. With trembling hands she held the back in place and tried to snap it back on. Damn, her brain was so scrambled she couldn't remember if it slid or clicked. Too bad; she gripped it hard and heard a solid snick. Then she checked the small screen. It still worked!

She frantically stabbed in 999 and waited for what seemed like forever as the connection was made. Somewhere in the distance, she heard a loud crashing noise, then moments later the furious blast of an air-horn.

✳

Palmer was nearing the bottom of the drive, running as hard as he could but knowing he could never catch up. He had burst out of the front door of the mansion in time to see the white van career out of a large garage on the edge of the car park and speed away down the drive. As it turned sideways on, he caught a glimpse of Quine and another man – Meaker or de Haan, he couldn't be sure – in the front seats. He swore. If only he'd thought to check the garage before entering the house. They must have deliberately locked the gates to suggest a deserted property and give themselves time to pack up and get clear. Right now it looked as if the strategy was going to work.

Suddenly there was an explosive bang and a tortured shriek of metal ahead of him through the trees. He didn't need to see what had happened; Quine had hit the gates full-on. As if to add colour to the sense of impending disaster, the air of the drive was hung with the blue haze of exhaust smoke, and the gravelled drive showed deep ruts where Quine had driven the van at a furious pace towards the road, clipping the verge on the way.

Palmer rounded the final bend and saw what was left of the ornate iron gates. The chain and padlock had given way first, but both gates had been ripped apart, mangled and twisted beyond repair. One of the ancient pillars had given way under the impact, leaving slabs of crumpled stone spilled across the driveway. Among the debris was the crushed chrome grill from the van, a sprinkling of broken windscreen glass and a section of plastic bumper, cracked and torn like paper.

Then an engine screamed in protest, followed by the thud-thud-thud of a damaged wheel on tarmac, and Palmer realised the van was still close by. He skidded past the lodge, knowing he had Quine within his grasp.

Suddenly, another sound intruded, this one the frantic blare of air-horns, closely followed by the hiss of air-brakes and a squeal of rubber. A huge shadow flashed past the open entrance, a charging hulk in dark green and yellow, dragging behind it a white-blue trail of smoke from tyres straining to get a grip on the road surface. The horns blasted again, wailing across the surrounding greenery and battering the trees.

Palmer stopped running and watched as the truck, laden with hardcore, thundered down the road and began a steady slide sideways as the driver stood on the brakes, desperately trying to bring it to a halt. For a split second there was an awful silence; no birds, no engine noise, no squeal of brakes. It was as if all sound was suspended, although it could only have been his own sense of dread at what was about to unfold.

Ahead of it, the white van seemed to get going again just in time, spluttering forward as if it was going to pull clear of the charging monster. But it was too late. With what seemed like a last frantic rush, the truck bore down on the van and scooped it up on its massive bumpers, carrying it forward with barely a sound before flicking it sideways off the road.

The truck took another two hundred yards to stop, grey smoke billowing from the wheels as the back slid round towards the verge. A scattering of hardcore sprayed off the top of the load and hit the surrounding vegetation like machine-gun fire, and the air-horn died away in a final wail. The van, meanwhile, under the massive impact of the loaded truck's weight, tore into the trees, ripping through branches and foliage before culminating in another violent crash.

Then silence.

42

Palmer jogged towards the spot where the van had left the tarmac, his eyes on the truck. There was no need to hurry now; the driver had been able to bring it safely to a stop. He couldn't see what damage had been done to the front of the cab, but the impact had been considerable. Then the door opened and a stocky figure dropped to the road, looking back with a stunned expression to where the collision had occurred.

Satisfied he was unhurt, Palmer veered off and jumped a ditch, following the trail of smashed branches and gouged earth littered with bits of metal and broken tinted glass. A box of Flowing Light pamphlets lay gutted in a patch of thick briar, and a computer terminal faced up to the sky, the screen broken and disgorging bits of circuitry.

The van had come to rest between two large trees, jammed tight and suspended three feet off the ground. One of the rear wheels was still spinning with a soft grinding noise, and a thin plume of smoke was rising from the exhaust. There was no sound of movement from inside, and no noise from outside. The smell of leaking petrol was very strong.

There was a click as Palmer opened the baton he had used at the arches. He stepped clear of the bodywork and approached the driver's door. It was badly buckled and revealed a man lying across the wheel, arms flung forward as though hugging the vehicle in a last fond embrace. His legs had merged with a third tree-trunk which had snapped off with the impact, the stump rearing up through the floor where the pedals had been. The man had short, cropped hair, and a pair of rimless glasses hung from one ear, one lens shattered. Quine. The man had suffered massive damage to the side of his head and body.

Beyond Quine was the bulky shape of de Haan in the passenger seat, his once-smart suit littered with leaves, shattered tree bark and a heavy splattering of blood. Palmer guessed most of it was Quine's. The pastor seemed unaware of Palmer, too intent on struggling to free himself from his seatbelt while uttering a high-pitched keening sound. But his struggles were hopeless. The belt was pinched hard back against the door pillar by a tree branch as thick as a man's leg; it had penetrated the side panel like a spear and stopped short of de Haan's body by millimetres. Everywhere there was broken glass and the smell of fuel.

He heard a shout from the road, and turned to see the truck driver hovering nervously at the edge of the trees. He looked stricken with shock but was holding a mobile phone in the air. Palmer ignored him; he guessed the man had called the emergency services but was unwilling to come any closer.

He clambered round to the other side of the van, stepping over broken and twisted saplings and branches. Through the open space that had been the windscreen de Haan watched him with a malevolent stare, still tugging at the seat belt. The pastor was muttering ceaselessly beneath his breath as if reciting a prayer, small bubbles popping from between his fleshy lips with each word. A trail of pink mucus was running down his chin and staining his shirt collar, and a larger bubble appeared from the side of his nose and blossomed like an obscene flower, pink and vivid, before popping and spraying blood down his cheek.

It was only when Palmer stepped up alongside de Haan

that he saw something he had missed from the other side of the van: the tree branch piercing the vehicle's bodywork and pinning the seatbelt had a secondary arm lower down. This had penetrated even further, pinning de Haan to his seat below the waist. A slick of blood was running down the fat man's thigh and puddling on the floor, staining it a deep, dark red.

"Get me out… get me out…" De Haan muttered repeatedly in a pitiful whine, his eyes flickering across Palmer's face. If he recognised Palmer, he gave no indication. He seemed short of breath, and the colour had drained from his face. "Help me, damn you…!" He flailed a pudgy hand against the seat belt, but to no effect. He looked towards Quine for help, and when he saw the man's open, faded eyes, he struggled even harder, as if aware that death was a mere moment away.

Palmer braced himself against the van and tried to ignore the sharp smell of fuel permeating the air around him. He reached in and lifted de Haan's face so the pastor could see into his eyes. "I'll help you," he said softly, "if you tell me about Katie Pyle."

"Wha… who?" De Haan's eyes seemed to slip sideways as he considered the question. Then he nodded eagerly and gulped for air, his whole body shuddering. "Bush…" he murmured. "… Jennifer Bush. She changed her… name."

"Why? What did you do to her?"

"Wha– nothing! We did… nothing. She… said she couldn't go home. Not our fault… people do what they want." He coughed up a small gob of blood and spat it out. When he spoke next, his voice sounded stronger. "We offered to take her home. She refused. She'd got pregnant by some kid at school… said it was a one-time mistake.

Her father wouldn't have understood, she said. It was her choice."

"She was just a kid. Scared and vulnerable." Palmer's voice was bleak, and something in the tone made de Haan flinch. "Did you arrange the abortion?"

The pastor nodded and looked away. "She was... stupid... she wanted to keep it. It was easier... not to. Too many questions. We did her a favour."

"Then you lost her, didn't you? You lost track of her."

"She wanted to leave!" de Haan hissed. "We couldn't hold her – why should we? She was no good to us!"

"So why did you take her in? Was she one of your unwitting Sirens – a lure for Nicholas Friedman?"

De Haan looked stunned at the extent of Palmer's knowledge. He shook his head. "I don't know what you... It wasn't like that. They were friends. He needed guidance and she... she agreed to help us."

"By pulling him in for you?"

"Call it what you like. They both did what they wanted to... nobody forced them."

"And afterwards? Why did she leave?"

"She wanted to. She said there was no going back, and agreed to keep quiet about... Friedman and to start a new life." He stared at Palmer. "She knew what she wanted, unlike some of them."

To Palmer his words had the hollow ring of self-delusion. If he could convince himself others were to blame, de Haan could do almost anything. "So why kill her after all this time?"

But de Haan had run out of words.

Palmer continued relentlessly, knowing he had little time. "Had Henry threatened to talk? To expose your scummy operations and get Katie to back him up? Is that why your men went to her mother's house – to find out where she was?" When de Haan remained silent, Palmer knew he had hit the truth. "What about the other kids who died? Like Nicholas Friedman. Were they a threat, too?"

De Haan rocked in his seat, obviously in pain, his jowls wobbling as he struggled with the seat belt. "They were weak, that's why!" he spat, eyes wild with fury. "They'd outlived their usefulness – is that clear enough for you? They would have died sooner or later, anyway, from drugs and… their filthy lifestyles!" He jerked his head sideways at the man in the seat beside him. "It was Quine who did it. Blame him! He managed to get into Pearcy's database and discover Katie's new name and address. He killed her, like he killed the others. He enjoyed it – always had done. I couldn't control him." He gave a sob and a trickle of blood oozed from his mouth. "Quine insisted… when the parents wouldn't pay up or the kids made threats against us, the only thing to do was silence them."

Palmer nodded. "And you went along with it."

"Yes, all right – I did!" De Haan's voice rose to a scream and his eyes took on a demented look that made the hairs on Palmer's neck bristle. "But so what? She was only a kid… she was nothing. *They were all nothing…!*"

Palmer stepped back from the van, his eyes stone cold. He could smell something burning, and a plume of oily smoke trickled past him into the air. He thought of the steady drip of fuel beneath the van and wondered if the truck driver had managed to call for help yet. Pray to God he hadn't.

"Wait!" De Haan's face wore his terror like a mask, and he began to struggle furiously when he saw the absence of emotion on Palmer's face. "You said you'd get me out of here! *You said you'd help me!*" De Haan's voice was hoarse with desperation. "I'll give you money…"

It was the last ounce of weight needed to tip the balance. When he'd considered the idea moments earlier, in a part of his mind capable of dealing objectively with such concepts, Palmer had decided he could never do it. But now it came down to it, it was remarkably easy.

Maybe later he'd have to deal with what followed.

"I lied," he said simply. He put the baton away, then turned and walked away through the trees.

"What's happening? Are they alive?" said the truck driver in a strangled voice. He was still standing on the edge of the ditch, holding the phone out like a talisman, as if it might have the power to reverse the damage that had been done. He stared in the direction of the van, then at Palmer, his eyes imploring him to say that everything was all right. "I tried to stop, honest… but they just came out of the gate. It was so sudden… I had a big load on and my brakes couldn't cope… " He dropped his hand to his side with a look of despair. "I don't believe this."

Palmer felt sorry for him. He would have to live with it forever, even though it hadn't been his fault. "Don't worry," he said softly. "I saw it happen. There was nothing you could have done."

"What?" The driver's look was of dawning comprehension, but still ready to clutch at any lifeline and avoid the unthinkable. He turned and stared towards the van. "Shouldn't we do something? There might still be a chance… "

Before Palmer could answer, there was a soft, muffled whump from among the trees, followed by a roar as the petrol-soaked ground around the van ignited. Vivid flames crackled among the lower branches and climbed around the smashed bodywork, and there was a loud crack as a surviving pane of glass broke in the heat. A lick of fire ate its way greedily up the length of a pine tree, and a dark column of smoke curled snake-like among the treetops and blossomed out into the air. Palmer thought he heard a shrill, intense cry of someone in agony.

But it might have been his imagination.

"There's no point," he said, pulling the driver away towards the road and breathing in a lungful of fresh country air. "They were already dead."

43

Riley watched the ambulance carrying Henry Pearcy move slowly down the drive away from Broadcote Hall, and hoped her former colleague would make it through the next few hours. The paramedics had remained neutral when she'd asked about his chances, but their manner had seemed quietly optimistic. It depended, one had said reservedly, on Henry's levels of mental determination as much as his physical strength. He had been badly beaten and was seriously dehydrated; he had plainly not been fed more than was necessary to keep him alive, and there could be underlying complications which only a full examination would reveal. Time alone would tell.

As the vehicle curved round a bend and out of sight, it passed a figure striding towards the house. She recognised Palmer's lean frame and felt a weight lift from her shoulders. Behind him and some distance beyond the trees bordering the road, a thick column of smoke pulsed into the sky, dragging with it a scattering of black debris like circling birds of prey. But there was no sound to indicate the extent of the fire, no hint at what might lie at its core. Further off, a siren whooped, heralding the approach of another emergency vehicle.

Palmer's face was grim and covered in dark smears. His jacket was torn and one shoe glistened with what looked like oil. In spite of that, he walked with his hands thrust in his pockets and a cigarette drooping from the corner of his mouth as if he was out for an afternoon stroll. Some stroll. Some afternoon.

He looked up and saw her, and gave a tired but

meaningful shake of his head. It told her all she needed to know. She also knew instinctively that if Palmer wanted to tell her any more – any more than he would tell the police, at least – about what had happened, he would do so in his own good time. Or maybe not.

In the meantime, she would go to where Henry had directed her while they'd been waiting for the ambulance to arrive. His voice barely audible, he'd told her of the place in the house where he'd hidden information about the Church of Flowing Light. There, he'd said, was more evidence about the extent of their operations and the people they had used and ruined. Information he had only realised the significance of far too late. His sense of guilt had been all too obvious. It was their need to guard that information which had made them so intent on finding him and Katie Pyle, and why, in the end, they had been prepared to kill them both.

All the missing details of the story Riley could now write.

After that, she decided, she would go away for a few days. Somewhere warm and, hopefully, safe. Somewhere she could file away the tragic stories she had learned over the last few days, into a deep and forgettable place, hope-fully never to take them out again. By the time she came back, her flat would be ready and she might be able to coax the cat back from Mr Grobowski's cooking. And give it a decent name.

Earlier on, while Henry was hovering half in and half out of consciousness, she had called Mitcheson's mobile number. His response had been instant, his voice relaxed and warmly familiar.

"I'm nearly finished here," he'd assured her, still in sunny Florida. "Three days max. Then I'm heading home."

By home, she reminded herself, he meant San Francisco.

"That's good." She had found herself suddenly tongue-tied, aware of the distance along the line and asking herself if it had been a bad idea calling.

"How about you?" he asked. "Anything interesting happening?"

She had looked down at Henry, his breathing hovering on the edge of fading altogether, and remembered her own bruises, and wondered if the crash she'd heard earlier had been anything to do with Frank Palmer. "No," she'd lied easily. "Not much."

"In that case," he'd suggested, "how about I stay down here and we do some catching up?"

It was no contest. She'd heard Florida could be nice at this time of year. But she'd given it several seconds before replying. Always better, her mother used to say, to keep 'em waiting. She told him she'd call him with her flight details.

"I hope," she said lightly, as Palmer came to a stop beside her and took a last drag of his cigarette, "that you haven't been smoking near petrol." She reached up and gently brushed a fragment of burned leaf from his cheek. It was the only thing she would say about what had happened, and hoped the attempt at dark humour would help with whatever he might be feeling right now.

"Nah," he said easily, and flicked the cigarette away into a small, half-dried puddle, where it sizzled and died. "I'm safety mad, me. Known for it, in fact."

More action-packed crime novels from Crème de la Crime

No Peace for the Wicked   Adrian Magson

ISBN: 0-9547634-2-4

Old gangsters never die – they simply get rubbed out. But who is ordering the hits? And why?

Hard-nosed female investigative reporter Riley Gavin is tasked to find out. Her assignment follows a bloody trail from a south coast seafront to the Costa Del Crime – and sparks off a chain of murders.

Riley and ex-military cop Frank Palmer uncover a web of vendettas, double-crosses and hatred in an underworld at war with itself for control of a faltering criminal empire.

The story soon gets too personal as Riley dodges bullets, attack dogs and psychotic thugs – and suddenly facing a *deadline* takes on a whole new meaning…

Praise for *No Peace for the Wicked*:
A real page turner… a slick, accomplished writer who can plot neatly and keep a story moving…
- Sharon Wheeler, Reviewing the Evidence website

…a hugely enjoyable roller-coaster of a thriller… adrenalin and heart-racing action... highly charged and explosive end…
   Macavity's Mail Order

A hard-hitting debut…
   Mystery Lovers

A Thankless Child   Penny Deacon
ISBN: 0-9547634-8-3

Family parties, calls from mother, home repairs… and dead bodies. Why does everything you most hate happen at once?

It's not long since Humility left Midway Port, determined not to return. Now she's back with a storm-damaged boat, and she's about to pay for her last encounter with ruthless patriarch Morgan Vinci. He wants her to find out why a man hanged himself on one of the boats in his new marina.

Just to complicate things, Humility's mother wants her to track down a thirteen-year-old runaway. But how do you find one child in streets full of homeless kids, terrified of whatever is coming out of the night and making their friends disappear.

When the missing children are linked to the hanged man's ferry company, his suicide needs a closer look. But good intentions count for nothing in a world where good wine is laced with poison, girl gangs guard their territory with knives and nightmares are terrifyingly real.

A storming follow-up to *A Kind of Puritan*, Deacon's acclaimed first genre-busting future crime novel.

Personal Protection   Tracey Shellito

ISBN: 0-9547634-5-9

Lapdancers at Blackpool's top erotic nightspot are being targeted, but the local police don't seem to care.

Randall McGonnigal, five foot five of packed muscle and a bodyguard, cares a lot. She's determined to track down the pervert who raped Tori, her exotic dancer lover.

Randall soon unearths murky secrets from the club's membership list – but she has to beat off attackers outside the club, and it becomes plain that she's getting too close. As she battles with her own dark side as well as the suspects who emerge from the woodwork, she lays her life on the line to protect the woman she loves – but will it be enough?

Dead Old   Maureen Carter

ISBN: 0-9547634-6-7

Blood-spattered daffodils stuffed in a dead woman's mouth: random violence by a callous gang - or hatred and revenge?

West Midlands Police think Sophia Carrington's murder is the latest attack by teen yobs – but Detective Sergeant Bev Morriss won't accept it.

To her the bizarre bouquet is a chilling message which will point straight to the killer – but Bev's reputation has hit rock bottom and no one is listening. Even Oz, her lover, has doubts.

The glamorous new boss buries Bev in paperwork and insults, and Birmingham's most gritty detective rebels.

Then the killer decides Bev's family is next…

Another gritty mystery for Bev Morris, Carter's hard-nosed female detective.

A Kind of Puritan
Penny Deacon

ISBN: 0-9547634-1-6

Jon was nobody – no money, no influence. So who killed him and dropped him in the river?

Bodies are bad for business, but Humility, a low-tech woman in a hi-tech world, isn't going to let go until she knows who killed the guy everyone said was harmless.

The mystery leads her to parts of the city where people kill for the cost of a meal – and help from the local crime boss exacts a high price. But her best friend's job is on the line, the battered barge she calls home is under threat and 'accidents' happen to her friends. She's not going to give up – even when one death leads to another, and the next could be hers!

Praise for *A Kind of Puritan*:
A subtle and clever thriller…
   – The Daily Mail

This novel manages to unnerve yet thrill, keeping a tight storyline with crisp descriptions and frightening visions of 2040… It's impossible to read a book of this standard without once thinking 'what if?' This is a great first title release.
   – Macavity's Mail Order

A bracing new entry in the genre … a fascinating new author with a hip, noir voice.
   – Mystery Lovers

An amazing style coupled with an original plot. I look forward to her next.
   – Natasha Boyce, Ottakar's Yeovil

If It Bleeds
Bernie Crosthwaite

ISBN: 0-9547634-3-2

There's only one rule in newspapers: if it bleeds, it leads.

Press photographer Jude Baxendale is despatched a grisly but routine job: snapping a young woman's body in a local park. But the murdered girl is her own son's girlfriend. Nothing in her life will be the same again.

Who stabbed and mutilated Lara – and why? Who hated her enough to dump her body in full public gaze? Jude and reporter Matt Dryden begin to unravel the layers of the girl's complex past. But nothing about Lara was as it seemed...

Finding the truth will risk Jude's job, health and sanity, and place her squarely in the killer's sights.

Some deadly truths are best left uncovered.

Praise for *If It Bleeds*:
A cracking debut novel... small-town atmosphere is uncannily accurate...
the writing's slick, the plotting's tidy and Jude is a refreshingly sparky heroine.
 - Sharon Wheeler, Reviewing the Evidence website

A Certain Malice
Felicity Young

ISBN: 0-9547634-4-0

Glenroyd Ladies' College has a reputation to protect – and a charred corpse in the grounds. Who wanted the caretaker silenced? And why did they set fire to his body?

Senior Sergeant Cam Fraser has just returned to the sleepy Australian town of his youth following the death of his wife and son in a fire. The burnt body brings back ghosts and grief.

Everyone in the community has something to hide: the two young teachers who seem very close; the waspish headmistress desperate to prevent a scandal; Cliff, who runs the local volunteer fire service and has dangerous friends.

Cam is close to the truth when fire rips through the evidence. He is already in more danger than he could imagine.

Praise for *A Certain Malice*:

a beautifully written book… Felicity draws you into the life in Australia… you may not want to leave.
- Natasha Boyce, Ottakar's Yeovil

a pleasant read with engaging characters
- Russell James, Shotsmag

Working Girls   Maureen Carter

ISBN: 0-9547634-0-8

Dumped in a park with her throat slashed, schoolgirl prostitute
Michelle Lucas died in agony and terror.

Detective Sergeant Bev Morriss of West Midlands Police thought
she was hardened, but Michelle's broken body fills her with cold
fury.

This case is the one that will push her to the edge, as she struggles
to infiltrate the jungle of hookers, pimps and violent johns in
Birmingham's vice-land. But no one will break the wall of silence.
When a second victim dies, Bev knows time is running out. To win
the trust of the working girls she has to take the most dangerous
gamble of her life – out on the streets.

Praise for *Working Girls*:

*Working Girls is dark and gritty… Carter's writing has energy and bounce…
an exciting debut novel, both for Carter and new British publishing house
Creme de la Crime.*
   - Sharon Wheeler, Reviewing the Evidence website

*Fans of TV from the Bill to Prime Suspect and the racier elements of chick-
lit will love Maureen Carter's work. Imagine Bridget Jones meets Cracker…
gritty, pacy, realistic and… televisual. When's the TV adaptation going to
hit our screens?*
   - Gary Hudson from the West Midlands writing on the Amazon
   website

*A hard-hitting debut ... fast moving with a well realised character in
Detective Sergeant Bev Morriss. I'll look forward to her next appearance.*
   - Mystery Lovers